Appointment in Samarra
The Doctor's Son and Other Stories
Butterfield 8
Hope of Heaven
Files on Parade
Pal Joey
Pipe Night
Hellbox
A Rage to Live
The Farmers Hotel
Sweet and Sour
Ten North Frederick
A Family Party
Selected Short Stories
From the Terrace
Ourselves to Know

Sermons and Soda-Water: A Trilogy
    The Girl on the Baggage Truck
    Imagine Kissing Pete
    We're Friends Again

Five Plays:
    The Farmers Hotel
    The Searching Sun
    The Champagne Pool
    Veronique
    The Way It Was

Assembly
The Big Laugh
The Cape Cod Lighter
Elizabeth Appleton
The Hat on the Bed
The Horse Knows the Way
The Lockwood Concern
My Turn
Waiting for Winter
The Instrument
And Other Stories
The O'Hara Generation
Lovey Childs: A Philadelphian's Story
The Ewings
The Time Element and Other Stories
Good Samaritan and Other Stories

GOOD SAMARITAN
and Other Stories

JOHN O'HARA

GOOD SAMARITAN

AND OTHER STORIES

RANDOM HOUSE · NEW YORK

Library of Congress Cataloging in Publication Data
O'Hara, John, 1905–1970.
      Good Samaritan, and other stories.
         CONTENTS: The gentry.—The sun room.—Sound View.   [etc.]
         I.   Title.
PZ3.O3677Go   813'.5'2   74–1483
ISBN 0–394–49070–3

Manufactured in the United States of America

98765432

First Edition

23581

FOREWORD

All of the fourteen stories in this volume appear to have been written during the 1960's—the decade in which O'Hara published six big collections containing 134 stories —and are on average much longer than those of his earlier years. In a Foreword he wrote in November 1955 for the forthcoming Modern Library *Selected Stories*, but which was displaced by Lionel Trilling's admirable Introduction and therefore never published, he referred to that past time:

> I don't think I'll write any more short stories. In very recent years I have been made sharply aware of the passage of time and the preciousness of it, and there are so many big things I want to do. But during the Thirties and the Forties these stories were part of me as I was part of those nights and days, when time was cheap and everlasting and one could say it all in two thousand words.

In spite of this negative prediction concerning stories, he did manage to write slightly more than one a month during the last ten years of his life, and a great number of them belong among his or anybody's best.

Of these stories from that decade, two were published

by magazines near the time they were written and one in the year of publication of this volume. None of them has ever before been published in a book.

"Christmas Poem" appeared in *The New Yorker* (December 19, 1964), just too late for inclusion in *The Horse Knows the Way*, which had been published in November; and it was apparently overlooked by the author when he made his next collection, *Waiting for Winter* (November 1966).

The last volume of stories O'Hara collected, *And Other Stories*, came out in November 1968, just before *The Saturday Evening Post* printed "Good Samaritan" (November 30, 1968), the last story to appear in a magazine during his lifetime. "The Sun Room" was accepted by *The Saturday Evening Post*, but was never printed because the *Post* suspended publication shortly thereafter. "Tuesday's as Good as Any" was declined in May 1968 by the *Post*, which accepted "The Journey to Mount Clemens" (written in 1966 or before) for 1974 publication.

Two of these stories were not given titles by the author: "George Munson" and "Harrington and Whitehill." On the typescript of the latter, in the position where he customarily put the title, he wrote "1963 Play." The meaning of this designation became clear when Matthew Bruccoli told me about a piece by Sam Zolotow in *The New York Times*, July 29, 1963, based on an interview with O'Hara and referring to two recently completed, unproduced plays: "The latest, still unnamed, deals with a husband-wife publishing team. Spanning the last twenty-five years, the drama follows the progress of the publishing house and the individuals involved."

No script of this play has been found, but "Harrington and Whitehill" is clearly a by-product, either preceding or following that dramatic project—a practice which the au-

thor followed more than once. Whether he regarded this
story or "George Munson" as final drafts, I have no way of
knowing, but they appear to me to be complete and to work
admirably as stories, whatever further intentions he might
have had regarding them.

"The Mechanical Man" has a curious history. O'Hara
included it in the typescript for *Waiting for Winter* (1966),
but when he received the galley proofs of that volume, he
phoned me to say that either we or the printer had lost the
end of the story. I did not believe this to be the case then,
and I do not now: I believe that any additional scene in the
conflict that is the subject of this story would mar it. Furthermore, it has, typed under the last line, in the center,
the mark # he so frequently put at the end of a story. I
stopped arguing, though, when I saw it would get me nowhere, and removed the story from the collection. Then
years later, when I saw for the first time "The Journey to
Mount Clemens"—which has kindred subject matter and
apparently derives from the same experience—it occurred to
me that probably at that moment his memory had confused
the endings of the two stories.

Concerning the six stories not mentioned in these notes,
there is no specific information, apart from the fact that the
format of the typescripts is that which O'Hara characteristi-
cally used in the 1960's. Since none of them were included in
the six big collections he made in 1961, 1962, 1963, 1964,
1966, and 1968—in which the majority of stories had not
been previously published in magazines—it is reasonable to
suppose that some of them at least were written in the last
year of his life, intended for a volume yet to come, rather
than excluded by him from previous collections.

ALBERT ERSKINE

CONTENTS

GOOD SAMARITAN
and Other Stories

THE GENTRY

In that winter George Campbell hardly ever missed a Sunday afternoon call on his father and mother. The old man and George would sit in the bay window from some time after two o'clock until the town clock struck five. With the coal stove burning and the windows tightly closed, the bay window was blue with the lingering smoke of their cigars, and what with the air that way and their having eaten substantial Sunday dinners, the father and son would sometimes sit in drowsy silence and sometimes both would doze off. But as soon as one opened his eyes and resumed rocking, or scratched a match to relight his cigar, the other too would open his eyes and neither man would comment on his own or the other's nap.

There were plenty of things to talk about when they felt the need of conversation. There were business and money things, and local and state politics, and the federal government in Washington. Road-building in and out of town was a favorite topic of conversation, and so was building and rebuilding of structures for private or commercial use. And then there were the passersby. Men and women out for a Sunday stroll—or, more likely, walking from one house to another house—could see the two men in the bay window, and nearly all the people would bow to the Campbells and the Campbells would return the greetings with bows and waves. "The Frankenheimers," the old man would say.

"Yes," George Campbell would say. "Guess they were over at the Schultzes'."

"More than likely."

"Burying Adam Tuesday afternoon. Wonder why they're keeping him that long?"

"Your mother says it's to give Adam's sister time to get here from Iowa."

"Wasn't that sudden. She could have been on her way."

"No, the way we heard it, Adam was showing a big improvement the early part of the week, then took a turn for the worse I believe it was Thursday night. Yes, Thursday night. They had the doctor in twice Thursday night. Got a tank of oxygen from the Outerbridge Colliery, but it was too late to do him much good."

"Well, Adam was one of those sickly fellows. He always looked on the verge of consumption."

"Yes, you remember his mother died of it, old Mrs. Schultz. It runs in the Schultz family. Marian's hardly more than skin and bones. And you look at Maude Frankenheimer. She'll be the next to go."

"Well, if she is I don't know what'll happen to that family. Felix Frankenheimer wouldn't be able to hold them together."

"Oh, Felix is a pretty good fellow."

"Oh, no, Pop, you don't know."

"You mean he gets liquored up? That's a well-known fact, George."

"I was thinking more of something else."

"Yes. Well, I guess not as many know about that, and

voices carry. Your mother's in the bay window right above us."

"Thought she was in your room, taking a nap."

"She was, but not now."

"I guess they could keep Adam another week if they wanted to."

"Yes, what the embalmers can do nowadays."

"Not only nowadays. The Egyptians had the secret two thousand years ago."

"I guess they did, yes. Those mummies. But that was wrapping them up in linen bandages, wasn't it?"

"In something, I don't know just what it was. They were way ahead of their time in textiles."

"I just as soon be cremated, but your mother won't hear of it. I was going to put it in my will, but she wouldn't have it."

At five o'clock George would rise and say, without fail, "We're having early supper, so I guess I won't keep Lucy waiting." He would put on his overcoat and derby, call upstairs, "Goodbye, Mom," and wait for her reply, then he would speak to his father. "May see you next Sunday, if not before. Goodbye, Pop."

"Goodbye, son," the old man would say, and another Sunday would be gone without George's having said what was on his mind.

So it went all through that winter. George would drop in on Sunday afternoon and he would be pleasant company for his father, but Oscar Campbell would often hope during the week that on the next Sunday George would unburden himself. He was a good son and, as far as Oscar knew, a good man. He was certainly a good husband and father. He seldom touched hard liquor, and considering that he was a good-looking fellow, he was extremely honorable about women. It was true that any deviation from the strictest observance of the marital vows would have put him in a conspicuously different category, and in Lyons there was little opportunity for adultery; but George was not even gallantly flirtatious. He had no special smiles for special women friends; he was equally polite to them all. And so Oscar Campbell ruled out liquor and women as his son's problem. George was in good health for a man near forty, putting on a little weight, but it was natural for a man that had a desk job to put on some weight. His children had gone through and were going through the illnesses of childhood, but nothing more serious that appendicitis had afflicted either child. Money worries? Well, everybody had money worries to some extent. Everybody wanted more money, to do the things he could not afford; to buy things for the house, to own a car or a bigger car, to save more for the children's education, to take out more insurance, to go away on a longer, distant vacation. There were not many men in Lyons who were better fixed financially than George Campbell; he pulled down a salary of $7500 a year, and he did not have the actual handling of money as a responsibility or a temptation. And George knew that in the event of some crisis, some emergency, he could always go to his father. At the same time Oscar knew that his son saved money, had a growing bank account, paid his bills promptly, had his wife and children looking neat and clean and nicely dressed for church and Sunday school. There was really nothing in God's world that should have been bothering George Campbell, but his father knew that something was eating George, and it was something either so piddling or so awful that he could not bring himself to talk about it.

The season for the Sunday afternoon calls came to an end with the arrival of warmer weather. They sat out on the porch now, and people would stop and visit with them, and in late May, George stayed away two successive Sundays and his father rightly guessed that his son would not resume the visits until they could sit inside again, just the two of them in the bay window. Maybe by fall whatever it was would have straightened itself out, and if not, maybe George would tell his father what his troubles were. It would not do to come right out and ask George if there was something bothering him; their relationship had been too long established as father and married son, heads of separate households, with separate family secrets and the son going his own way. Oscar Campbell was glad in a way that the summer came when it did: without the summer interruption he might have let his curiosity get the better of him and said something that would reveal to George that he had been noticing all winter that George had a problem on his mind, and that was the last thing he wanted to do. Surely, too, the last thing George would have wanted.

Immediately after the Fourth the elder Campbells closed their house and went on the trip to California that they had been planning most of their married life. They had postponed the trip four years earlier, when George went in the Army and was sent overseas. They had put it off again in 1919 and 1920 because Oscar had been worried about the state of the Union; it was no time to just pack up and leave the business and go sailing off to places three thousand miles away. If George had elected to work for his father instead of becoming superintendent of the stocking factory, the Campbell Hardware & Supply Company would have been in safe hands; but Oscar fully understood why George had made his decision. He wanted to be on his own, and there certainly was a bigger future with Acme Mills than with the Campbell store. Acme had small factories scattered all over the coal regions, where the women were

willing to work for low wages, and promotion in the Acme
organization was said to be rapid. In ten years, by 1931,
George might expect to be working in the main office in
New York City. Campbell Hardware & Supply offered no
such inducements, and Oscar Campbell had his eye open
for a buyer. It was a good business, he had made money at
it, but he wanted to be able to sell it for a top price. Now
he had two young fellows, local talent, interested in buying,
and with two fellows interested, he decided to make believe
he was not eager to sell. It was the right moment to go on
a long trip . . .

When Oscar Campbell and his wife returned from
California they had George and Lucy and the children over
for Sunday night supper. The children were in excellent
health: Andrew was brown from the sun, had grown nearly
an inch taller since June, and had won the boys' ladder
tournament at the tennis club. He was no longer the little
boy who loved to tap his grandfather's cheek to make smoke
rings. Fay, the granddaughter, had changed even more. She
was excited and apprehensive about going away for the final two years of school; a boarding school would be so different from High. They were good-looking children. Lucy
had brought them up well. After supper Oscar's wife and
Lucy and Fay did the dishes, and the three males sat on
the side porch behind the mosquito netting.

"Grandpa, why don't you put in wire screens instead of
this netting stuff?" said the boy.

"Because your grandmother doesn't like the look of
wire screens, not on this porch. She wishes this porch was in
the front of the house and the front porch was back here."

"Why?"

"Well, I guess for show."

"Women have funny ideas," said the boy.

"Sometimes," said the old man.

"When I have a house I'm going to have a porch all the way around, full of swings and chairs and things. Upstairs, too. I'm going to have all sleeping porches."

"Do you expect to sleep outdoors all year round?" said the old man.

"Sure. That's healthy. Then you jump out of bed in the morning and go inside to a nice warm room. When I get rich I'm going to have my breakfast brought to my room every morning. In the winter I'll have waffles and maple syrup, or else some mornings I'll have fried scrapple and apple sauce with a lot of cinnamon. And every morning I'm going to have a glass of orange juice as big as a glass of milk. Every morning. Do you know the McMillans, Grandpa? The new people? They all have a glass of orange juice every morning. They just moved here from East Orange, New Jersey."

"Maybe that's why they drink so much orange juice."

"Oh, Grandpa, quit your kidding."

"I know some people live in Coaldale, but they don't eat coal for breakfast. Do you know how much a dozen oranges cost?"

"No, how much?"

"I think around forty-eight cents a dozen, somewhere around there. Do the people in Chestnut Hill eat chestnuts for breakfast?"

"Oh, Grandpa. Just because I said the McMillans came from East Orange . . . We live in Lyons, but we don't eat lions. Do you get it?"

The old man laughed. "All right, boy. Go help your mother and grandmother. I want to talk to your father private."

The boy left, and his grandfather said, "He's growing awful fast, George."

"Like a weed, but he's on the go from morning till night."

"Well, just as long as he gets his rest."

"He gets plenty of that. Is he hard to get out of bed in the morning? My Lord. When he said that about jumping out of bed into a warm room. That was a good one. Lucy and I have to call him three times to get him out of bed in time for school. I wish I could sleep like that."

"You did, when you were his age."

"Well, I'm not his age now."

"Why can't you sleep? What keeps you awake?" The old man was pleased that the conversation had taken this turn, but he knew he had to be carefully casual.

George hesitated only slightly. "Oh, I guess I oughtn't to drink coffee at night."

"I guess not. I'm only allowed the one cup a day, at breakfast. Some people it affects but others can drink it just before going to bed and they go right to sleep." The old man was voluble to cover up his inquisitorial moment, but he was not sure he was deceiving George.

"I used to love to sleep," said George. "I don't know just when I stopped getting enough. I guess when I was away at college. I guess that was it. Not that we had to get up any earlier at Spring Valley than I was accustomed to at home, but at home, in high school, you and Mom made me go to bed earlier. That was it. At Spring Valley, living at the Phi Gam house, we used to play pool till ten o'clock, then we were supposed to put the cover on the pool table and turn out the lights. That was a house rule, and the year I was king of Phi Gam I had to enforce those house rules. But then we'd sit up and talk till one, two, three o'clock in the morning, and that wouldn't leave us much time to sleep. You know, I never thought of that before."

"No, you never told me Spring Valley was like that."

"A lot of things you don't tell your father at that age. All ages, I guess. Andrew doesn't tell me much. He asks a lot of questions, but telling me things is a different story."

"Well, before you know it he'll be off to Spring Valley, and new friends and a whole new life, and you won't see much of him. That's the way it was with you. I'll never forget that year you didn't want to come home for Christmas. I thought your mother would cry her eyes out."

"For a girl in Detroit, Michigan. Adeline Halliday, Joe Halliday from Phi Gam's sister. Married a missionary and lives in China. I don't even know her married name. But you know, Pop, if you hadn't put your foot down and made me come home that Christmas, chances are Adeline and I would have gotten married. And who knows, I might have studied for the ministry. She had a lot of influence over me, Adeline."

"You weren't cut out to be a preacher."

"I certainly wasn't, but Adeline could have made me into one."

"You're much better off with Lucy. Lucy's the perfect wife for you, George."

"Yes. Yes, I know she is." George Campbell did not enlarge upon his compliment to his wife, and apparently wished to say no more about her. "I'm going to send Andrew to Mercersburg for his last two years of high."

"Well, I guess that's no more than fair. You're sending Fay."

"No, that isn't why. We don't expect Fay to go to college. But I'm not sure Andrew is going to Spring Valley. He wants to go to some place bigger, and if I get transferred to the main office we'll be living somewhere around New York and around there they never heard of Spring

Valley. This McMillan, the new man in town, he went to Williams and I think he's been telling Andrew they have good tennis teams at Williams."

"Williams. Where would that be?"

"In Massachusetts. Oh, it's one of the best, but it's going to cost a lot more money than Spring Valley. But of course if I get transferred to the main office that'll mean more money for me."

"Well, you know there's nothing I'd rather spend money on than my grandchildren, so don't let that bother you. But on the other hand, you're not going to send Andrew to a college because it has a good tennis team."

"I might."

"You would?"

"Well, I might. I don't say I would, but if people know who you are, say you're a good tennis player, they like to do business with you."

"Well, you're his father, so I'll leave that up to you. But I couldn't tell you the name of any famous tennis player."

"That's because you don't read the sports pages."

"A waste of time."

"Not any more, Pop. In business nowadays you have to be up on things. The last time I was in New York the company took us all to a ball game and then we had a big dinner at the Commodore Hotel and they had entertainment."

"That's nothing new."

"A cowboy spinning a rope and making jokes about the government and Europe and all that? If you didn't read the papers you didn't get the point of half of his jokes."

"The sport page?"

"Well, I guess not the sport page so much, but things are changing in the business world, Pop. You ought to see the difference in bookkeeping. We don't even make out our own timesheets any more. We send the time cards to the main office and they send back the paychecks, all made out."

"I know. I've cashed some of them at the store."

"Efficiency."

"I don't call it efficiency to send a boy to college to learn to play tennis. I call it just the opposite. But your grandfather had the same doubts when I sent you to Spring Valley. 'How is that going to help him sell dynamite to the mines?' he said. And he was right. You're not selling dynamite to the mines. You're making stockings for some Jews in New York City."

"As long as they treat me right I don't care what they are. Jews or Christians."

"Oh, I have nothing against Jews. Some of them are fine people. But I wish you were going to stay around here, George. You have your roots here and your children belong here, not in some little town near New York City, where they won't know anybody and nobody will take any interest in them."

"Pop, there's nothing for them in Lyons, or for me. We're too dependent on the mines. The collieries close down for a couple of weeks, and if it wasn't for the stocking factory and the tap-and-reamer, where would a lot of our people be? I have eighty-five women and girls at my factory, and the tap-and-reamer has maybe sixty men working there. When the collieries shut down, or there's a strike, you know how it can be in Lyons. Seventy-five hundred a year isn't the most I hope to earn, but that's as high as I'll ever go if I stay here."

"Well, I'd like to see you get the promotion, but it'll be lonesome around here when you and the children and Lucy all move away," said Oscar Campbell.

"I've *got* to get away!" said his son. He spoke with such startling vehemence that the old man expected more to follow, but George Campbell had said all he was going to say. The old man avoided looking at him.

"Oh, I want to show you some picture postcards we collected on our trip. There's a whole stack of them in on the mantel, George. To the right of the clock, I believe I left them." He wanted to give his son a chance to recover from his outburst. Whatever was to be learned, he did not want to learn it until his son was ready to talk, for he was now convinced that George's trouble was not a piddling one. He was sure, too, that George's story would be a long one. "Bring along a couple of cigars, on your way back, George," said the old man.

"Just one for you, Pop. I'd rather have a cigarette if you don't mind."

"Well, then never mind the cigars. Just bring me the postcards. On the right of the clock, a whole stack of them in an elastic band."

"On the right of the clock."

"Yes, and while you're getting them I think I'll take a walk down to the end of the yard. My bladder's giving me a little trouble."

"Maybe you ought to let Sam Merritt have a look at you."

"Oh, it's just those six days and nights on the train. No exercise. If I don't get in a mile every day my whole system pays the penalty. I'll be back to regular after I'm home a few days."

The young and old spent the remainder of the evening over the postcards. "I didn't know California was so full of Catholics," said Lucy.

"I didn't notice that particularly. Did you, Mom?" said Oscar Campbell.

"We didn't see any," said Mrs. Oscar Campbell.

"But all these missions, and all those towns beginning with Santa," said Lucy.

"Oh, those are from the Spanish days. The Catholics don't cut much ice any more," said Oscar Campbell.

"Then why don't they change the names of the places?" said Lucy. "All those Catholic names would keep me from going there."

"Oh, you're always harping on Catholics," said George Campbell.

"Well, those missions are very pretty, *there*," said Mrs. Oscar Campbell. "They don't belong here, but out there they fit into the landscape and the climate. Here they'd look out of place, of course."

"I hope it doesn't get much hotter there than it does here sometimes," said George Campbell. "We're getting dog days again."

"Out there you don't seem to mind it as much. I guess it's dryer," said Oscar Campbell. "A lot of their land is real desert."

"That's where the twenty-mule team comes from," said Andrew. "They have to carry their own water. They have a cart as big as the borough sprinkler or else they'd die of thirst."

"I'd love to go there sometime," said Fay. "I'd never come home. I hate cold weather."

"You can play tennis all the year round out there. That's why they're such good players. McLoughlin. The cannonball serve. Whack! But Tilden is better, I have to admit that. But if I lived in California I'll bet you I could beat anybody around here, even Mr. McMillan," said Andrew.

"Stop boasting," said Lucy Campbell.

"It's not boasting, Mother. And anyway you wouldn't

mind living in California. You said you'd rather live any place but here. I heard you."

"Well, I don't take that back," said Lucy.

The younger Campbells went home at nine o'clock. "I wonder what's going on there," said Mrs. Oscar Campbell.

"Why?" said her husband.

"There's something pestering Lucy. I don't suppose George let on what it was?"

"No."

"There's something pestering her, you must have noticed it. I had the feeling all last winter that there was something, but I didn't want to say anything. Not so much with Lucy as George, here every Sunday. But tonight Lucy was the one. And Fay, too."

"Fay? I didn't notice anything with Fay."

"You didn't happen to be looking in her direction when she said that about California and never coming home. She meant it. They're *all* acting different, except Andrew. I'm going to see what I can find out."

"Now don't you go asking a lot of questions or you'll start people wondering."

"Now don't you tell me what to do, Oscar. I know how to go about a thing like this."

"The best way is to not go about anything. You do no good stirring up a lot of curiosity."

"That's your way, not my way. Your way didn't find anything out all winter from George."

"My way didn't make a mess of things, either, and that's what you're liable to do. Don't start asking people a lot of questions." When he spoke in that tone, which was seldom, she did not oppose him.

They got through the dog days, and Fay went away to her boarding school, and it was Indian summer, and Andrew was picked for the high school varsity football team, and the older men changed to their long underwear. But George Campbell did not resume his Sunday visits to his parents' house. The father and son encountered each other on the street and George said, "You have a nice window for hunting season."

"Yes, we received a lot of compliments."

"Who did it?"

"Young Bob Frankenheimer."

"Well, he did a better window than I ever did."

"He used some of your ideas," said the old man. The Campbells had always been proud of their window displays at the hunting season and Christmas. Even after he went to work for the stocking factory George Campbell continued to do the hunting season window.

"No, mostly his own. I forgot all about it this year. Why didn't you remind me?"

"I thought you'd be too busy so I gave the job to young Bob."

"No, if you'd have reminded me I'd have done it, but I guess it's a good idea to break in a new man. And he deserves a lot of credit. How many guns did you sell so far?"

"Well, I know we sold five pump guns."

"Five? Boy, that's the most pump guns you ever sold."

"Three or four double-barrelleds. The single-barrelled are very slow this year. I think we only sold one. They all come in wanting to see the pump guns."

"You know why. The dummies young Frankenheimer had in the window, they all had pump guns. What else did you sell a lot of?"

"Three rifles. The high-powered Savages."

"Three in one year! We didn't use to sell that many .22's, or just about."

"No, there was some years we didn't sell a one of the high-powered rifles."

"You know why, Pop? That's young Frankenheimer again. He got hold of those deer heads. Where did he get them from?"

"I don't know."

"I used to have to get the loan of the moose head from the Moose Lodge, and they always made me have a card in the window, courtesy Loyal Order of Moose. I notice you didn't have the head in this year."

"No. Bob said he was going to do without those cards this year. No advertising cards, no courtesy-of. Just try to make it look like a hunting camp, as much as possible."

"Yes, I always used to have a lot of revolvers and axes and compasses and all that stuff lying there. His was more like a real camp. I recognized those dummies. They came from the clothing stores. But I always had to have a little card saying courtesy of the stores."

"Well, I know what he did there. He told Forrest Brown and Herb Hoffmann that any time they wanted to borrow guns from us they could, and we wouldn't insist on a card."

"I should have thought of that," said George Campbell. "Well, tell Bob for me, he did a darn good window."

"He'll appreciate that. You know it looks like I'm going to sell to him."

"I know."

"But he can't call it Frankenheimer's as long as I'm alive."

"Well, he'd be foolish if he did. You've been in business a long time."

"Yes, but his folks say he ought to be allowed to change the name. They don't want the town thinking you're a silent partner. They don't have anything against you personally, but they want Bob to start out with his name on the sign-board."

"Is that what's holding up the deal?"

"No. What's holding up the deal is that I don't know what I'll do if I retire."

"Well, you've been talking about it a good many years, Pop."

"Yes, but when the time comes you don't want to. It'd be different if I could hand the business down to you and Andrew."

"Now, Pop, don't try to sell me that bill of goods. I'm leaving Lyons as soon as I get my promotion."

"Why do you and Lucy want to leave here in such a hurry?"

"What made you say Lucy?"

"Well, it's Lucy as much as you, isn't it?"

"It's both of us . . . I gotta go to the bank before it closes. So long, Pop."

It was a poor excuse; the bank was open until three, and it was only half past two. In the evening Oscar Campbell said to his wife, "I saw George today."

"Our George?"

"Sure."

"Did he have anything to say for himself?"

"No, why should he? You mean because he hasn't been here?"

"Well—he certainly stayed away all fall," she said.

"Well, is that against the law? If he doesn't want to come, he doesn't want to come. He will when he wants to. But I think he misses working at the store, down deep. He noticed young Frankenheimer's window."

"Is that what you talked about?"

"Mostly."

"Listen to me, Oscar. Don't you start trying to get him

to stay here in town. As soon as he gets his promotion, I want you to do everything you can to help him get settled wherever he's going to live. If it looks like he needs money, you give it to him. And I pray it'll be soon."

"Woman, did you go and do the opposite of what I told you? You've been poking your nose into things that don't concern you."

"If you don't tell me about my own son, I'm going to have to find out for myself."

"I don't know anything *to* tell you."

"Then you better start finding out."

"What?"

"You won't get anything out of me. And don't accuse me of poking my nose into anything. What I found out was told to me without me asking anybody anything."

"About George? What?"

"No sir, not another word out of me. Find out for yourself."

It was now his turn to be respectful of her anger, as she had been of his. In the forty years of their marriage they had learned such things; how far one could go in taunting the other; when to keep silent; when to yield. In twenty years neither had struck a blow at the other, and in those years of controlled anger long silences had taken the place of the slaps and punches that were not uncommon among the couples of their acquaintance.

This long silence lasted for three or four days and nights. Except for nights spent in travel and just before and after her two accouchements he had always slept in the same bed with his wife, and he continued to do so now; but their sleep was not restful, and in the mornings they were tired and peevish. Oscar Campbell was the greater sufferer because he was a home man, never one to discuss family matters with outsiders; with no friend so intimate that he could make inquiries about his son, he could not now suddenly begin asking questions, to find out for himself.

Then on the fourth day of their silence he came home from the store and she was crying. She was sitting in the upstairs bay window and she called down to him. "Oscar?"

"What?"

She came downstairs and said, "What are we going to do?"

He was hanging up his coat and hat in the closet under the stairs. "About what?"

"You didn't hear about her? Stella Valuski?"

"Who is she? Paul's wife?"

"Daughter. She hung herself."

"Well, I'm sorry for Paul. He's a good honest man."

"Sorry for Paul? Be sorry for us. For George, and *his* wife and children."

"Are you saying there was something between George and this girl?"

"Oh, God. Do I have to tell you that too?" she said.

"George carrying on with a hunkie girl?"

"She's one of the girls at the stocking factory."

"Oh, God. I thought he was above that." He reached for his hat and coat.

"Where are you going?"

"To find George."

"Wait. Don't go there. Leave them alone. They don't want us interfering now. Wait till he comes here and then talk to him, but for God's sake let him and Lucy be by themselves now."

Oscar Campbell put his coat and hat back on the hooks. "I don't know what to do," he said—having made one decision. "Let's go out in the kitchen and sit."

They did so, and he got a cigar but did not light it.

"The last thing I hoped my son would ever do. Monkey around with one of those factory girls. Did she leave a note? Tell me about it. How did you know she was his strumpet? Where did you hear she hung herself?"

"If you'll let me tell you, I will. You can always hear gossip in this town if you're willing to listen."

"I want to know, without you going into a long story, who connected up George and this Valuski girl? Do you have any proof?"

"Nobody connected them up. They didn't have to."

"You mean it's only guessing on your part? Nobody told you she was his woman, but you know it anyhow?"

"Some things you don't have to have the proof for. Some things you know."

"Good God, woman. You must be losing your senses." He now put a match to his cigar. "It's all in your imagination."

"Stella Valuski hanging in the boiler-room at Acme, that's not my imagination."

"Where do you connect that up with our George?"

"You'll see, you'll see."

"Not a single person said anything about George and this girl. Is that right?"

"Yes, that's right. But they've been saying things about Stella Valuski. Where does she get the money for stylish clothes, on a factory girl's pay."

"There's a thousand other men in this town besides George."

"There's a thousand other men, but how many of them were worried sick about something for over a year, and now one of the girls in his factory hangs herself. You're trying to look in the other direction because you want to."

"To think that I was on the verge of going over to George's house, accusing him of the Lord knows what all.

And all based on your crazy guessing. And you his mother, worst of all."

"You know there's something bad, only you don't want to admit it. Well, we'll see who's right."

They buried the Valuski girl in unconsecrated ground, without a requiem Mass. The town heard that the autopsy showed her not to have been pregnant, a discovery which added to the mystery of her death; but in the kindlier view she became a flighty girl, who smoked cigarettes during lunch hour, who wore silk stockings in the factory, although she could have bought cotton for wholesale; a flighty girl who laughed off the casual indecent invitations of the men in the factory; a flighty girl who may have been wild, and being wild, a bit crazy. In the town the final judgment was that she *was* crazy, and among the Polish element an effort was being made to obtain permission to have her buried in the Catholic cemetery. Among the other, non-Polish townspeople she had ceased to exist, ceased to have had an existence. In a month she was forgotten. No one wanted to remember a crazy young girl who had tied a rope around her neck and hanged herself from a steam pipe in the boiler-room of the stocking factory.

And yet in those first weeks Oscar Campbell could not bear to see his son, and he was relieved that George had not resumed the Sunday afternoon visits of the previous winter. No more was said between Oscar Campbell and his wife about the Valuski girl; indeed, they avoided mentioning George's name. She had been wrong, wrong, wrong about George, but Oscar Campbell was not a man to rub it in. She loved George as much as he did, and forty years of marriage taught you when it was best to keep still. You did not taunt a woman who had made such a shamefully wrong judgment of her only living son.

It was Lucy's family's turn to have her and George

and the children for Thanksgiving dinner. At the store the clerks were working nights unpacking the Christmas goods. At church the women were busy in the basement selecting and wrapping clothing for distribution among the poor. The miners were pleased that they would be getting some over-time. The holiday season, everyone said, would be on you before you knew it.

And so it was, with its comings and goings and greet-ings and good wishes. And then it was over, the bells and the carolling and the three days of snow, and Fay gone back to her boarding school; and the January winds came down the valley and even on the brightest days no one was on the streets who could remain indoors. The paint sales-men were around, getting orders for spring, and the men who sold gardening tools and fishing tackle. There was skating in the Glen, and a tramp was found frozen to death under the railway freight platform. Farmers reported deer in their barnyards, and you could have venison and pheas-ant if you did not ask too many questions. There was a lot of pneumonia around, but not as much other sickness. Peo-ple somehow took better care of themselves in the winter-time. They bundled up warm and they ate good substantial meals. And they slept better.

THE SUN ROOM

The butler who came to the door was English and correct, down to the black four-in-hand tie and gold watch-chain. "Good afternoon, sir," he said. "Mr. and Mrs. Barlow?"

"Yes, we're expected," said Henry Barlow.

"Yes, if you'll just follow me, please," said the butler.

"We're a little early," said Barlow. "We thought we'd have more trouble finding it."

"Very good, sir. If you'll just have a seat in here," said the butler, and bowed in the direction of a small room. Henry and Wilma Barlow sat down and the butler disappeared.

"A butler, yet," said Wilma Barlow.

"Yes," said her husband. "His name is Kenneth Kingsley. Didn't you recognize him?"

"Why should I?" said Wilma Barlow.

"Well, maybe you shouldn't. He's been in seventy-five thousand pictures."

"You know him?" said Wilma.

"No, but I recognized him," said Henry. "He never got to be a Leo G. Carroll or Arthur Treacher, but he worked."

"I guess I didn't notice butlers," said Wilma.

"That's why he worked. He wasn't supposed to be noticed. But he probably went right on year after year, making his fifteen or twenty thousand—and saving it. He probably owns some nice real estate."

"Then why would he be doing this?" said Wilma.

"Because Eileen asked him to, and because he couldn't say no to the money she offered him. How the hell should I know?"

"Funny he didn't recognize you," said Wilma.

"Why should he? He probably never saw me before, and believe me, movie butlers were never impressed by movie writers. I just happen to have an extraordinarily good memory for bit players and dress extras. I should have had a job at Central Casting."

"It worked out better this way," said Wilma.

"The pay was better this way," said Henry.

The butler returned. "Miss Elliott will see you in the sun room," he said. "This way, please." He now led the Barlows through corridors on varying levels and finally to a large, glass-inclosed porch. "Mr. and Mrs. Barlow," he announced.

"Of course, Henry and Wilma, you're so prompt," said Eileen Elliott. She gave them both hands and presented her cheek to be kissed. "What delicious intoxicant can I offer you?"

"A very light Scotch and water for me," said Henry Barlow.

"Oh—a vodka and tonic, if I may," said his wife.

"You may anything," said Eileen. "Let me bartend, I want to." She thus dismissed the butler, who bowed and vanished.

"Didn't he used to work for someone else?" said Henry.

"Some very old families named Fox and Goldwyn and Warner. Also the Paramounts and the Metros, and no doubt the Republics. His name is Kenneth Kingsley, and he's an old dear. I've been in any number of pictures with him. He won't come if I'm having a director friend or one of the old-time stars. It would embarrass him and embarrass them. But a writer is different. Didn't you recognize him, Henry?"

"Well, as a matter of fact, I did," said Henry.

"It was nice of you not to let on. He comes because he adores me. He doesn't need the money, the old fox. He owns a motel out in the Valley. He's as queer as a jaybird, but there was always a certain type of pansy that watched every single penny. If you were nice to them, you could always go to them for money, if they had any reason to think you'd pay them back. Kenneth lent me the money for my first abortion, that's how long I've known him. I couldn't go to the father, because he was a star and I was very much on the make for him, and he'd have dropped me like the proverbial hotcake. He did anyway, the stupid bastard. Why stupid? Because I kept him out of a picture when *I* became a star. And there you have the story of my first three years in Hollywood. I'm dying to know why you wanted to come to see me."

"I said in my note, I wanted Wilma to meet some of the real people," said Henry.

"That's subject to several interpretations," said Eileen. "I'm sure you know, Mrs. Barlow, that your husband and I had a torrid romance lasting two months."

"Three," said Henry.

"Was it three?" said Eileen.

"Yes, I knew," said Wilma.

"We were both very young, of course," said Eileen. "I was practically a virgin, having had only one abortion. And Henry was an innocent young writer who tried to lay every girl in Hollywood, and very nearly succeeded."

"I missed out on a few," said Henry.

"But we always stayed friends," said Eileen. "You could, you know. More than once, as I've gotten older, I've found myself admiring some middle-aged man and had to remind myself that there was a *time*, there was a *time*. We were so full of sex, and so active, that it left no impression whatever. Anyway, you'd go out of your mind re-living all your old romances. If a man wasn't an out-and-out fairy, and you weren't too tired, you'd say, 'All right, come on over,' and who cared whether you went to bed with him or didn't? If you didn't, he was almost sure to say you did. And if he was a big enough star, *you'd* say you did. I was married four times. I had a son by my first marriage, and he's over forty. He and his father live in my home town back in Ohio. Both married, have families of their own, and the only time I ever hear from them is when some friends of theirs wants to visit a studio. My son was brought up by his stepmother, and she and his father have managed to convince him that I abandoned him for a career in pictures. The fact is that my first husband used to beat hell out of me whenever he got tight, and I did run off to Detroit with a band leader. My husband kidnaped my son and left me with the band leader, and I came to Hollywood with him. I could sing a little, but what made the difference was that I had a shape. A lot of girls had shapes, but that was during the flat-chested look, the tight bras. Not for me. I had them, and I showed them, and boy did the women hate me! But not the younger ones, and they were the ones that were going to the movies. In droves. The men liked me, and the young girls liked me, and I got paid ten thousand dollars a week. Five for the right one, and five for the left one."

"Oh, the face helped a little," said Henry.

"Thank you, dear," said Eileen. "You see why we had

our mad romance, lasting three months? He remembered that I had a face too."

"It was a nice face. It had real sweetness," said Wilma.

"You must have been one of the younger ones," said Eileen.

"Well, not much younger."

"Did you belong to one of my fan clubs?"

"No. But I was a fan," said Wilma.

"You never wrote me for a picture, enclosing twenty-five cents to cover cost of mailing?"

"No, I didn't."

"The odd thing was that girls used to send me pictures of themselves, to prove that their bust development was as good as mine. Needless to say, I never rushed into a producer's office with one of those pictures. Right into the wastebasket they went. And the better the bosom the quicker the wastebasket. What kind of a damn fool did they think I was? Ten thousand a week. I wonder what ever happened to it—as if I didn't know."

"Are you broke, Eileen?"

"Make me an offer. No, I'm not broke. I have a nice income. It's no ten thousand a week, and it isn't as much as they pay the President of the United States. But Honest Andy Anderson—do you remember Honest Andy?"

"Sure. The agent," said Henry Barlow.

"Honest Andy made me go into the studio retirement plan, and it's paying off now. Also, I go back every summer and do the straw hat circuit for ten weeks, and that pays very well. And once a year I go to Vegas for two or three weeks. I'm not filthy rich any more, but I live nicely and I pay the taxes on this house. One of these days this house is going to make a lot of money for Eileen."

"It's beautiful, isn't it?" said Wilma.

"And I'd sell it at the drop of a hat, but I have to get my price. Would you like to buy it?"

"No, we're settled in Vermont," said Henry Barlow. "Wilma writes, too."

"Not really. I'm a teacher," said Wilma.

"She teaches creative writing, and so do I."

"And your books make money, don't they?"

"They do pretty well. We don't need much," said Henry. "I never got up to ten thousand a week."

"But you got two," said Eileen.

"No, fifteen hundred was my top. But I used to get as much as twenty-five for an original, and a six-weeks' guarantee for working on the screen play. For a man of limited talent I did all right."

"Are you and Wilma going to write about me?"

"I hadn't thought of it," said Henry.

"Oh, what a liar," said Eileen. "Every writer that comes here goes away and writes something."

"Some of them have, there's no doubt about that," said Henry. "That's why I wanted Wilma to see for herself. But we're not going to write about you, so relax."

"Well, why *don't* you write about me? What you don't know, I'd be willing to tell you. And I wouldn't sue."

"I don't think people care that much any more," said Henry.

"Maybe you're right. There's practically nothing left to the imagination on the screen, so why should they want to read about it? Do you remember when we used to look at dirty movies at parties?"

"Yes," said Henry.

"I used to love them, frankly. But I saw a feature picture a week ago, two big present-day stars that got a half a million apiece for this picture. In our day they'd have got fifty dollars for just about the same thing. I mean, what they left out of this picture the other night I'm sure is on film. Because what they started, they had to finish, you know? We did one on 16-millimetre at Malibu. The works. It was practically suicidal to let that get around. The studio sent for me and I went to J.B.'s office and of course denied everything. The only trouble was, he had a print right there, and it was a dirty movie all right. So I broke down and admitted it, and waited for the ax to fall. The morals clause. Well, it was the morals clause that saved us. How the hell were they going to tell the American public that they were firing four of their biggest stars for being in a dirty movie?"

"What finally happened?" said Wilma.

"They got rid of one girl that they were going to get rid of anyway. They simply didn't renew her option. The rest of us got away with it, although it cost the studio a fortune to buy up the prints and the negative. I understand they're planning a remake of the picture."

"Oh, come on," said Henry.

"Oh, not with the original cast," said Eileen. "Actually, when I was in England shortly after the war I met a duke, who told me he had seen me in a film that not many people had seen. It was the dirty movie we made in Malibu, and the studio had shown it to a select few V.I.P.'s in New York. 'How was my makeup?' I said. I wasn't going to take any crap from him, duke or no duke."

"How *was* your makeup?" said Henry.

" 'Outdoor Number 7,' I think I used," said Eileen. "Not taking any crap from you either, Henry."

"I'd forgotten Outdoor Number 7," said Henry. "There's so much I don't remember about picture business. But I did remember Kenneth Kingsley. Why did you have him here today? Not to impress us."

"Not exactly impress you, but yes, to impress you if you were going to be condescending."

"We're not in the least condescending, and anyway, how could we be? You're still Eileen Elliott."

"You can bet your sweet ass I am. Anybody that thinks they can tear that up and thereby make me into nobody—they soon find out. They can laugh at the scrapbooks and the souvenirs, but I have them. Some little jerk pretends to pity me, with my memories and my mementoes, but I can always say, 'And how many kings did you know, mister? How many presidents did *you* have *your* picture taken with?' And I'm not talking about college presidents. I'm talking about presidents of the United States. Coolidge, Hoover, F.D.R., Truman. Eisenhower, when he was a general but not when he was President. By that time I wasn't getting top billing, a hundred percent of the main title. I had some pushy little woman come and ask me to donate some money to some charity she was heading up out here. She said Mr. Eisenhower was honorary chairman and gave a strong hint that the major contributors would get an autographed picture. 'You mean *this* Eisenhower?' I said, and showed her a picture of Eisenhower and me during the war. Any autograph I don't have, I don't want. How many Lyndon B. Johnsons will you trade me for my Wallace Reid?"

"Wasn't he a little before your time?" said Henry.

"In his heyday, he was, but the poor junkie, I asked him for one anyway," said Eileen. "Tell me about your job, teaching at the University of Vermont."

"Anticlimax department," said Henry. "Well, it isn't the University of Vermont. It's a smaller college called Whitefield, privately endowed."

"That sounds rich," said Eileen. "Or are you here to put the bite on me?"

"We didn't have that in mind, but I'm sure a large donation would be gratefully accepted," said Henry. "No, it was started a few years ago by the Whitefield Foundation, mostly the heirs of the late Benjamin Whitefield and his brothers. They were in the textile business, and the Foundation started with twenty million but became worth a lot more. We have about five hundred and fifty students. Small, by present-day standards, but our entrance requirements are fairly high."

"You mean they don't let in any Jews, Henry?"

"I wouldn't say that. No restrictions based on race, creed, color, or national origin. Only on the individual's potential."

"I was wondering," said Eileen. "And Wilma teaches creative writing there?"

"I give a course in creative writing," said Wilma. "I don't like to say I *teach* creative writing."

"I guess if it's creative, it can't be taught. Is that what you mean?" said Eileen.

"Exactly," said Wilma.

"They wanted me to give a course in acting at one of the local universities. I thought about it. One week I'd lecture on bust development, which was such a great help in my career. The next week I'd demonstrate the technique of the casting couch, which was also a great help in my career. I could spend several weeks on that. Then of course the art of reading contracts. The man that came to see me about it was inclined to think I wasn't taking the thing seriously enough, but I assured him that I was. If he was talking about acting for the movies, it was a damned sight more important to know how to handle producers than it was to give out with the pear-shaped tones. But he wasn't talking about movies. He was talking about *films*. He called them films, and I called them movies. I never learned to call them anything else, try as I might. Always movies. Never films. And never, never cinema. Those people that call them films, and cinema, they're the kind of people that talk about the art of some little broad that makes a sexy mouth and every man, woman and child in the world gets the message. That's art? Who's kidding who? The poor little broad begins to believe it, and the next thing you know she's late on the set, and fighting with the director, and coming out against poverty. She ought to be in favor of poverty. If it wasn't for poverty, who'd want to go to the movies? They used to say it was Mr. DeMille that popularized the bathtub. Nuts. It was the ordinary set dressers with ordinary tubs, not Mr. DeMille and a pool full of slaves. You might as well say Mr. DeMille popularized slavery. People who worked for him wouldn't give you an argument there. But I don't know that that was more true of Mr. DeMille than a lot of other directors. Give anybody too much authority and you have a slave-driver. I'll bet you can be a son of a bitch with your pupils, Henry."

"Students. I don't call them pupils," said Henry.

"*I* don't call them *students*," said Wilma.

"Well, you have to have some name for them," said Henry.

"Enrollees," said Wilma. "Time-passers. Excuse-makers."

"You gather she hates her work," said Henry.

"I really do," said Wilma. "But I'd never say so in Vermont."

"All work is disgusting," said Eileen. "Ten thousand dollars a week doesn't make it any the less so. But it's nicer to be paid ten thousand a week for doing something you don't like than fifty dollars a week for something you don't like. My idea of heaven was getting full salary for doing nothing. The home office used to call from New York and raise hell. 'When is that Eileen Elliott picture starting shooting?' And the supervisor, as we used to call them then, would say we were having script trouble. It almost never occurred to them to have the script ready ahead of time. And as far as I was concerned, it didn't make any difference. I was getting paid anyway. *Then.* When I began to slip a little and wasn't getting ten thousand fifty-two weeks a year, I began to feel the pinch. Only the pinch didn't come from the big producers. The pinch, or the feel, came from elderly English actors. I could always tell when I was beginning to slip. That was when the English actors began to make up for lost time. They wanted to be able to put it in their memoirs that they had put it in me. And I may say that one or two of them did. They weren't much different from the cloak-and-suiters, but they could make adultery seem high class. Adultery! What a word! What a fancy word! I don't think I ever stopped to think that I was committing adultery. The only time I was conscious of committing adultery was when I ran away with the band leader, and I wouldn't have thought of it then if my husband's lawyer hadn't reminded me. Legal language can take the fun out of anything. I'm still not sure what sodomy is. Is that when—well, never mind. I'd rather not know."

"Oh, you know, Eileen," said Henry.

"As a matter of fact I do," said Eileen. "But I have to stop and think. When I was a girl back in Ohio I thought it was one thing, and then I found out it was something else. Sodom and gonorrhea was the way I associated them. Does this remind you two of your conversations back on the old campus?"

"You should hear the conversations back at the old campus," said Wilma. "Those kids all know what sodomy is."

"Well, I should hope so," said Eileen. "They're supposed to be educated, aren't they? My son is a college graduate, and if he doesn't know what sodomy is, I wasted a lot of money. Oh, yes, I was allowed to pay for his education. His stepmother and his father didn't want me to abandon him *that* much. They thought it would embarrass me to come to his graduation, but I wouldn't have been a bit embarrassed. I could have brought the bills along to show I had a right to be there. Do I sound bitter? I don't mean to. If you want to know the truth, I'm confused. I haven't been able to figure out why you came to see me. Why did you?"

"No angle, no hidden motive," said Henry. "As I said before, I wanted Wilma to meet one of the real ones."

"The real what, Henry?" said Eileen. "The old-time movie star, waiting for the phone to ring? The broken-down glamor girl with a pansy actor for a butler? You have plenty of curiosity, or you wouldn't be here. So I'm entitled to some curiosity of my own. You say no angle, no hidden motive, but that's only what you *say*. Wilma, did you think it would be sort of fun to make love to me, or me to make love to you? That would be a good one to tell back in Vermont."

"I never thought of it," said Wilma. "Why did you?"

"Why did I? Because I always think that women that dress like you, those black blouses and tan cotton skirts, and those ballet slippers—they all look as if they spent a lot of time with the head-shrinker."

"I was in analysis," said Wilma.

"I was sure of it," said Eileen.

"Weren't you ever?"

"Of course I was, when it was the thing to do," said Eileen. "You either bought a Picasso, or you were psychoanalyzed. Sometimes both, but if you were making two thousand a week you did at least one. You *had* to. You were nothing if you didn't. I didn't know anything about art, so

I settled for the couch. Well, now, I want to tell you, I
went to that guy for two months, and what I didn't know
about him at the end of two months simply wasn't worth
knowing. But then we all got interested in the Hollywood
Canteen, war work. Have your picture taken washing dishes
and doing the Lambeth Walk with the service men. Loddy
da-da loddy da, loddy da-da loddy da. I was just getting
around to the interesting part, how I fell in love with the
iceman's horse when I was ten years old, and I had to tell
the head-shrinker that they wanted me in the war effort.
So he slapped me with a nice fat bill for professional services and I guess no one will ever know about me and the
iceman's horse. I go back to the day when there *were* ice-
men and they had *horses*. I cover a lot of American history.
My father-in-law had a Haynes. Do you know what a
Haynes is? Or was? It was a big car that people bought in
Ohio. My father-in-law had one that he drove us to church
in on Sunday. My husband washed it every Saturday so it'd
be nice and shiny on Sunday, for church, and it was just
about the only God damn time we ever got a ride in the
God damn thing. My father-in-law was the meanest old
bastard in the State of Ohio, and the only thing he ever
loved was that Haynes car. He'd sit there on the side porch
and watch my husband washing it. 'Don't get any water on
the upholstery. It's bad for the leather,' he used to say. He
was Presbyterian and I was brought up Lutheran, on top
of which my father worked with his hands, and wore over-
alls. No trade, no steady job. Anything he could get. He
played the cornet in the town band, and that was his way
of getting free beer. Hard liquor he liked better, but beer
was free for the men in the band. You see I had a musical
background, what with my father and the man I ran away
with. He also preferred hard liquor. In fact I never saw him
take a glass of beer, not even to be sociable. But he was

sweet. He really was. When he got tired of me and wanted
to get rid of me for good and all, he did his best to pass
me on to his tenor sax player, the highest paid man in the
band. That's what I call sweet, don't you? If you don't, you
don't know musicians."

"You were never much of a drinker, were you?" said
Henry.

"Not then, and not now," said Eileen. "You'll see me
put away a few scoops of vodka, or gin, or tequila as the
day wears on. But it has very little effect on me except it
makes me drunk. No, I wouldn't call myself a drinker. What
the hell do you mean, I was never much of a drinker? I
started hitting it when I was in my early twenties, and the
only reason I'm alive now is because I never stopped. Some
women, most women put on weight when they drink. It just
so happens that I don't. We all have a different chemistry,
and I don't put on weight. I may get disagreeable, or I may
wake up and wonder who that is I'm in bed with, but I
don't get fat. I weigh now just about what I weighed when
they were paying me ten thousand a week, a hundred and
twenty-eight pounds. I never diet, I never go on the wagon,
I've never given up smoking, I don't take any exercise. They
ask me what the secret is, and I tell them. Do what you
please, and keep out of jail. I said that in an interview once
and the studio had a hemorrhage. I was denounced from
every pulpit, a man made a speech in Congress, and the
women's clubs threatened to march on Hollywood. I was
going to be boycotted all over the world. But it had the
opposite effect. The grosses on my next picture were bigger
than ever and it was a lousy picture, but my little announcement of my personal philosophy saved it. It isn't the
public that cares whether a movie actress is having an affair
with a married man. It's the studios. They have some idea
that if they put the pressure on you morally, they can keep

putting it on when option time comes up. As far as morals
are concerned, I'd still be making ten thousand a week. But
the one thing you can't beat is youth. Not age. Youth. Youth
is another word for new faces. Not new figures. New faces.
We all know how a woman is constructed, and why. But
about once a year a new face comes along, and there's no
way to fight it, and I can prove it. I could go out now and
round up a dozen car-hops with figures as good as mine
ever was. But I can't turn them into movie stars by just
photographing their shapes. The kisser, the face is what
counts. But they get hired for their shapes, the way I was.
Why? Because they're hired by men, and men see the shape
first. I've come to the conclusion that every studio should
have a committee of Lesbians and fairies to pass judgment
on the new talent, because they actually look at the faces.
The only trouble with my idea is that the committee would
be hiring all their little chums, and the queers go for some
very strange mutts. The queers only go for people they can
feel sorry for, feel superior to, masculine, feminine, or neu-
ter. They can spot a weakness right away, and that makes
them feel good. If you want to be popular with the queers,
you'd better have a weakness. In my case, they liked me
because they could make jokes about my shape, which they
turned into a kind of a weakness. Fortunately, the normals
didn't see it that way, and I became a big star. But I stayed
popular with the queers because my morals were bad and
I was always getting into trouble with the studio. You want
to know, if I was popular with the queers, were the queers
popular with me? Well, if you mean was I one of them—
no. Did I play around with them? Maybe a little around
the edges. A little. You go through phases in this town, and
I guess I went through most of them, but my queer phase
didn't last very long. A jealous man I can understand, but
a jealous Lez is sort of ridiculous, as if she were carrying

the masculine bit too far. At least that was what happened
to me. I had a Lesbian girl friend—and believe me, when
they take over, they take over. She ran my house for me,
and gave me financial advice, and got rid of some of the
people that were sponging off of me. She was the same as
a husband, except of course in the one department. And
that was the whole trouble. I like an occasional man—a
habit I got into when I was about fifteen and was never
able to break myself of. Nature invented the male sex, and
I refused to deprive myself of them. But my girl friend was
very jealous and she finally said it was either them or her.
Out of politeness I gave the matter some serious thought,
like counting up to two, and came to my decision. She
spread some nice stories about me, but how can you top
the fact that for about a year she was living here with me
and everybody knew it? How do you ruin a reputation
like mine?"

"I never thought of your reputation as being especially
notorious," said Henry.

"You take that back or I'll sue you!" said Eileen. "The
only thing I was never accused of was murder, and I came
pretty close to that. Not that I ever killed anybody, but I
was on a party where a silly broad shot herself and everybody there was questioned. Do you remember Dolly
Duval?"

"I do, but I don't think Wilma would," said Henry.

"She was—let's face it—one of those dime-a-dozen not-
quite stars that had to shoot herself to get publicity. That
may sound heartless and cruel, but it's the truth, and she'd
have shot someone else, anyone else, if it would have done
her any good. There've always been girls in picture business
that would do anything for the publicity, but no matter
what they'd do, the newspaper people wouldn't print it.
Dolly was one of those. Another thing about them, they're

always publicly in love with guys that aren't in love with *them*. They're what used to be called professional torch-carriers. Some guys would go to bed with them, thinking it was a one-night stand, and a couple of days later she'd be on the phone to the columnists saying that this was it, this was the only guy she ever loved, et cetera. Meanwhile the poor chump was in blissful ignorance of any romance, and the first thing he'd know about it was if one of the columnists called up to check. 'What's this about you and Dolly Duval?' they'd say. 'Dolly *Duval*?' he'd say. 'Come on, pal, you've got to do better than that.' But you'd be surprised at some of the big names that she got mixed up with. It finally got so that guys avoided her like Typhoid Mary, although she wasn't bad-looking and she had a nice little shape. She'd come to press parties alone, uninvited, and usually she'd go home with one of those correspondents for the foreign papers, the great free-loaders of all time. Even they were wise to her, but she was buying the dinner, also providing the other entertainment, and some of those creeps were hard to please."

"She was pretty. I remember her," said Henry.

"How well?" said his wife.

"Not *that* well," he said.

"No, Henry wasn't a star, and he was never one of those free-loaders. Dolly Duval wouldn't have gone for Henry—lucky for Henry," said Eileen. "This one night, there was a big opening, a world pre-meer at the Cathay Circle. Searchlights. Radio interviews. All the hired limousines. The bleacher seats for the fans. This one Dolly was invited to, because she had a small part in the picture, and her studio saw to it that she had an escort. He was a creature named Rod Something. Rod was a New York actor who usually played gangster parts, and hung around the Vine Street Derby. Rod Rainsford, he called himself, and he also had a part in the picture. Well, what do you know but he damn near stole the picture, and on the way out they were all talking about a new Cagney, a new Tracy, a new George Raft. And nobody was talking about Dolly Duval. Nobody. In those days everybody went to the Troc after every opening, and Dolly had reserved a table to make sure she got one. But when she and Rainsford arrived at the Troc he was whisked away by the studio big shots, and given a seat at their table between the head of the studio and Marlene Dietrich. I've never known anyone for being there at the right time like Marlene, and of course she was a bigger star than Dolly Duval. And where was Dolly? Dolly was at her own table, with a couple of bit players. In fact, one of them was Kenneth Kingsley, my temporary butler today. Kenneth looked well in tails, and he never got drunk, but he wasn't the lion of the hour. The lion of the hour was at the big shots' table with Marlene. After the Troc there was a party at somebody's house in Beverly, to which all the cast were invited, and Dolly couldn't keep away. She arrived alone, having sent Kenneth and the other person home, and she then proceeded to drink it up. Up to that time she'd stayed sober and on her good conduct, but she had a few things to say to Mr. Rainsford and she was going to get them off her pretty little chest."

"I remember. It was a pretty little chest," said Henry.

"It seems to me you remember too well," said Wilma.

"Go on with your story, Eileen," said Henry.

"Try and stop me," said Eileen. "One thing about our Mr. Rainsford, some of the people he hung out with at the Vine Street Derby were genuine hoods, and one of them was called Al Cummings. He was a gambler, a bookmaker, mixed up in the rackets, and altogether a very bad boy. I imagine Rainsford owed him money, because Rainsford was the kind of guy that owed everybody money, including hoods. It was easier to borrow money from hoods, because they charged high interest, and they liked to have people like Rainsford in hock to them. Cummings always carried a large bankroll, and he always carried a medium-large revolver. They were sitting there when Dolly arrived, and she had a big double bourbon and went over and sat beside Cummings. 'Hello, Al,' she said. 'What are you doing wasting your time with this small-time hambo? I thought you had better taste.' Something like that. She was really burned up at Rainsford, and began making passes at Cummings, in the course of which she came across his revolver. 'What's this?' she said, and took it out of his pocket. 'Give it back,' said Cummings. 'No, let her play with it,' said Rainsford. 'Let her blow her silly brains out.' And now I want to tell you something, because I was there, and only about from here to you away from them. That girl put the revolver to her ear and did just that. She pulled the trigger and blew her brains out. Ugh. Ugh. The whole half of her head, the whole left side was scattered all over. The yelling and screaming that went on, and at the same time the laughing, because the room was half full of people that didn't realize what had happened."

"She just put the gun to her head and shot herself?" said Henry. "Because Rainsford told her to? That seems incredible. Why would she want to do that?"

"There you start going into something that there's no real answer to," said Eileen. "How did she get into that state of mind? It goes 'way back, I guess. She didn't do it because Rainsford told her to, but that's exactly why she did it. Rainsford was nothing to her, but who was? It came out later that Al Cummings was one of her many boy friends, but only one of many, and never anything big. The procession of guys that had to go to the district attorney's office was a parade of actors and agents and cheating hus-

bands and chiselers and wolves and some nice guys that
happened to be in Dolly's little book. Girls like Dolly Duval
always keep a little book. Never fail. Alongside of some
guy she's been sleeping with will be the name of the Japa-
nese gardener or her foot doctor, but they're all in there.
It would save a lot of trouble if they said who was what. I
used to keep a diary, pretty hot stuff it was, too. But that
was separate from the names of my foot doctor and the
man that cleaned out my swimming-pool. Although one fellow that repaired my pool filter was in both. *There's* one I
haven't thought of in years. He was absolutely beautiful, so
consequently I was always having something the matter
with my filter. You can take that any way you like, I don't
care. You can knock California and I won't object, but
where else could you call up the swimming-pool repairman
at ten o'clock in the morning and at half past ten a beautiful
blond Swede arrives to spend the day? He was an Olympic
swimmer, or maybe a diver. Olympic I'm sure of. He's
probably nothing now, but I suddenly remember him with
great tenderness. He took my mind off Dolly Duval, and
Kenneth Kingsley was never able to do that."

"Probably not," said Henry.

"They're always saying we had too much sex in Hollywood. But on the contrary, we never had enough," said
Eileen.

"Do you mean on the screen, or off?" said Henry.

"Either. Both. On the screen the best they could do was
once in a while in a mob scene they could sneak in a long
shot of a man and a woman going at it, but that was always
in some Roman orgy and you couldn't even be sure unless
you had them rerun the footage. Even then you couldn't be
positive. What they should have done back in the Thirties
was show a couple of big stars going to bed together, the
whole works. Close-ups. Two-shots. They'd have got a lot

better acting, I can tell you, because it was all some of them
could do. As a matter of fact they did get some good acting
out of some of the men, who had no more desire to kiss a
woman than I have to kiss a pig. Some of those male stars
were so queer they'd come off the set after a love scene
and be shaking with fright, afraid they were going to murder the girl. One of them told me once, 'Eileen, it isn't
against *you* personally. It's because I can't stand to have a
woman touch me.' But the director knew that, and he made
us do our love scenes over and over again because he'd get
one scene that he could print, and the actor would look
like the most passionate lover in the history of the world.
Why? Because real hate and real love are hard to tell apart.
Dolly Duval loved herself and hated herself, which is why
she blew her silly brains out. Or why any of us would. I
never reached that stage, but I may yet. I'd hate to think
my feelings weren't as deep as Dolly Duval's, but maybe
that's why I'm still alive. If I were more sensitive, and more
passionate, I could give myself a pretty good argument for
knocking myself off. But I was never really passionate. Hot,
but not passionate. You're my witness, Henry. Was I really
passionate?"

"I thought you were, but maybe you were only hot,"
said Henry.

"I'm passionate, and not very hot," said Wilma.

"I was hoping you'd say that," said Eileen. "It was the
way I had you figured. Henry wouldn't know the difference."

"There isn't any difference," said Henry. "You two just
like to think there is."

"That's how much you know," said Eileen. "You've
stayed married to a passionate woman, whereas the hot
number that *I* was lasted a couple of months. Henry, you
were more passionate than hot."

"That's not the way I remember it," he said. "But I could argue either way."

"And would, just for the sake of argument," said his wife. "The blond that came to fix your swimming pool—what was he?"

"Passionate," said Eileen.

"Because he'd stay all day?" said Henry.

"You're damn right," said Eileen.

"That wasn't passion, that was vitality, or virility," said Henry.

"You're damn right it was," said Eileen. "He could have stayed a week. Wilma, it was a pity you and he never got together, two passionate people."

"I probably would have taken an instant dislike to him. He probably looked too Nordic for me," said Wilma.

"He looked Nordic, all right. But you wouldn't have been the first Jewess I knew to go for a Nazi," said Eileen.

"Oh, he *was* a Nazi?" said Wilma.

"I don't know what the hell he was. Nordic, Nazi. When you say one you mean both, don't you?" said Eileen.

"Pretty much, I guess," said Wilma.

"Wilma could never have fallen in love with a Nazi," said Henry.

"Who said anything about love?" said Eileen.

"Have you got a picture of him anywhere around?" said Wilma.

"A *picture* of him?" said Eileen. "The man that took care of my swimming pool?"

"It wasn't all he took care of," said Henry.

"Why, I haven't even got a picture of *you*," said Eileen.

"That doesn't surprise me," said Henry. "But I was never Olympic, at anything."

"Don't be *too* modest, Henry. I don't want to have to boast about you in front of your own wife."

"Go right ahead. I might learn something," said Wilma.

"So might I," said Henry.

"Yes, we all might," said Eileen. "I could put myself into some kind of a trance and remember every man I ever had any kind of relations with. And sometimes I do. But I'm probably wrong half the time. Did you ever have your appendix out, Henry?"

"Yes, when I was in high school."

"Did I?" said Eileen.

"Well, I don't remember," said Henry.

"You see?" said Eileen.

"Yes, but we weren't looking for appendectomy scars," said Henry.

"I remember some," said Eileen. "My swimming pool man had a beaut."

"Yes, I guess there's not much about him you don't remember," said Henry.

"You sound just a trifle jealous. How nice," said Eileen. "But don't be. He was all body. Tight blond curls. Big shoulders. No hips. Wilma, you really should have seen him. I'd have lent him to you. I was never stingy about that, and you must have had a nice little figure."

"Would that have made any difference?" said Wilma. "He sounds like he'd have done anything you told him to."

"That was more or less true," said Eileen. "More or less."

"I wish you wouldn't try to get my wife all steamed up about some stud horse you had an affair with thirty years ago," said Henry. "It isn't good for her."

"I've really taken a tremendous dislike to this man," said Wilma. "In fact, I'm not even sure he ever existed. Are you sure he isn't all your fantasies rolled into one?"

"I never had much time for fantasies, Wilma," said Eileen. "I was much too busy with action."

"A fantasy doesn't take long. You can have one while the action is going on," said Wilma.

"You shouldn't have said that," said Eileen. "I know it, and you know it, but Henry won't like it."

"Men have fantasies," said Henry.

"We know that too, but you don't like us to have them," said Eileen.

"How old-fashioned can you get?" said Henry. "Wilma has been having an affair with Benjamin Disraeli since she was in high school."

"George Arliss must have spoiled it for her," said Eileen. "If there was ever a stuffed shirt it was George Arliss. I used to see him on the Warner lot. But I don't know who I'd have gone for in history. I can't think of anybody. Daniel Boone. He was a sort of Tarzan if you stop to think of it. Lafayette might have been fun, but I don't know much about him. Franklin—wasn't he quite a chaser?"

"I loved Disraeli, and he would have loved me," said Wilma.

"She really means that, too," said Henry.

"Arliss. That's all he is to me," said Eileen.

"Do you ever talk about anything but sex?" said Wilma.

"I guess I never get very far off the subject," said Eileen. "Maybe you'd rather talk about politics, but how long would it be before you got back on sex? Was Hitler a fairy, or wasn't he? He always seemed to be having a good time with that doll he was shacked up with but out here everybody insisted he was a queen. On the other hand, if it was so bad for him to be a fag, what about Marcel Proust?"

"Marcel *Proust?*" said Wilma.

"Yes, I heard of him, Wilma."

"You don't speak of him in the same breath," said Wilma.

"I do. I just did. I'm sitting right here with the first

person that ever tried to get me to read Marcel Proust. Your husband."

"You tried to make her read Proust?" said Wilma.

"Yes, I tried," said Henry.

"And what's more, I did," said Eileen.

"And how did you like him?" said Wilma.

"Don't look down your schnoz at me, pal," said Eileen. "I didn't like him, but I didn't say so till after I read him. I know plenty of people that said they liked him, and hadn't read as much of him as I did. Don't look down your schnoz at me. Did you read him in French?"

"No, did you?"

"No, but I made ten thousand dollars a week. What did your father do for a living?"

"My father? He was in the textile business. And he *didn't* make ten thousand a week," said Wilma.

"Why not? That's what he was in it for, wasn't he? He wasn't in it because he liked the feel of cotton ginghams, was he? Or maybe he liked the feel of a size-ten model. Maybe we'd better get back on sex."

"Were we ever off it?" said Wilma.

"Not while I'm around," said Eileen. "I'm trying to be a good hostess, because I know damn well you and Henry came to see a sex freak. You came to the right place, all right. Now I think it's time you went back to Vermont and talked about Marcel Proust. But don't forget how I got my introduction to him. In a triple-size bed, with Mr. Henry Barlow, who wanted to improve my mind."

"We're being asked to leave, Henry," said Wilma.

"Oh, Henry can stay if he wants to," said Eileen.

"You bitch," said Wilma.

SOUND VIEW

Mrs. Gray's house was the one at the end of Sound View Lane, the last house and the only one that had a fence. The fence started at the very edge of the cliff and went back inland about a hundred yards. Mrs. Gray owned everything west of her fence—her house, her garage, her swimming pool, her tennis court, her grounds—and the fence discouraged picnickers and trippers who could instantly see that Mrs. Gray's property had the best view anywhere in the neighborhood. It had, as a matter of fact, a 270° sweep, to the east, to the south, to the west. Back of her house, to the north, there was nothing much to see, only some rocky land between Mrs. Gray's property and the top of the bluff. Mrs. Gray owned that land, too, but it was practically worthless. Her taxes on it were only twenty-five dollars a year, and as long as she owned Sound View nobody would want to spend a fortune to develop land that offered nothing but a good look at the backside of the Gray estate. Some day she would die, and the whole place would go; her cottage, her beautiful lawn, her gardens. She knew, because they had made her fabulous offers, what they wanted to do with her property. And they were quite right; they merely wanted to do what her husband's grandfather had

said could be done when he bought the land and built the
cottage. "Worst comes to worst we can always turn it into
a hotel," he had said, although he knew that it was not
likely that that would happen in his lifetime.

It had not happened in his lifetime, and his son had
made so much more money that Sound View seemed like a
conspicuous example of Yankee thrift. The Grays could
have had any marble palace in Newport, people said, but
there they stayed, right there at Sound View. Electricity
came in and kerosene went out, the stable was torn down
and the garage put up, the surface of the lawn-tennis
court was changed from grass to clay to a fast-drying com-
position, and the first tiled swimming pool was rebuilt, en-
larged, and remade of cement. But the acreage remained
the same as it had been at the original purchase, and the
cottage was probably the last remaining monument to its
architect's plans, with a continuous porch on three sides,
bay windows at both ends of the southern elevation, a
widow's walk, a porte-cochere. And even the garage was as
much like the stable as a garage can be like a stable, and
as harmonious with the cottage. It had one whimsical detail
that was different: instead of the gilded horse on the weath-
ervane, there was a miniature electric coupé, a touch suggested by the second of the rich Grays, who made more
money than his father had made but also had more fun
while making it.

First there was S. C. Gray, the Samuel Charles who
founded the fortune, and who said they could always turn
Sound View into a hotel. His pessimism was well grounded
in his early failures, which included the loss of an inherited
Vermont farm; the collapse of a hay, feed and grain partnership; and the bankruptcy of a planing mill. He was fond
of saying that he never made a nickel till he left his home
state and stopped working with his hands. As long as he

did not have to touch what he sold, he was all right. He went to New York City and got a job as night clerk in a hotel and took a course in accounting that he mastered so quickly and so well that he was soon teaching the course. He bought the hotel, sold it at a good profit, and became a loan shark. By the time he was thirty years old he was a successful speculator in rail stocks, and at forty he was a director of a dozen small railways in New York, New Jersey, and Pennsylvania. He sent his son to Yale and his three daughters to Miss Hume's Select Academy on East Twenty-first Street, and he built Sound View because his son Charles Samuel had a friend whose family owned a summer place nearby. Two of the daughters married well and the third—in the language of the day—stayed home and kept house for her father and mother.

Charles Samuel Gray had acquired all the bad habits at New Haven, and his intimate friends shared his liking for cards, liquor, actresses, and expensive clothes. His father (and the other fathers) were hopeful that the young men would settle down on or about their twenty-fifth birthdays, but such was not to be the case. They went to work, they married, but the regeneration did not occur. They were living in a period when most of the great capitalists were men of large appetites, who were mistrustful of their sober contemporaries. Young Charley Gray possessed not only native intelligence, but he had the self-confidence of a man who enjoyed his excesses, and the combination attracted the admiring attention of the older men. He was, moreover, a large man; taller than most, broad-shouldered, and the beneficiary of generations of plain living and fortunate breeding. He was beautifully homely, with a hard, loud voice that seemed to proclaim a forthright spirit. To see him and to hear him was to discount the importance of his dissipations, as though they were tiny peccadillos in a big and vigorous and guileless man. He made money for himself and his friends, and he did it, as one friend said, while eating a dozen oysters on the half shell. He married the rather mousy sister of a Yale classmate, but no one expected him to submit to domestication—nor did he do so. It was fairly common knowledge that he was the father of an illegitimate child who was born a couple of months after the birth of his first son. Charley went to Vienna to see his bastard daughter and her mother, and to settle a hundred thousand dollars on them. He thus behaved according to the best convention of the time, influenced by neither embarrassment nor stinginess, and the older men in the financial community were pleased that their early judgments had been confirmed. Louise Gray's brother stopped speaking to Charley, but Ted Burling was a cautious roué who had not objected when his sister announced her engagement to Charley. He had never objected to anything until the story of the Vienna trip became widely known, whereupon he took a public stand that only made matters worse for his sister.

Louise Gray had a second son by Charley, a fact which was taken to indicate that she accepted—if not condoned— his attitude toward their marriage. But several years passed without further issue, and the theory was abandoned in favor of some guesswork that Louise had had the second child as a token of a reconciliation that did not last. If so, it was an all too apt token: the boy died of diphtheria, and Louise and the surviving son remained permanently at Sound View.

During the years of Sammy Gray's boyhood he became accustomed to a way of life that did not disturb him, since it was the only way he knew. He had a succession of tutors until he was eight years old and from the tutors and the children in the village school he became convinced that he had to be brought up that way because his father and mother were rich; his father, in order to be rich, had to work in an office in New York, and could only come to see him after he had made a lot of money. One boy in the village school had a father who was a traveling salesman and he only saw his father once in a while. Sometimes the boy's father would be away for months at a time. There was another boy whose father worked on the railroad, and that boy's father would be gone for two or three days at a time, but that was not as interesting as a man who would be gone for months at a time. There was a girl in the school whose mother and father were on the stage, and she lived with her aunt and uncle and did not see her mother and father all winter, not even at Christmas. She could have been interesting, but she was a show-off and Sammy did not like her. Sammy did not like many children. The kids who came to the village in the summer were all right, he guessed, but he did not miss them much when they went home, even those he knew best. They were all right when they came to Sound View to swim in the pool or go for a pony ride, but he did not like to go to their houses. Their fathers and mothers, especially their mothers, wanted him to sit and talk instead of having fun. He could always tell, with some of them, that they were going to ask him how his father was and when was he coming up to Sound View, but most of them did not know his father and hardly any of them ever came to Sound View. The ones that did know his father never were the ones that asked about him. The fathers would ask him if he was going to go to Yale, and that was just about the only thing they ever did ask him. But the others would ask him how often his father came to Sound View, and he didn't see that that was any of their business, really. But he had to be polite to them because they were grown-ups.

His father's visits were never very long, and during them Sammy spent little time with him alone. His father would arrive on a Friday, often while Sammy was having his supper. He would hear the crunching sound of the car wheels on the gravel of the driveway as it moved slowly past the breakfast-room. Doors would be opened and closed, but there was never any sound of greeting. His father would come to the breakfast-room, a giant of a man he seemed in that room, with its small-sized table and chairs. "Hello, there, son," his father would say.

"Hello, Father," Sammy would say.

"Use your napkin before you kiss your father," Mrs. Jones would say. Mrs. Jones was always the one to give him his supper on the nights of his father's arrivals; his mother stayed in the sitting-room on those nights.

"How've you been?" his father would say.

"Very well, thank you."

"Are you studying hard?"

"Pretty," the boy would say.

"Doing what your mother tells you?"

"Yes, Father."

"That's good. You must always do what your mother tells you. Well, you finish your supper and then come in and say goodnight."

After supper Mrs. Jones would take him to the sitting room and his father and mother would be there, occupying chairs that were not very close together, and his father would seem like a visitor, like Mr. Parsons the parson, or Dr. Medwick, or Uncle Jim Draper, who was not really his uncle. His real uncle, Uncle Ted Burling, was never there when his father was visiting, but Uncle Ted was always much more at home than the others and he stayed longer, sometimes for two or three weeks.

"He's come in to say goodnight," Mrs. Jones would say.

"Ah, well. Then off to bed?" his father would say.

"Yes, Father. Goodnight. Goodnight, Mother."

"Goodnight, dear." His mother would kiss him.

"Goodnight, boy." His father would bend down to have his cheek kissed.

The next day his father would be gone until supper-time, playing golf at the new club, but he would be back in time to repeat the previous night's visit to the breakfast room. On the Saturday, however, his father had less to say, having asked him about his studying and his obedience to his mother. Sammy would wait for his father to say something new or different, but that only created silence. The next day, Sunday, his father would play golf again and after his golf game he would often have to hurry to catch his late afternoon train back to New York. "Can I go to the station with you, Father?" Sammy would sometimes say.

"Whatever your mother says."

"No, dear, not this time," she would say—every time.

Nearly always, after one of his father's visits, Sammy would be having his supper when Uncle Jim Draper arrived to have supper with his mother. Uncle Jim and his mother would be in the sitting-room when he went in to say goodnight, but it was very different from when his father was there. His mother would be laughing and talking and Uncle Jim would be having just as much fun as she was having. And no wonder. Uncle Jim *was* fun. He always had some kind of joke or riddle. "Sammy," he would say, "what kind of noise annoys an oyster? Hmm? Give up? A noisy noise annoys an oyster. You knew that, didn't you? Sure you did." Uncle Jim was always cheerful, and when he was in the house Sammy's mother was more cheerful too. He played the piano and sang Yale songs, but he also played the harder pieces. When he played them they sounded better than when Sammy's music teacher, Miss

Turnbull, played them. He could move about on the tennis court, too, although he had what he called a corporation, a rather large tummy, and he was a very good swimmer. He had once had a wife of his own, but she died, and now he lived in New London and was a lawyer, but not a rich one. He drove a Ford car with rust stains on the radiator and holes in the isinglass windows of the side curtains. "My tin Elizabeth, the champion puddle-jumper," he called his car. He had a little joke that Sammy took a while to understand: he would point to the pedals of the piano and say, "Clutch, reverse, and brake."

Sunday after Sunday Uncle Jim came for supper, winter and summer, and on most Saturdays he would come for lunch and tennis and a swim, but on the Saturdays he came with other people. He did not shine when there were a lot of other people; he could beat them at tennis, but he was not as funny as when there was no one there but Sammy and his mother. Then, when Sammy was ten or eleven years old, he first began to understand that Uncle Jim was in love with his mother, and that he saved his best jokes and stuff for her. When other people were there Uncle Jim was more like the other people; pleasant, polite. But not a bit funny, really. Company manners. And Sammy's mother had on her company manners with everyone but Uncle Jim. She even treated Uncle Jim differently when there were other people there, and it was hard to believe that on Sunday nights they were the same two people who had been together at lunch on Saturday.

When Sammy had been at St. Bartholomew's a couple of years he had learned enough about life to be troubled by the precise nature of his mother's relationship with Uncle Jim, and as a Third Former he discovered that the same problem had been bothering his Uncle Ted. They were having lunch at a hotel in New York during the Christmas holidays, and Uncle Ted said, "Tell me, Sammy, what's your opinion of Mr. Draper?"

"Uncle Jim Draper?"

"Uncle Jim? You call him that?"

"Ever since I can remember, sure."

"I'll be damned. That mother of yours. Uncle—Jim. Then I guess it's no use asking. You like him."

"Sure. Very much."

"Let me get this straight. You've been calling him Uncle Jim for how long?"

"My whole life, I guess. I never called him anything else."

"Then you've known him all your life, at least that you can remember."

"Sure."

"What would you think if your mother married him?"

"She can't. She isn't divorced."

"But if she got a divorce?"

"If she loved him."

"Do you think she does?"

"Why don't you ask *her*?"

"Don't get flip with me or I won't buy you dessert. Seriously, would you like Jim Draper for a stepfather?"

"I couldn't think of him as a stepfather. I guess that's what he'd be, but I don't know."

"Has your mother ever said anything about marrying him?"

"Honestly, Uncle Ted, I wish you wouldn't ask me these questions."

"All right. But you wouldn't mind if your mother married him?"

"No, I wouldn't mind."

"It might make a difference in your financial welfare,

your future. Kid, have you any idea how much money your father is worth?"

"I know it's a lot. Several million."

"I'll say it's several. He could give you a million and your mother a million, and never miss it. But you're old enough now to face a few facts. Your mother is entitled to more than one or two million, and so are you. You shouldn't let your father get away with that, giving her a million or two."

"How would I have anything to do with that?"

"Ah, an interesting question, my boy. If your mother does decide to get a divorce and marry Jim Draper, that's going to cost you both a hell of a lot of money. She'll just about have to take what your father feels like giving her. And it won't be much, I can tell you that. One man your father could never put up with is Jim Draper. Rightly or wrongly, your father thinks Jim kept him out of a senior society at Yale."

"Too bad."

"You can say that now, but wait till you get to New Haven. And after you graduate. Especially after you graduate. Your father is convinced that the only thing that kept him out of a certain bank was not making a senior society at Yale. And he blames Jim Draper for that. And if you want my opinion, he's dead right on all counts."

"I thought you didn't like my father, Uncle Ted."

"That's neither here nor there. Matter of fact, I don't like him, and that's why I don't want to see him short-change your mother. But he will if she's planning to marry Jim Draper, as I hear she is. Five or six more years you'll be twenty-one. Which would you rather have? One million or ten?"

"Ten."

"I was afraid you were going to say it didn't matter."

"Well, it doesn't if my mother wants to marry Uncle Jim. I don't need ten million."

"Oh, hell, you're hopeless. What are you planning to be when you get out of college?"

"Be?"

"Be, or do?"

"I'd like to go to Oxford."

"Why?"

"Well, Uncle Jim said a year at Oxford would be good for me."

"Then I hope Uncle Jim has the money to pay for it. But I doubt that very much. Very much indeed. Why Oxford?"

"Because he said I ought to take as much time as I can before I decide what to do."

"What are you smiling at?"

"He said to be like you, Uncle Ted. Take forever. He didn't mean it as a slam."

"The hell he didn't. But I care precious little what opinion he has of me. In his eyes I'm a loafer. But in my eyes he's a perennial undergraduate, the kind that shot their bolt at Yale and never got started again. I could name a half a dozen from my class alone."

"Did Uncle Jim keep you out of a senior society?"

"He couldn't. I got the one I wanted, and it's not the one he belonged to. We've never been impressed by fellows like Jim Draper."

"Then why didn't my father join yours?"

"Well—let's just say that his father didn't go to Yale."

"I may not go there either."

"Where else would you go?"

"I don't know. Maybe some smaller place."

"Oh, no. You mustn't do that, Sammy. A lot of boys

from your school go to Harvard, but a good percentage go
to Yale. No, Yale is the place for you. You know your father's given them quite a bit of money, and you wouldn't
want to see that go to waste. He was never sore at Yale,
only at one senior society, and one member of that."

"I don't know. I have three more years to decide."

"But meanwhile, you better think about Jim Draper
and your mother—and all that money. I'm quite serious
about that."

His uncle's concern made his own seem both imperti-
nent and disloyal to his mother, as though his uncle's curiosity were an intrusion. At the same time he was troubled
by the disloyalty of keeping the conversation a secret from
his mother, and before the holiday ended he had it out
with her.

She was in her sewing-room on the second story. "What
are you doing?" he said.

"Knitting a muffler."

"For Uncle Jim?"

"Yes, why?"

"Are you thinking of marrying him?"

"Good heavens." She unclipped her pince-nez and
looked at him. "Then that's what's been on your mind. I
thought it was a girl. Sit down. Smoke a cigarette if you
like."

He confined his report of the conversation as much as
possible to its financial aspects, and she did not interrupt
him.

"Finished?" she said.

"Yes."

"Oh, dear. What a tangled web we weave, et cetera.
But I don't know how I could have told you this before."
Unconsciously she began to wind the yarn about her fore-
finger, and she looked out at the choppy waters of the

Sound. "You always knew you had a little brother," she said. "But you never knew that you had a half sister. Yes, your father had a love affair with an actress, an Austrian woman, and they had a child. A daughter. I was madly in love with your father, Sammy. A lot of women were, and probably still are. I was so much in love with him that I forgave him, or thought I did. But it isn't easy to forgive a thing like that, not when there's a child and so many people know about it. Your father went abroad to see the mother and the child, and he took care of them financially. But when your little brother died I found that I hadn't really forgiven your father. If I hadn't still been in love with him I could have forgiven him, but I was in love with him and I stayed in love with him for a long time. I left him, that is I came here with you and refused to live with him in New York or go anywhere with him. He offered to give me a divorce, but I refused that. He wouldn't have been giving me a divorce, I would have been giving it to him, and I didn't want to give him anything. I had to punish him, to have my revenge, and my way of getting it was to stay married to him and make it difficult for him to see you. And I certainly did that. Even when he came here to visit us in his own house, he might as well have been a stranger. You never heard me say a word against him, but I took care that I never said anything to you that would make you miss him or want to see him or be grateful to him. And I did something else that I know was sinful, but I did it, which was that I never told him when you were sick. Never told him anything about you that would make him want to come here or be with you. He'd ask me if you missed him, and I'd say no. Yet he kept coming here all those years, in the hope of somehow making you love him. But every time he came here it was the same. He didn't know what to say to you, and you didn't know what to say to him. I know that

that's a terrible thing to do, to deprive a boy of a father, and a father of his son, but I was very careful that no one could ever say that I refused to let him see you. The only thing was, the more you saw of each other, the older you got, the more awkward it was. He was nothing but a visitor to this house, and not one that you looked forward to his visits. And consequently you've known your father all your life, seen him, and he's seen you, but you never learned to love him and he's never learned to understand you. I'm sure he loves you, in his way, but you two have never even been angry with each other. He's never punished you, and he's never been able to reward you. Presents, yes. Lots of presents. But you never cried when you broke anything of his, or lost it. You always knew I'd get you a new one to take its place. I wonder how much of this you've figured out for yourself. Some of it, surely. You've always been a thinking child."

"I guess I knew some of it. I didn't know you were doing it intentionally."

"I was, though. In fact it became second nature to me, to prevent you from ever getting attached to him."

"And you, when did you stop loving him?"

"I have no idea. Do you realize that you never saw your father kiss your mother? I made sure of that, too. You want to know when I fell in love with Uncle Jim Draper. Well, I could say never, and I'd be telling the truth. On the other hand, I loved him before I ever met your father. And he loved me. But then I did meet your father and nothing else, no one else mattered. I can't tell you. I couldn't tell you even if you were older. If I heard someone just say his name, Charley Gray, I'd love that person. Your Uncle Ted used to tease me, say the name over and over again to make me blush. And then to think that the time would come when the sound of his name was like a stone falling in a pond.

Thud. A stone in a pond. That's the way it is now, an un-
mistakable sound of deadness. And he is dead to me. Why?
Because he did it to me. He made it just as impossible for
me to love anyone else as I have for you to love him. I love
Uncle Jim, and I could have been happy with him, but I
fell in love with your father. And there's someone else to
consider before you pass judgment on me, dear. Jim Draper.
Not always the fat little man you've always known. He was
in love with me, then I gave him up for your father and he
married another girl. She died, yes. But he could never
make her believe that he loved anyone but me. The answer
to your question, or your Uncle Ted's question—no. I'm
never going to marry Jim Draper."

"Why not?"

"Because I'd ruin him. He can't bear to think of what
your father did to me. But if I married him I'd be his wife,
and it'd be his wife that Charley Gray had done those
things to. I wouldn't like to see Uncle Jim turn into a hater.
He can't hate Charley Gray as long as I'm Charley Gray's
wife. This is a lot for a young boy to think about in his
Third Form at school. I hope it isn't too much, but we do
learn some things sometimes before we're quite ready."

"Yes."

"Perhaps I was never ready, for that kind of love. Poor
Jim Draper. And poor me, for that matter."

He took a headful of thoughts back to school with him
that year, and they were disturbing thoughts. He found,
for instance, that he did not like Uncle Jim Draper as much
as before, but he liked his father a little better. He knew
that his mother had tried to be completely fair, but in trying
to be so fair she had been too fair, with the result that his
father came out of their conversation a man who had been
punished too much, too long. Uncle Jim, on the other hand,
began to seem ineffectual, unmanly. His mother had not

intended Sammy to have these thoughts, but then she herself had not come out of the conversation unchanged. He
understood her better, but she would never again be the
one person in the world who was above criticism. She had
revealed herself to be a human being, with some of the very
faults that she had always cautioned him against. She could
hate, she could be vindictive, she could be vacillating, she
could be insincere, and she could be weakly susceptible to
the charm of a man like his father and ungenerous to a
man like Uncle Jim Draper, who loved her. And throughout
the creation of her self-portrait she was unconscious of the
revelation that she was a strong and determined woman.
Until then he had never thought of her as either determined
or strong, but only as his quiet, gentle mother. He could
see, too, that there was some resemblance in deviousness
between his mother and his Uncle Ted. It was not much of
a resemblance, but it was there, and it was finally the most
disturbing thought of all. He would go on loving her, the
different her, but with his eyes open.

There was a three-hole golf course at St. Bartholomew's, and during the next term Sammy abandoned tennis
for golf, so that when his father came to Sound View on his
first visit of that summer, Sammy invited himself to join
his father. "I thought tennis was your game," said his father.
"Not that I don't want you to come along."

"I took some golf lessons this spring," said Sammy.

"Well, fine. We have a foursome, but you come along
and show us how it's done."

Sammy whiffed the first tee drive, but his second try
was long and straight, almost as long as his father's.
"Charley, where've you been hiding this boy? You've got
another Francis Ouimet," said one of his father's friends.
During the remainder of the match Sammy was longer off
the tee than anyone but his father, and his medal score

was a 91, the second best score of the five. His father had
an 84. At dinner that evening Charley Gray said to Louise,
"Would it be all right if Sammy spends next weekend with
me? I'd like him to play Piping Rock."

"Why, yes, if he'd like to," said Louise. "Where would
he stay? With you?"

"Naturally. Why?"

"Just as long as it's not at the Rainsfords'. I wouldn't
like him to stay there."

"I had no intention of having him stay at the Rainsfords', Louise," said Charley Gray.

"I'm glad to hear *that*," she said.

On his visit to Long Island Sammy kept expecting to
meet the Rainsfords. He and his father stayed at the club
on Friday and Saturday night. "I guess you don't get invited to the coming-out parties," said his father.

"Not yet," said Sammy.

"You will be, soon enough," said his father. They were
having dinner at a roadhouse. "Have you got a girl, a special girl?"

"No."

"Soon enough for that, too. I suppose you've often wondered about your mother and me."

"I used to. Not any more."

"Oh?"

"Mother told me."

"How long ago did she tell you?"

"Last Christmas."

"And what did she tell you?"

"Why you live in New York and we don't. The real
reason."

"The real reason. I won't spar with you, son. You're
referring to the child I had in Vienna?"

"Yes, Father."

"Well, there'd be no use in trying to deny that. You have a half sister and she's just about your age."

"What's she like?"

"I don't know. She's at school in Lausanne. That's Switzerland. I haven't seen her or her mother in the last five years. Her mother got married. Married a musician and the girl took his name. I had to agree not to see them again, the mother or the daughter. So now when I go abroad I have to stay away from Vienna. And Lausanne."

"You *want* to see the girl?"

"Yes, very much. Why not? She's my daughter. Why, did you think I'd be ashamed to see her?"

"Well—I guess so."

"She's as much my daughter as you are my son, Sammy."

"She is not!"

"Oh, yes she is. And she's your half sister, whether you like it or not."

"She is like hell."

"Don't talk to me that way, Sammy. Just when we're beginning to get along with each other, you have to take me the way I am."

"No I don't. And we don't have to get along with each other, either."

"That much is true. We *don't* have to get along with each other. That's been seen to."

"Why don't you say what you mean? You mean Mother has seen to it."

"All right, I'll say it. She has."

"You think more of that bastard in Vienna than you do of me."

"Not more, but not any less. Get *that* straight. And don't call people names. She is a bastard, that's true. But what is a bastard? A bastard, the way you say it, is me, not the child. If you want to call anyone a bastard, or a son of a bitch, call me one. I'll know what to do."

"What?"

"Knock you on the floor. And I would, in case you're thinking of taking that risk."

Sammy got to his feet. "You know what you can do," he said.

"Sit down!" said his father. The boy obeyed slowly, and his father summoned the waiter and got the check. He left a large bill on the salver, got up, and said, "Come on."

Sammy followed his father to his grey Rolls-Royce phaeton. "I'm taking you back to the club. In the morning you can get a train into New York. You can take a taxi from the Long Island to Grand Central. I'll telephone your mother to let her know you're on your way." They continued the ride to the clubhouse in silence. "You know where your room is," said Charley Gray, still behind the steering-wheel.

"I can find it," said Sammy.

"I won't be seeing you in the morning—or any other time, I guess. I'm sorry, son, but I guess we didn't have much to go on. Golf isn't enough. Goodnight."

"Goodnight, Father," said Sammy.

His father looked at him quickly, with his hand on the gear shift. He seemed about to say something, but he faced forward and put the big car in gear and drove away.

In the morning Sammy knocked on his father's door. When there was no answer he carried his suitcase to the club station wagon and was driven to the railway station.

At Sound View his mother was not expecting him. "Why are you home so soon, dear? I thought you were—"

"Mother, I'd rather not talk about it, please, if you don't mind."

"I was afraid there'd be something," said Louise.

"Mother, please," said Sammy. He went to his room and changed his clothes. He put on white ducks and sneakers and an old white shirt and sat at the edge of the cliff, he knew not how long, and watched without interest the racing boats on the Sound. Then his mother came and sat beside him.

"What was it, Sammy?" she said.

"*Please*, Mother," he said.

"When did you last see your father?" she said.

"I don't know. Why? Ten o'clock. Half past ten. Whenever he brought me back to the club."

"Last evening?"

"Of course," he said.

"Sammy, I have some very bad news for you. For both of us."

"Spill it," said Sammy. "I don't care."

"Your father died about an hour ago."

"Died? You mean he's dead?"

"Yes, dear. He was in an automobile accident last night. His car caught fire and he was very badly burned. He died in the hospital a little over an hour ago. They telephoned."

"My father was burned to death?"

"And the other person in the car. A Mrs. Rainsford. I'm afraid it's going to be in all the papers, Sammy."

"What's there to be afraid of? They're dead, aren't they?"

"Sammy? That's not like you, to say a thing like that. It's your father."

"What did you expect me to do? Cry?"

"I don't know. I'll be in my sewing-room if you want to talk to me."

She left him, and knowing that she would be watching him from her sewing-room, he sat stiffly, letting the tears flow without wiping his cheeks, without changing his position. He swore then that he would never let her see him mourn his father, and she never did, that day or any other day. If he shared his tears with her, they would belong to her, and they did not belong to her. They belonged to the man who had wanted to say something to him and had not said it, the man in the big grey Rolls, the bastard who would have knocked him on the floor.

He joined the aviation branch of the Signal Corps in 1917, the year he graduated from Yale, and his mother invited three hundred people to a farewell dance at Sound View. "I hope I'll see you over there," said Jim, no longer Uncle Jim, Draper.

"You? What would you be doing over there?" said Sammy.

"Don't be surprised if you do see me. I have my application in for Y.M.C.A. secretary. A little overage, but I know the right people. And they'll knock off five years because I can play the piano."

"They'd better knock off more than five years," said Sammy. "How about that corporation of yours?"

"I'm in training. This is my second highball in over a month and my last till they accept me."

"I can just see you, Jim. All the brave soldier boys gathered around the piano, and you banging away. 'Pack Up Your Troubles in Your Old Kitbag.' "

"Well, I want to do something, and the Red Cross is all filled up," said Jim Draper.

"Stay home and take care of Mother. Or let her take care of you, would be more like it."

"God, you're fresh. I think of the nice, polite boy you used to be, and the scamp you turned out to be. I wanted your mother to send you to Andover, where they'd have taken the guff out of you. But St. Bartholomew's made you just about unbearable. Unbearable. Maybe the army will cut you down to size."

"Then you ought to join the army, to cut you down. You could spare a ton or two."

"I've lost twenty-two pounds."

"Well, it doesn't show," said Sammy.

"Sammy, if I don't get over, and I don't get in the Y.M., you know where you can always reach me. Anything at all I can do for you."

"I know that, Jim. I still don't see why the hell you and Mother don't get married. Nobody knows how long this damn thing's going to last, and you two ought to as they say keep the home fires burning."

"That's what I've been trying to tell her for twenty years, damn near. Maybe if *you* try."

"Oh, I can't convince her of anything. She's a very determined woman."

"Yes, she is. And you haven't really tried to convince her of anything much, have you?"

"Why do you say that?"

"Do I have to draw a diagram? Sammy, I don't want to sound morbid, but men get killed in a war."

"So they do."

"And I don't want to sound gushy either. But you're all she has, you know. She has nobody else, not a soul. All that bitterness with your father, and the quarrel with her brother Ted. She should have let him go to prison. And all these years in this house, seeing fewer and fewer people. There are more people here tonight than have been at Sound View, all told, in the past five years. And you know what I'm leading up to."

"And maybe you ought to lead away from it."

"No. You used to call me Uncle, but I felt more like a

father, and I have some rights and privileges. Age, if nothing else. You must, you've *got* to convince your mother in the next twenty-four hours that you don't hate her. That's what she believes, Sammy. And she doesn't know why. This could be your last chance."

"Well, maybe she's right."

"Why you cold-blooded son of a bitch. Would you like to step outside?"

"Yes. But alone."

"Alone. Alone is right, Sammy. That's what you deserve to be. I feel sorry for a man like you. I really do. I give up."

"Then it's all right for me to go back to my party?" said Sammy.

"As far as I'm concerned, you can go to hell, and I mean that from the heart," said Jim Draper.

For the rest of the night Sammy avoided his mother and danced with a girl named Nancy from Boston. Shortly before three o'clock he took Nancy away from the party to a steam yacht that lay at anchor half a mile off Sound View. The yacht was a detail of the party that was not in Louise's plans but had been chartered by Sammy and three friends for such a contingency, although Nancy was less a contingency than a certainty. In the morning he returned to Sound View for formal breakfast with his mother, at which nothing was said that created a memorable emotion, until he lit his cigarette.

"You had a long talk with Jim, I noticed," said Louise Gray.

"We had quite a long talk. He's going with the Y.M.C.A."

"No, he isn't, Sammy. He's going to marry me."

"Oh, really? You must have had a very busy evening, Mother."

"About as busy as yours, I guess."

"Busier. I'm not planning to get married. He must have swept you off your feet."

"He did. I was wondering how much of it was due to your talk with him."

"Well, I did say he ought to stay home and take care of you, or you take care of him. Keep the home fires burning."

"That wasn't what convinced him, though."

"Oh? What did?"

"That he's all I have in the world."

"That *he's* all you have in the world?"

"Yes."

"Then he must have repeated our entire conversation."

"He did, just about."

"Mother, why do you have to be so indirect about things? If you knew the whole conversation—"

"Because you had a lot to drink last night, and I was hoping you had said things you didn't mean. If you hadn't remembered them, I was planning to tell Jim I'd changed my mind. But you do remember."

"Everything I said."

"And meant everything."

"Yes."

"Then I'm going to marry Jim next month. You expect to be sent overseas by then."

"Unless we've all guessed wrong. Some of us might be sent to Texas, but in any case I won't be anywhere near here, and I have no more leave coming."

"Do you want this house? Your father left it to me, but I can't sell it without your consent."

"No, I don't want it. Do you want to sell it?"

"No. I want to stay here, but I'd move away if you had any objection to Jim's living here."

"I have none if he hasn't."

"Jim will live wherever I want to live. Whatever happy memories I have are associated with this place. When you were little."

"Well, I never expect to live here. After the war—who knows? I might want to live in South Africa. China. Considering that I don't know where I'll be a week from now—but this house is yours, as far as I'm concerned."

"Thank you," she said. "Well, I'm afraid I hear the car in the driveway."

"Yes, you do."

"Kiss me goodbye, Sammy. I am your mother."

"I was going to."

"I'm glad. Goodbye and good luck. Take care of yourself, and write to me when you feel like it."

"I will. And I think you're doing the right thing, marrying Jim Draper. I mean that."

"Thank you, dear."

He hastily shook hands with various servants and got in the car. He did not look back.

He need not have. A week later, in Texas, while instructing a cadet in takeoffs, he went into a ground loop with his two-place biplane. The cadet, who froze at the stick, was killed; Sammy Gray came out of the crackup alive, but with compound fractures of both legs and one arm, a brain concussion, and what were called possible internal injuries. For most of the following year he was in army hospitals, and his mother was always somewhere in the neighborhood. During the entire year she never mentioned Jim Draper, who was with the Y.M.C.A. in England, and wrote her at least once a week.

For Sammy Gray it had been a year that was half tedium, half pain. The army doctors and nurses represented pain, his mother represented the tedium. The tedium was some relief from the pain, but then it would become so overwhelming that he would almost welcome the discomforts of the medical attentions. He would never be any use to the army, but they would not let him go. He suspected them of using him as a guinea pig and he was certain they were binding him in red tape to thwart his mother's efforts to get him out of the army and take him to civilian doctors in Philadelphia and Baltimore. In the end it was Jim Draper's appeal to a former President of the United States—a member of his senior society at Yale—that got him his release from the army. By that time Sammy was ready to accept favors from Jim Draper or anyone else. Anything to get away from the army hospitals, even though the immediate destination was Sound View.

The war was still very much on, but for Sammy it was over, and he would sit on the lawn at Sound View and watch the ships and boats. The crazy, cubistic camouflage of the deep-sea vessels and the sub-chasers kept him from quite forgetting about the war, but he was not only a noncombatant; he was a non-participant. The friends in his squadron who had been sent overseas wrote him letters that were intended to cheer him up, but the letters had no such effect. No matter how they tried they could not keep a slightly patronizing note out of their letters, and the most offensive of all—without meaning to be so—was Jerry Brandon, who had shot down his five Germans and was thus a qualified ace. "If I had been as good a flyer as you," he wrote, "they would have made me an instructor & sent you over here." The worst part of that was that it was exactly true, but meanwhile the Sunday rotogravure sections printed Jerry's picture, with his D.S.C.—the medal, not the ribbon—and his Croix de Guerre with four palms, wearing his uniform blouse with the collar open and folded to look like a British tunic; Sam Browne belt, breeches and high laced boots. When Sammy had seen that photograph for the fifth time in various publications, he stopped reading the newspapers.

He was in a Philadelphia hospital on Armistice Day. Buzzell, the great orthopedic surgeon, came into his room and sat down wearily on a white iron chair. He had been operating all morning. "Well, now it's all over, I guess," said Buzzell.

"So it seems," said Sammy.

"Would you like to go out and celebrate?"

"I suppose I will, later. Have I got anything to celebrate?"

"Well—yes and no. Depends on how you look at it. I don't want to operate on you, Gray. The left leg is going to be about three-quarters of an inch shorter than the right. Mind you, I could operate, but I don't want to put you through that for the sake of preventing a slight limp. If I did prevent it. You'll have full use of the leg, but you will have a slight limp. And you mustn't blame the army doctors. They had to do a hurry-up job on you, and it could have been a great deal worse. In fact, you could have lost the leg."

"Is that what they call professional ethics, Doctor?"

"If you mean, am I covering up for the army doctors, no. Bear in mind that I didn't have to say anything at all, but I didn't want you to go through life blaming the Medical Corps. You have the leg, so be thankful for that. And now that the war is over, young man, I suggest that you get yourself something to do. Stop thinking about yourself. You did more than your share, more than most of us, more than a lot of them that got overseas. But if you don't snap out of it this war'll go on forever, as far as you're concerned."

"Thank you. I'm sure that's very good advice."

"I have a good notion to charge you a little extra for that sarcasm. I just operated on a ten-year-old boy that's so much worse off than you are that there's no comparison. Ten years old. How old are you, Gray?"

"Twenty-three."

"Then thank the good Lord for the twenty-two years you had before your accident. And if you want a free lesson in spunk, go down to the children's ward before you leave and ask to see a boy named—I can't think of his last name. But his first name is Bobby. But don't ask him how *his* leg is. I took it off this morning."

"Is there anything I can do for him?"

"Not in your present state. Unless you want to leave a nice fat cheque. I'll see that his family gets it."

"Instead of charging me for the sarcasm?"

The doctor laughed. "There's some hope for you, I guess." He rose. "You can leave here any time you want to. Your mother's staying at the Bellevue, is she not?"

"Yes."

"I'll ring her up when I get to my office."

"How did you know she was in town?"

"Friend of mine that knows her told me she'd most likely be here. Jim Draper, from New London. Classmate of mine at Andover. You know him, I'm sure. At least he seems to know you."

"Oh, sure."

"I hadn't heard from old Jim in twenty years. We were fraternity brothers."

"At Andover?"

"Why, yes. Theta Phi Upsilon. We had fraternities at Andover. Where did you go to school?"

"Little church school called St. Bartholomew's."

"Little church school, huh? Like Groton, another little church school. Putting on the dog in reverse. Well, Gray.

Check out of here, and join the celebration. It'll last all day,
I'm sure of that. And give my best to old Jim Draper if you
see him."

"I'll most certainly see him," said Sammy.

Time stood still at Sound View, or at least it was easy
to take a present moment and match it with one in the distant past, when Sammy could look down from the porch
and see his mother and Jim Draper, in deck chairs on the
lawn, sipping lemonade and engaging in their frequently
interrupted but never really ending conversation. As a taci-
turn boy he had sometimes wondered what they found to
talk about; now, as a man who had become articulate, he
had no curiosity for the substance of their conversation,
but he could wonder what it was that they jointly possessed
that stimulated the durable phenomenon of their dialog.
How could they meet so often and after so many years—
nearly his own lifetime—and be impatient only to resume
their talk? For it was not a companionship of the sort that
was punctuated with silences, such as two men can have.
And yet Sammy knew that when his mother and Jim Draper
talked they were not exchanging mere nervous chatter.
Over the years he had learned that Jim Draper's ability to
make his mother laugh was only a small part of his conversational appeal. He had seen them together for hours at a
stretch during which she had not even smiled. Did they ever
settle anything? Apparently not, or if they did, the matter
was immediately succeeded by something else that required
their diligent conversational exploration. In a vague way he
understood that some of their talks dealt with subjects that
automatically provided continuation. Sometimes Jim would
arrive at Sound View with a volume of verse, a work of reference, that he would open at a marked page as he sat down
with her. Louise Gray was not an educated woman, but she
had an active mind to go with her deviousness and deter-

mination and the other less demanding demonstrations of
the intellect. Jim Draper, on the other hand, was a brain.
He had not made much money as a lawyer, but he exercised
his mind for the pleasure of it, as he exercised his body.
Indeed, the physical exercise was not a vacation from the
mental. In his tennis he was an alert tactician, in his swimming he was constantly analytical of the timing of his
breathing and his strokes. In his bachelor existence in New
London he played auction bridge with men who did not
regard it as a pastime. In his piano-playing he was always
giving himself harder pieces to play, pieces that were beyond his technical mastery but that kept his mind at work.
He was a failure in life, recognizably a mediocrity by the
standards of professional accomplishment and of social ad-
vancement. Nevertheless he had made himself indispensable
to one human being, and Sammy Gray, in the final months
of his convalescence at Sound View, was beginning to com-
prehend the importance of that achievement.

He recalled now the years of his father's spaced-out
visits to Sound View, and he saw with a new clarity that his
mother could not have resisted his father without the support of Jim Draper. It was possible that the determination
and the deviousness—and the revenge motif—had been
superintended by the round little man who made her laugh.
Perhaps she had understood it, too, and submitted willingly.
Hadn't she once said that she did not want Jim Draper to
hate his father? Had she meant that she did not want him
to hate Charley Gray even more than he already did? In
any event she had been submissive; she could have ended
the companionship any time she wished. She could even
have ended it by marrying Jim Draper, and she had not
done that. They were a pair, all right. Sammy wondered if
his mother was secretly afraid of Jim Draper—and having
had the thought, he knew he had arrived at a truth. All

these years his mother had been living in a state of terror, and it made no difference whether it was the fear of losing Jim Draper's companionship, fear of losing his love, fear of loneliness without him, or fear of his fat little hands at her throat. It was fear, and it was exciting, and she did not even have to know it was fear.

The discovery was Sammy Gray's first major experience in the observation of human subtleties, the art of finding more than met the eye. And the discovery would not have been made if he had not had that year of tedium and pain. Until his accident he had found expression for his restlessness in mild imitations of his father's collegiate debaucheries, in fast driving on the Boston Post Road, in taking his speedboat outside the channel markers. He had not liked himself while doing these things; they were only temporary release, and they went against his natural disposition, which was for caution and calm. He had not wanted to be an aeronaut, but he had gone along with those of his friends who drove fast cars and raced speedboats, and aviation was as inevitable for him as the cavalry for his friends who played polo at Narragansett and Point Judith. He was not yet ready to admit that his crackup could have been caused by the fear that jabbed at him every time he climbed into an aeroplane. Did the fear not vanish as soon as the plane gained altitude, and had he not been one of the first of his group to solo? His old caution now protected him from the damaging admission of his responsibility for the crackup; he would postpone that until he was far enough away from it and ready for it. For the present he would content himself with the discovery of fear in others, beginning with his mother's subjugation by Jim Draper.

He looked every day for confirmations of his theory, and they were not hard to find. He began by spending more time in their company, and his deluded mother told him

how pleased she was that he was getting over his animosity
for Jim. They lunched together two or three times a week,
and he was encouraged to take part in their perennial conversation. It was no surprise to Sammy to find that their
conversation bored him; it was a course in culture and
current events. Some days it would be the poetry of Elinor
Wylie and Edna St. Vincent Millay; other days Jim would
be holding forth on the activities of a man named Kerensky.
They had welcomed Sammy, but they had become so used
to talking to each other that after a few luncheons they fell
back into their own conversational habits and he was all but
ignored. He, however, was an attentive listener; they both
commented on this quality, never, of course, suspecting that
he did not give a damn about the lady poets or the Bolshe-
viki. But he was fascinated by his mother and Jim Draper,
who were really just the same as *they* had always been but
were fascinating because *he* was not the same. One simple
discovery had made the difference. It was like having a
special pair of glasses to see them with. No. It was like
nothing. It was what it was, and not like something else. It
was simply knowing that his mother was quietly and not
unwillingly terrified of a man who had probably never had
a villainous thought in his life, who was goodness personi-
fied, the enemy of evil, a Kewpie doll with a Phi Beta
Kappa key.

GOOD SAMARITAN

Her first words to her first guests were, "Weren't we lucky with the weather?" Then she added, because it had rained most of the morning, "I mean, think of how it looked at eleven o'clock. You know? Were you caught in any of it?"

"George was," said Carrie Reed. "He was soaked."

"I was literally soaked," said George Reed. "I was playing the fourteenth. About as far from the clubhouse as you can get, and by the time the station wagon got there I was drenched to the skin."

"Then quick have a glass of strong drink," said Mary Wood.

"Oh, I saw to that all right," said George Reed. "I had a hot shower and a slug of bourbon—or a slug of bourbon and a hot shower and another slug of bourbon. Where's our host?"

"I don't know," said Mary Wood. "And I really don't."

The Reeds were winter friends as much as summer friends, and Mary Wood was sorry to cause them embarrassment.

"You mean you don't know where he is? He isn't here, in the house?" said Carrie Reed.

"I haven't seen him since the day before yesterday," said Mary Wood. "He's completely disappeared."

"Leaving no word?" said Carrie Reed.

"Leaving no word with me or anyone, and leaving me with twenty people for lunch. I don't suppose you have any clue, George?"

"Well, the temptation is to make some kind of a joke of it, but this may be serious," said George Reed.

"Don't you want to call off your lunch?" said Carrie.

"I can't, now. I've been expecting him to show up at the last minute, but this *is* the last minute," said Mary.

"How do you want to play it?" said George Reed.

"I'm just going to say he had to go to Washington. With twenty people here, buffet, he won't really be missed," said Mary.

"I think you're being very brave," said Carrie. "You're really worried, though, aren't you?"

"I don't know," said Mary. "I'm damn good and annoyed, I'll say that much. I think it's God damn inconsiderate."

"To say the least," said Carrie. "If that's all it is."

There was a simultaneous arrival of six guests, then four, and then the rest, and in the babel of greetings and drink orders the absence of the host was noted perfunctorily when it was noticed at all. For half the people it was the time for the first nervous drink of the day, and some of the others had not waited so long. The fact that Willoughby Wood had not put in an appearance required no elaborate explanation, and it may even have occurred to one or two guests that he might be nursing a hangover upstairs, hiding until they drank and ate and went away. The only guests who had a deeper concern were Carrie and George Reed, and Mary Wood hoped they could keep their information to themselves.

They were all people who knew each other well or very well, and in a couple of cases, too well in years gone by, so that those who had been lovers in the past could now no longer find anything to talk about or the desire to sit near each other. They were the ones who could sustain polite conversation by taking turns listening to the latest developments in the lives of children and grandchildren. But the month of August was more than half gone, and the fund of such news was exhausted. At half past two Mary Wood's luncheon had become so tedious that she would gladly have dropped her own little bombshell to put some life in it, but she was beginning to believe that there might be a genuine sensation in the news she was withholding, and it was too good to toss away. She was relieved therefore when three of the men and their wives announced that they wanted to see the last few holes of the golf tournament that had been held up by the morning rain.

The departure of six guests set off the departure of all the others except George and Carrie Reed and Agatha Surtees, who was a notorious stayer. "Send me home whenever you want to," said Agatha. "You know me." It was what she always said, and there were those among her friends who considered it a form of bullying, as though she were daring them to take her up on her offer. But now Mary Wood did take her up.

"Well, the party *is* over, Aggie," said Mary Wood.

"Oh. I see. You want me to go," said Agatha Surtees. "Where are you three going that I'm not invited?"

"We're going to stay right here and talk," said Mary.

"What on earth are you going to talk about that you can't talk about in front of me?" said Agatha. "God knows you've said everything you can about me. Say, what happened to Willoughby today? I never did hear why he wasn't here."

"He's having some brain surgery," said George Reed. "Go on, Aggie. We want to talk private."

"Brain surgery? Willoughby? What will they have to work on?" said Agatha Surtees. "All right, you stuffy bastards. I know where I'm not wanted."

Mary accompanied her to the door. "I'll see you Thursday," said Mary Wood.

"Maybe you will and maybe you won't," said Agatha. "I don't like being put out of a friend's house."

"Very well, then, suit yourself about Thursday," said Mary.

"That isn't true about Willoughby, is it? The brain surgery?" said Agatha.

"He had to go to Washington," said Mary.

"On a weekend? Nobody goes to Washington on a weekend. Come on, Mary."

"It has happened, though," said Mary.

"Maybe, but not to Willoughby Wood," said Agatha.

"Well, if we decide to change our story we'll let you be the first to know," said Mary.

"You know perfectly well I couldn't care less," said Agatha.

"That's good. And goobye," said Mary. She watched Agatha, who was not allowed to drive a car, take off in her hired limousine.

"She's a pest," said George Reed.

"Well, you didn't always think so," said Carrie Reed.

"You have to have a hell of a long memory to remember when I didn't think so. Forty pounds and forty years ago," said George Reed.

"Aggie is fifty-two," said Mary Wood. "She has other problems."

"And she's all too willing to share them," said George.

"Suddenly I seem to be doing the same thing," said Mary. "This is my first cigarette since I stopped."

"Then don't start," said Carrie.

"Oh, the hell with it, why not?" said Mary, and lit it.

"The hell with it is right," said George Reed. "If you feel like smoking, why not?"

"Because it tastes so awful," said Mary, and crushed it out.

"So far the only help you've got from us was George's telling you to go ahead and smoke," said Carrie.

"You come up with something more constructive, dear," said George.

"The thing is that damn inconsiderate son of a bitch said absolutely nothing," said Mary Wood. "There s the phone. Do you suppose that's him? George, will you answer it?"

"Me? All right," said George. But before he could get to the telephone Mary's maid entered.

"It's the sheriff's office wishes to speak to you, ma'am," said the maid.

"The sheriff's office," said Mary. "All right, thank you, Elizabeth. George, will you get on the extension in the library?"

The man said, "Am I speaking to Mrs. Willoughby T. Woods?"

"This is Mrs. Wood."

"This is Lieutenant Hackenschmidt, Sheriff's Patrol, Midhampton. There's a man here says you can identify him. He says he's your husband, Willoughby T. Woods."

"Well, what makes you think he isn't? What's going on, for heaven's sake? Is he all right? Has he been injured?" said Mary.

"Maybe you better come over to the sub-station," said the man.

"Will you answer my question? Is he all right? What's this all about?"

"We have a man here, he's not under arrest, but maybe

if you describe your husband it'd save you a trip," said the man.

"My husband? He's fairly tall, just under six feet. He weighs two hundred and five, two hundred and ten. Age fifty-nine. Blue eyes. Brown hair, partly grey."

"That's him, all right."

"Why is he there, at the sheriff's office?" said Mary.

"Mrs. Woods, I think you'd save a lot of trouble if you came to the sub-station," said the man.

"Let me speak to my husband," said Mary.

"That wouldn't do any good," said the man. "I promise you, we're trying to be helpful, and this is one of our busiest days. Do you have a car, or someone that can escort you?"

"All right, I have a friend here, Mr. George Reed. George L. Reed. He'll escort me."

"Oh, well, we know Mr. Reed. That's the president-of-the-hospital Mr. Reed, right?" said the man. "George L."

"Lieutenant, this is Mr. Reed, on the extension. What can you tell me now?"

"Well—mentally, he's in pretty bad shape. We picked him up around four o'clock this morning, aimlessly wandering around in the vicinity of the East Quantuck Steak House."

"East Quantuck? What was he doing over there?"

"You got me, Mr. Reed. He wasn't intoxicated. He was well dressed, but his clothes were somewhat the worst for wear. Also, he needed a shave. He didn't have any money on him, or a watch, or any identification. He was probably rolled. You know, his money and watch stolen. He didn't show any bruises or anything, but the doctor said he might have a slight concussion. We didn't take him to the hospital. It isn't all that easy to get a man in the hospital if he isn't an emergency case. At first he wouldn't tell us his name, but finally he told me that much and I found it in the phone book. I asked him was there anybody would identify him, and he said he *presumed* his wife would. He presumed. He had some kind of a blackout, Mr. Reed, that's about as much as I can say. Some kind of a mental blackout. You know, he's not some kind of a criminal type, and he wasn't dressed like one of these kooks. We got plenty of them this summer. He was kind of a, you know, upper-class, elderly-business-man type. She says fifty-nine but he looks over sixty."

"Well, thank you, Lieutenant. We'll be right over," said George L. Reed.

"What do you think?" said Mary Wood.

"Nervous breakdown, I guess," said George Reed. "Gone since Friday. Didn't take his car. No message. Is there anything you ought to tell us, Mary?"

"Is there!" she said. "How far back do you want to go? A week? A year? Ten years? Is there anything *you* could have told *me?*"

"Yes, who wants to open whose can of worms?" said Carrie Reed. "Not in our set, thank you."

"Except that when it happens, it happens," said George. "I suppose we're all borderline cases."

"Name one that isn't," said Carrie. "Do you want me to go along with you to the sheriff's office? Or would it be better if I didn't? I was thinking of the effect on Willoughby if all three of us trooped in."

"Maybe it *would* be better if just Mary and I went," said George Reed.

"I'd just as soon be left out, frankly," said Carrie. "I'm not as touchy as Aggie."

"All right, we'll go in my car and I'll drop you on the way," said George.

They let Carrie off at the Reeds' driveway. "Call me when you know anything," said Carrie, and turned in.

"She wanted to come," said Mary.

"Sure she did," said George.

"Oh, you knew that?" said Mary.

"Of course I knew it. My God, Mary, I knew it at the time. Twenty years ago."

"It wasn't very serious, really," said Mary.

"No? Willoughby thought it was, and you must have. And I did. And she still thinks so. At this moment she's probably in floods of tears."

"I don't think of Carrie as giving in to floods of tears," said Mary Wood.

"Trickles, then. Rivulets."

"Rivulets," said Mary Wood. "I'd hate to think that Carrie was more capable of emotion than I am. And yet she may be. At least over my husband. He hasn't affected me that way. I want to help him out of his jam, whatever it is. But I'd do that for anybody. My true feeling at this moment is that once again Willoughby Wood, in his own, self-centered, special way, has managed to revive my hatred of him. And just when it had simmered down to a calm, cool dislike. Would you be my lover, George?"

"I've often thought of it," he said.

"It would be a damn nuisance, no question about that," said Mary. "And you probably have somebody already."

"Yes, I have," he said. "At our stage of the game it's just as well she lives in Detroit, and I don't get to see her very often."

"Well, you wouldn't have to overdo with me either."

"I might want to," he said.

"No, if it was only that, I'd find some stud horse. But I'd like to have you as my lover, that I could think of as my lover as much as actually go to bed with you. I'd be good in bed with you, George. I promise you that. Whoever this bitch is in Detroit, I'd have nothing to fear from her. But it would be so nice to be your mistress, and so convenient. That is, I'd give you sex whenever you wanted it, and the rest of the time you'd give me someone to love. I wouldn't be surprised if I always have loved you. I certainly love you now."

"Yes, we've always loved each other, you and I."

"Incestuously, you might say," she said.

"I guess that goes for all of us that have known each other all our lives and never gone to bed," he said.

"I once actually slept with Norman Gregory. We got undressed and had complete sex, and the next week I was a bridesmaid in his wedding. And never again as much as a kiss."

"Why did you sleep with Norman Gregory?"

"Because he wanted me to and I wanted to see what it would be like, and Judy was my best friend, and the whole atmosphere was so full of sex that—oh, I don't know why. But I did, that once, and I may say he's hated me ever since, for fear I'd tell Judy. And I hated him for the same reason. The two of us with guns at each other's heads. I never told anyone."

"Why are you telling me at this late date?"

"Oh, I thought I'd start out by telling you everything, and the best way to start is with the one I never admitted, poor old Norman, with his three wives and numerous concubines."

"It's a good start," said George Reed.

"We don't have to decide this minute," said Mary. "But I'll be much nicer to Willoughby if I know I can count on you. I'm going to need all the help I can get to take care of him. I'd much prefer to let him rot in a police station, and if I had any real guts I would. But think what people would *say*. Just *think* what they'd *say*. Instead of which they're going to have to say, 'Oh, isn't that Mary the kindest, the most devoted?' And the real credit will belong to you, for making it possible."

"I make it possible by becoming your lover?" he said.

"Oh, maybe you won't become my lover. But I hope you do. If you ever want to, you can. And if you ever want to stop, you can. And if I ever want to stop, I will. It was just an idea that came into my head. Willoughby is going to give me a lot of grief, and if I had you to console me, it wouldn't be quite as bad."

"Why is it going to be bad, Mary? You must have reason to think so," said George Reed. "Has he been acting strangely?"

"For about ten years," she said. "Ever since his father died, and he came into that money, he's had one crazy scheme after another. The first thing he did was quit work, which wasn't altogether surprising, in view of the fact that he was never more than a figurehead. Then Marietta got married to a boy that Willoughby insisted was a fairy, although they have managed to have two children. The boy has never made any secret of the fact that he can't stand Willoughby, and that's why they live in California. So Willoughby never sees Marietta, and whenever I go to California he pretends to think I go there to have an affair with somebody. I did, once, and stayed longer than I had planned. When I got back to New York he had done the house over from top to bottom, and put all my things in storage. I literally couldn't find anything. It cost him seventy thousand dollars to spring that little surprise on me. I didn't spend a single night there. I went to a hotel. I told him the best thing he could do was talk to his lawyers. But he didn't. He talked to me instead. He put the house on the market, and that was when we bought that apartment on Seventy-first Street. Financially, it was one of the best deals he ever made. Everybody thought he and I had worked it out together, but that's the true story of why we sold the house and took an apartment. We got credit for a very astute move, but what it really was was Willoughby trying to punish me, and I wouldn't punish. Since then he's been afraid to make any grand gestures like that. He was so absolutely sure that I'd live in that house, constantly reminded that I was being punished, that it never occurred to him that I wouldn't. For the first time in our marriage he realized that I wouldn't be bullied. And it was such an *elaborate* scheme, such a fancy way to get his revenge. I know he was very proud of that part of it. He's always thought of himself as a man with great imagination. It just this minute occurred to me that this trouble he's in now could be another elaborate scheme."

"I don't think so," said George Reed.

"Well, no, I don't either," said Mary. "But I'm going to keep my eyes open."

"We're almost there," said George Reed. "We'll soon be able to tell."

The sheriff's sub-station was a small building that resembled those cottage-like non-residences that are used as offices on real estate developments. It contained one large room with benches and chairs, a flat-top desk, and a switch-board-radio apparatus which was carrying the sounds of short-wave conversation, presumably between a station and a police car. To the rear of the large room were two smaller rooms, one with the door open, the other with a closed door. A youngish man in uniform, wearing a revolver holster and well-filled ammunition belt, got up to introduce himself. "Hello, Mr. Reed. I'm Lieutenant Hackenschmidt."

"Yes, I remember you, Lieutenant," said George. "This is Mrs. Wood."

"My pleasure," said Hackenschmidt. "We got Mr. Woods resting in there. It's a cell, but we only have him in there because he wanted to lie down on the cot. You want to come in my office?"

He led the way, and he pointed to a couple of chairs. "No, we don't have Mr. Woods under arrest. He's here strictly on a voluntary basis and for his own protection. He could walk out of here any time he felt like it. We don't have him booked on any charge whatsoever, you know?"

"Right," said George Reed.

"Okay," said the lieutenant. "But I'd rather hold him on some technical charge rather than see him go out of here and start wandering around aimlessly. Like he could walk in front of a car, or fall into a ditch, or any number of things. Then he'd be our responsibility, you know what I mean."

"Oh, yes," said George Reed.

"When you see him you'll put two-and-two together," said the lieutenant. "Oh, God, it sounds like he got awake. Yeah, he's awake. Hello, Mr. Woods. D'you have a little nap?"

Willoughby Wood, his fine blue linen suit rumpled and spotted, his collar open and his necktie missing, a two-day stubble on his chin, looked at his wife and George Reed. "Uh, is this the rescue party?"

"So to speak," said George Reed. "We came to bring you home, Willoughby."

"Is that with your approval, Mary? Or is George taking me to his house?"

"To your house, our house," said Mary Wood.

Willoughby Wood ran his fingers over his chin. "I'm not exactly Prince Philip, am I? Well, am I free to go? I mean, are there any formalities, things to sign? Bail? This very nice young man has assured me that there are no charges against me, but I've been in a room with barred windows. Probably something I may have to get used to."

"Nonsense, Willoughby," said George Reed. "Well, Lieutenant, we'll be on our way. And thank you very much."

"Yes, thank you *very* much," said Mary Wood. "We came in George's car, Willoughby."

"I'll sit in back," said Willoughby Wood. "If somebody will give me a cigarette?"

"I haven't any," said Mary. "George, have you got cigarettes?"

"Right," said George Reed, and handed her his case. "You must have been calm about the whole thing, if you didn't start smoking again, Mary. I congratulate you," said Willoughby.

"I wasn't very calm, I assure you, and I did light one but it tasted awful," she said.

"How was your luncheon?" said Willoughby.

"Oh, you remembered," she said.

"It's all coming back," said Willoughby.

"Don't talk about it if you don't want to," she said.

"I don't mind. Apparently I drew a blank the night before last. I seem to have lost my wristwatch and my money, my signet ring, my silver cigarette lighter, and my bifocals. I can imagine giving everything away but my bifocals, which leads me to believe I was robbed. But where all this happened I don't know. I don't know how I got to the police station. Maybe I don't want to know."

"What you need now is some rest. A nice warm bath and some shut-eye," said George Reed.

"A doctor came and had a look at me. No bones broken, and I refused to let him take me to the hospital. In fact I was very uncooperative with the doctor. He was a fresh young squirt, and I told him if I had to have medical attention I had my own doctor in Southampton. I imagine they were glad to get rid of me, although I rather liked Lieutenant Haggenschmaggen or whatever his name is. I owe him some money for coffee and doughnuts, and I suppose I'll be getting a bill from the doctor. Who won the golf tournament?"

"They're playing the finals this afternoon," said George Reed. "Postponed on account of the downpour this morning. Billy Cox and Martin Hammond are in the finals."

"Billy Cox? I hope he loses," said Willoughby Wood.

"It's pretty even," said George Reed.

"If I were more presentable I'd go out and watch them play, just to root against Billy Cox," said Willoughby Wood.

"What's this new thing against Billy Cox?" said Mary.

"There's nothing new about it, I can tell you that," said her husband. "I don't always parade my likes and dislikes. That fellow you had the affair with in California, I'm always extremely polite to him."

"We can lay off that, Willoughby," said George Reed.

"Oh, all right. I didn't hold it against him anyway," said Willoughby. "You know how it is, a woman has certain biological requirements, and she gets lonely all the way out there in California."

"Oh, shut up, Willoughby," said Mary.

"Why? In another day or two, who knows? You might miss me so much that you'd ask George to help you out in that department."

"You've gone far enough, Willoughby," said George Reed.

"I don't know. I've always thought I could count on Carrie," said Willoughby. "There used to be a time when I could, and I'm a little disappointed in her today. I was sure she'd be in the rescue party. Didn't she offer to come along?"

"You may think you're getting away with murder, but don't push your luck," said George Reed.

"I'm not well, you know," said Willoughby Wood. "I may have to be put away for a while."

"Stop taking advantage of it," said Mary Wood. "I don't care what you say to me, but leave George out of this."

"George is *in* it, as a volunteer member of the rescue party. I didn't ask him to come, but he's here," said Willoughby Wood. "For all he knew, I might have turned violent. That's the chance he took. The good Samaritan. Are you planning to have me put away for a while?"

"It shouldn't be too difficult," said George Reed.

"Unless I make a fuss," said Willoughby Wood.

"Even if you do make a fuss," said George Reed.

"I noticed you seemed to know that lieutenant. He'd be on your side, wouldn't he? Yes, he would. You're so full of good works and things like that. The hospital. The Boys Club. They'd all be on your side. But how would it look if I could prove some kind of a conspiracy to have me put away? There was a case like that a while ago. It got to be very messy. And you don't want anything messy, George. The head of the hospital. The big leader in the Boys Club. And not to mention the senior partner in Chickering and Reed. No, if I were you I'd give up the idea of having me put away. I don't want to be put away. I want to be right here where I can see everything that's going on. You know, people have never been very fond of me, although I tried very hard to be nice to them. Mary married me because I made her see how hard I was trying to be nice to people. That was my reward. But it didn't seem to do any good, so I gave up trying. My own daughter, for heaven's sake, deliberately picked an entirely unsuitable young man and married him. And went out of her way to find a lover for her mother. They tell me that the whole State of California was in on that one. I tried to give Mary the hint, that as far as I was concerned she could stay in California. But the man is about five years younger than Mary, and I understand his wife's family have oil. I sometimes wonder whether oil has been a good thing or a bad thing. It helps prevent friction, that's true, and it provides us with fuel and so forth and so on. But oil money has had a worse effect on the human race than gold. Gold is at least pretty, and oil is only messy. I've never met an attractive oil millionaire. Never. And they know it, too. I think it's because they're so conscious of being oil millionaires and they expect everybody to overcharge them. And Mary's friend in California wasn't even the real thing. He had to marry oil. Did you like him, Mary? I mean, aside from his fulfilling the biological requirements? Which could have been just as well fulfilled by the driver of an oil truck."

"I wish we had a tape recording of this," said George Reed.

"Yes," said Mary Wood.

"To be used in evidence against me, obviously," said Willoughby Wood. "Well, if you two ever try to have me put away, I'll say things for the record that aren't going to sound any better. They may make me sound crazy, but all the same people are going to relish every juicy morsel. No matter what I say, you know, people are going to believe at least half of it. That's the damn trouble with people, even one's dearest friends. In fact, it would be rather fun to have you try to put me away. What are we stopping for, George?" The car pulled over to the side of the road.

"This is where you get out," said George Reed.

"Don't be silly. We have a half a mile to go," said Willoughby Wood. "Or are you putting me out?"

"That's the idea," said George Reed.

"I don't think I can walk that far," said Willoughby Wood.

"Then thumb a ride," said George Reed. "Go on, get out. I'm sick of listening to you."

"Would you throw me out, in my weakened condition? Yes, I believe you would," said Willoughby Wood.

"Oh, boy, would I!" said George Reed.

"Well, come on, Mary," said Willoughby Wood.

"No, Mary stays," said George Reed.

"Are you staying, Mary?" said Willoughby Wood.

"Yes, I think I am," said Mary Wood.

A MAN TO BE TRUSTED

When I was growing up there was one house I always liked to go to. It was in a town about fourteen miles away by the country roads, and though there were two ways to get there, neither way totally avoided the crossing of a mountain. Consequently I had never been to the town before my father bought his first automobile, in 1914. It is hard to believe now that a town only fourteen miles away was so remote or inaccessible and yet in the same county as the town where I lived, but that was how things were when I was a boy, before we had a car and roads were paved. We lived in Gibbsville, which was the county seat, but people in Batavia who had business in the court house mostly had to take a railroad train to a station in the next county, change trains, and in effect double back to get to Gibbsville. There was no direct rail communication between Gibbsville and Batavia, and as Batavia was a good five miles to the west of the river and the canal, the two towns might just as well have been in different counties. It just happened that Batavia was in Lantenengo County instead of Berks County, and Batavia people found it easier to go to Reading, the next big town, than to Gibbsville. I

would be inclined to guess that Batavia people felt that
they had much more in common with Reading than with
Gibbsville, and not only because of the fact that it was
easier for them to get to Reading. Traditionally Reading
was a Pennsylvania Dutch town, while Gibbsville was a
mixture of Yankee, English, Welsh, and Irish that together
outnumbered the Pennsylvania Dutch. And on court days
the Batavia people would also be encountering the Poles
and Lithuanians and Italians who worked in the coal
mines and the mills and car shops, whom Batavia people
called foreigners. There were no foreigners in Batavia, although Pennsylvania Dutch was their second language and
in the case of some of the older people, their only one.

To this town, late in the nineteenth century, had come
a man named Philip Haddon and his wife Martha. She was
the daughter of old Mike Murphy, who had come up the
hard way in the steel business in Ohio and had made
enough money to send Martha to school in the East and
then to Switzerland. The Murphys owned a big house in
Cleveland, but Martha and her mother and sister preferred to live in New York, in a house that was less os-
tentatious but more elegant than the one in Cleveland.
Martha Murphy was a handsome brunette, tall enough to
wear her hair in a pompadour, and rich enough to attract
titled Europeans who were her co-religionists and some
American Protestants who could supply her with Knickerbocker names. But she fell in love with Philip Haddon
and he with her, and he turned Catholic and married her.
To the delighted surprise of Mike Murphy his new son-in-
law went to work for Wexford Iron & Steel, which was
named after Mike's home county in Ireland, and Philip
was put in charge of a Wexford subsidiary in the town of
Batavia, Pennsylvania. "It's nothing big now, mind you,"

said Mike Murphy. "But it's twice as big as when I bought it and there's over fifty second-generation puddlers on the payroll. It's got a future, Philip."

Martha would have lived anywhere with Philip, and Batavia looked nothing like a steel town. Indeed, it was not a steel town. It was a town on the edge of the Pennsylvania Dutch farming country that happened to have an iron foundry at one end of it. The foundry, as it continued to be called, filled special orders; deck plates and turrets for the Navy, parts for the independent manufacturers of automobiles and trucks; jobs that were too small to engage the facilities of the big mill at Wexford, Ohio. Philip Haddon ran the Batavia foundry efficiently and profitably, and was rewarded by his father-in-law's decision to promote him to an important post in the Wexford mill. Now Mike Murphy got his second surprise from Philip Haddon: Haddon told Murphy that he preferred to remain in Batavia, that he had no desire to move to Ohio, and furthermore had no ambition to be Murphy's successor as the chairman of the board of Wexford Iron & Steel. To a man like Murphy, who had fought his way up, Haddon's lack of enterprise was incomprehensible, and he did not hide his disappointment. He had a talk with his daughter Martha, hoping to persuade her to influence Philip to change his mind, only to discover that Martha was in agreement with Philip and was herself content to stay in Batavia. "Well, if that's the way you want it," said Murphy to his daughter.

"It's the way we want it, Daddy," said Martha.

"You're not saying why. In ten years Philip could b a rich man. In twenty years he could be as rich as me "

"Yes, he probably could," said Martha.

"He's not a lazy man. It's just that he don't have the ambition," said her father. "Maybe instead of a gentleman you'd have done better to marry one of my lads in the oil shanty, a fellow with more get-up-and-go."

"But I didn't. I married Philip, and you should be proud of him for making a success of Batavia."

"Batavia wasn't all his doing. He took over a going concern. He got no test of his abilities there. But if that's as far as he wants to go, he's not the man I thought he was. What I don't understand is why the two of you are content with Batavia. I gave you a million when you were twenty-one. He wouldn't have to work at all. How much of this is your doing, Martha?"

"Half of it, maybe a little less, maybe a little more," she said.

"I give up, I give up," said Mike Murphy.

"If you want Philip to resign from Batavia, he will. But if he does, you'll never see *me* again," said Martha.

"There's things you're not telling me, there's more to this than meets the eye."

"There always is, Daddy," she said. "There always has been."

"Now what do you mean by that remark? You're not resurrecting that old trouble between your mother and I."

"I'm not resurrecting anything, am I? You've always had someone else, and the whole world knew it."

"Your mother had a better understanding of that than you'll ever have."

"Acceptance of it, not understanding," said Martha.

"Ah, you're afraid that Philip'll get too big for you. Is that it, girl?"

"No, that's not it, Daddy."

"If he got as rich as me, you'd lose him. Is that it?"

"No. I'll never lose him. Or he me," she said.

"Well, that's something to be thankful for, isn't it now? To be so certain of everything the future holds for you. No temptations and deviations and allegations and fascinations and affiliations. Not to mention some other -ations I could think of."

"Yes, you left out fornications," she said.

"So I did, didn't I?" said her father. "Well, my girl, being's you have your future all worked out for yourselves, as your loving father I can only hope and pray that the good Lord concurs with your plans. It'd be a pity if ten or twenty years from now your husband belatedly suffered an attack of ambition. Belated ambition could be as bad in one thing as another for a man, whether it be business or pleasure. The time to pull a heat is neither too soon or too late."

"I'm sorry you're disappointed in Philip, Daddy. Maybe what I ought to be sorry about was that I had a sister instead of a brother. Then you'd have had a son and you wouldn't have counted on my husband."

"At that Margaret is more of a man than he is," said Murphy.

"Don't you believe it," said Martha. "Margaret's as feminine as I am."

The old man was too malleable to become misshapen by one defeat, and he sought and found a man of Philip Haddon's age whom he could train to succeed him at Wexford. The man he found was not a gentleman, and Mike Murphy lured him away from Pittsburgh and married him off to his other daughter, Margaret. It apparently made little difference to Margaret, who was unhappily married to a concert violinist of limited talent and strange ways. I was never sure what money changed hands in the process of Margaret's obtaining an annulment of her musical marriage and her union with her father's hand-picked successor. I was too young to know about such matters, and besides I never laid eyes on Margaret. In fact I was quite grown before I knew or cared that Martha Murphy Haddon had a sister. As far as I was concerned, Martha Haddon was the beautiful wife of Philip Haddon, and they lived in Batavia, fourteen miles from my home town, and I always liked to visit their house.

The Haddons had visited my house twice before we owned a car and paid our visit to Batavia. I must explain here—and especially now, in the seventh decade of the century—that the first meeting of the Haddons and my parents came about because my mother had gone to a Sacred Heart school. The Sacred Heart nuns are an order whose influence is world-wide, often compared to the Jesuits, but smaller in number and far subtler as a power elite. The children of the poor do not go to Sacred Heart schools, in Paris, in London, in Montreal, in New York, in Philadelphia, in Mexico City, in Madrid, in Vienna, and money alone was not an automatic qualification for admission to one of their schools, nor was membership in the Roman Catholic Church. What I might ironically call a freemasonry existed among Sacred Heart alumnae, and when Martha Haddon settled in Batavia, Pennsylvania, she got a letter from a Madame Duval, of the Sacred Heart order, who told her that my mother lived in Gibbsville. My mother likewise got a letter from Madame Duval, saying that one of her girls, Martha Murphy Haddon, had recently moved to Batavia. In due course my mother invited Martha to a ladies' luncheon at our house, and the ice was broken. My mother was older than Martha, and they had not been to the same Sacred Heart school, but they had friends in common among Sacred Heart alumnae in various parts of the world, and I suppose the two women looked each other over like two old Etonians who are thrown together on a rubber plantation in the Straits Settlements. Philip Haddon owned a green Locomobile phaeton, which was driven by a chauffeur without livery. We were accustomed to seeing Locomobiles and Pierce-Arrows and Packards, owned by mining superintendents and driven by men in business suits, and so I guessed that the Haddon car went with his job. I was about nine years old, impressed but not overawed.

A few months later my father bought his first Ford, and he and my mother and my sister and I returned the Haddons' visit. Batavia was a pretty town, much more countrified than I had expected, with great walnuts and chestnuts and elms on the principal streets. The foundry was at the southern end of the town, not noticeable from the Haddons' house except for a tall stack from which issued a thin trickle of smoke, the day being Sunday. "We usually go to Mass in Reading," I heard Mr. Haddon say to my father. "There's a priest that says Mass here every fourth Sunday, but the rest of the time we drive down to Reading."

"Oh, are you a Catholic too?" said my father.

"Yes, I became one when we announced our engagement."

"Well, I'd better be careful what I say. Converts are stricter than we are," said my father. The two men then talked about guns and shooting, and Haddon invited my father to spend the night when the season opened. Quail, and some pheasant, and always a good bag of rabbit.

"This young man isn't quite ready for that, is he?" said Philip Haddon, putting his hand on my shoulder.

"He's getting a .22 for Christmas, if he's a good boy," said my father.

"Well, would you like to go down in the cellar with me after dinner? I have a couple of .22's you might like to try," said Haddon.

"Me?" I said.

"I believe your father thinks you've been a good boy, don't you, Doctor Malloy?"

"Sometimes," said my father.

"Splendid. Dinner'll be ready in a few minutes," said Haddon.

"Oh, boy, thanks," I said.

"Not *thanks*. Thank *you*, Mr. Haddon," said my father.

"Thank you, Mr. Haddon," I said.

We had not finished dinner when the telephone rang. "It's for you, Doctor Malloy," said Haddon.

"Who could that be?" said my mother.

"I can guess," said my father. "Excuse me."

He came back from the sitting-room. "It's the hospital."

"Oh, dear," said Martha Haddon.

"Mr. MacNamara?" said my mother.

My father nodded.

"Won't you even have time to finish dessert?" said Martha Haddon.

"I hate to say it, but we have to go right away," said my father. "I apologize for this interruption—"

"Oh, not at all, Doctor Malloy," said Philip Haddon.

"Isn't that always the way, though?" said my mother. She was already standing, and my sister and I were rising.

"May I offer a suggestion?" said Haddon. "Why can't Mrs. Malloy and the children stay, and I'll drive them back to Gibbsville in my car?"

"In your Locomobile?" I said.

"Well, Katharine, it's up to you. I'm going to have to go straight to the hospital."

"Oh, no. That wouldn't be right. No, we'll go with you," said my mother.

"It's no distance at all, and the doctor's going to be busy all afternoon, I can see that," said Haddon.

"Well, you're right about that. I'm going to have to operate," said my father. "If it wouldn't be too much trouble, but I have to leave this minute. Katharine, you and the children finish your dinner and come home with Mr. Haddon."

"Good. Good work, Doctor Malloy. I can see that your mind is on more important things already. You just leave it all up to me," said Philip Haddon.

He was the first person I had ever known to make audible comment on my father's habit of distracting himself. We might not know which patient or which operation he was thinking of, but we knew the signs that his attention was elsewhere. Philip Haddon had recognized the signs, and what's more he had made so bold as to be frank about it. It was a rare thing when anyone made a personal remark to my father. Most people were afraid of him, in awe of him, but Philip Haddon was not. To a boy of nine it was an instructive experience to see someone unhesitatingly change my father's plans, and my father's submission. The moment my father left for the hospital a party-like atmosphere prevailed. We finished our dessert, the two women and my sister went upstairs, and Philip Haddon took me down-cellar to his rifle range. It was a gun room as well as a shooting gallery, with rugs on the concrete floor, glass-paned closets for his rifles, shotguns, and handguns, and framed pictures on the panelled walls. That room was my first real introduction to Philip Haddon, and for the rest of the afternoon I kept learning things about him that added to my information and respect.

I remember that that day he was wearing a brown tweed suit and brown spats over wing-tip brogues. My father went in for tweeds but not for matching spats. Philip Haddon had an American face and gold-rimmed glasses, no moustache, smoothed-down light brown hair parted not quite in the middle. He was taller than my father, probably about six-feet-one, and built like an end. He had been to West Point. "Is that where you learned to shoot?" I said.

"Well, that's where I learned the army way, but I've always been fond of shooting," he said. "I must have been about your age when I started. What are you, ten?"

"My next birthday I'll be ten," I said.

"Good. Then you started earlier than I did," he said.

I was an inquisitive boy, especially if given the encouragement of sensible answers. "Why did you go to West Point? Did you want to be a soldier?"

"I didn't have much to say in the matter," he said. "My father and four of my uncles went there. But no, I didn't want to be a soldier. I wanted to be a painter."

"That paints pictures? An artist?"

"Yes. Do you want to be a doctor?"

"No," I said.

"What *do* you want to be?" said Philip Haddon. "Have you decided?"

"A state policeman," I said. "Or maybe own the circus."

"Yes, owning a circus would be fun," said Philip Haddon. "I'm not so sure about being a state policeman. Most of them were in the army, and I've *been* in the army."

"Why didn't you like it?" I said.

"Well, I suppose because I'm not very good at taking orders. As far as that goes, I didn't like giving them either. But that's something you can't avoid."

"You could run away," I said.

"Not really. You can't really run away."

"I'm going to. When I get bigger. When I'm twelve," I said.

"You're going to run away when you're twelve? Where to?"

"Out West. Wyoming, maybe. I can work on a ranch. Have you ever been there, to Wyoming?"

"Yes, I have, in the army. Twelve is a little young to be working on a ranch. Not that I want to discourage you, but I think you ought to wait a bit longer. Fifteen or sixteen. They have blizzards in Wyoming, and it gets awfully hot in summer. Much colder and much hotter than it gets here. Why a ranch? Do you like horses?"

"I'm a good rider," I said.

"Have you got a pony?"

"No, I have a horse. My sister has a pony but she doesn't know how to ride. She's too little, and she's scared."

"Well, she may get over that," said Philip Haddon. He opened one of the gun closets and handed me a Winchester .22 with a nickeled octagonal barrel. "Let me see you handle it."

"Can I fire it?" I said.

"You're on your own," he said. He was watching me carefully. I took it off safety, aimed at the target, and pressed the trigger. "Good. You proved the piece. You've handled guns before."

"You bet. Since I was little," I said. He handed me a box of ammunition. "I know how to load it, too."

"It's all yours," he said.

I fired fifteen shots, the full load, uninterrupted by him. "Very good," he said. "Your grouping was good, once you got the feel of it."

"I never got a bull's eye," I said.

"No, but you got some 5's and 4's, and only two worse

than a 3," he said. "Naturally you have a lot to learn, such as breathing, but you have the makings of a good shot. If it weren't Sunday we could try a revolver, but they make too much noise. Now I think it's time we joined the ladies."

"Thank you very much," I said.

He ran a cleaning rod through the rifle barrel, and I picked the empty shells off the floor and put them in a wastebasket, in imitation of his neatness. We smiled at each other. "We're going to get along fine," he said.

"Do you have a little boy?" I said.

"We did have, but he died. Diphtheria. Your father's a doctor, so you've heard of diphtheria."

"Yes, my brother had it. They had to put a silver tube in his throat," I said.

"But he got well. That's good."

"I had anti-toxin. That *hurt*," I said. "A needle in my back. But I didn't cry. My sister cried, but I didn't. All the kids in our neighborhood had anti-toxin, and I was the only one that didn't cry."

"You must be very brave," he said.

"My father said I had to set a good example. But it hurt that night and I cried then. It hurt as bad as the needle, only different. But I didn't have to set an example then, so I cried."

"It's very important to have to set an example," he said.

His wife called from the top of the cellar stairs. "Philip, Mrs. Malloy thinks it's time to go."

I wanted to stay, but the immediate prospect of riding in the Haddons' Locomobile was attractive. "Can I sit up front with you?" I said.

"Well, of course. Ladies in the back, gentlemen up front," he said. "Come with me while I get the car."

I accompanied him to the stable, where the green

Locomobile, spotless and facing outward, occupied space on the ground floor. The car had Westinghouse shock absorbers, twin spotlights bracketed to the windshield, and a double cowl in the tonneau. Right there as it stood was one of the most beautiful cars in the world, and I was about to go for a ride in it. "*Some . . . car!*" I said.

"You approve?" said Philip Haddon.

Then I saw the box stalls at the other end of the barn. "Look! A white one and a sorrel," I said.

"Mrs. Haddon rides the white one, I ride the sorrel," said Philip Haddon.

Everything was so neat and orderly; each horse's halter hung outside his stall, half a dozen bridles and saddles—English and McClellan—were on pegs against the wall; brooms and buckets, curry combs and brushes, soap and harness oil and sponges were where they ought to be according to someone's plan. "The sorrel wants to go out but he ought to know better. We never ride on Sunday," said Philip Haddon.

"I do," I said.

"Yes, but you don't live in Batavia," said Philip Haddon. "Well, off we go." He started the motor, let it turn over for a minute or so, and we moved down the slag driveway to the porte-cochere. In the half hour that it took us to drive to our house I said not a word. Philip Haddon and his wife and my mother carried on a conversation that did not concern me, and besides I had things to occupy my mind: the location of electric switches and buttons and dials and meters, and an enameled-brass St. Christopher medal that said something in French, and a small brass plate that was marked "Built for Philip Haddon, Esquire."

My first day with Philip Haddon came to an end, and I had so many things to tell my friends that I did not know where to begin. The next day, at school and after school, I decided I would not tell anyone anything. Mr. Haddon and Mrs. Haddon—she was pretty and nice—were not to be shared with my friends.

Months passed before I saw them again, and the next time I saw him he was in the hospital, where my father had operated on him for appendicitis. "I'm taking you over to see Mr. Haddon," said my father. "He said he'd like to see you, I suppose he was only being polite. Anyway, you can only stay a few minutes. He had a close call."

Mrs. Haddon was sitting in a white iron chair. "I brought you a visitor," said my father.

"Oh, it's my friend," said Philip Haddon. He was weak and not wearing his gold-rimmed glasses, which made him look weaker and older. He put them on.

"I brought you some flowers," I said.

"Oh, are they from your garden?" said Philip Haddon.

"No, *they're* all *dead*," I said.

"Well, I almost joined them," he said. "I can thank your father that I didn't."

"I'll be back in a jiffy," said my father, and left us.

"Does it hurt?" I said.

"No, not really," said Philip Haddon. "But it did."

"We were very lucky that your father was here," said Mrs. Haddon. "He was just getting ready to leave the hospital when I called. Dr. Schmeck and I drove Mr. Haddon to the hospital, and they had the operating room ready when we got here."

"Oh, yes. Peritonitis," I said.

"You know about peritonitis?" said Mrs. Haddon.

"I know that's what happens with appendicitis," I said.

"I notice you and your father pronounce it *eetis* instead of *eyetis*," said Philip Haddon.

"That's the way they pronounced it when he was in medical school. Appendic*eetis*, periton*eetis*."

"It must be the correct way, but I'll never get used to it," said Philip Haddon. "Well, how is school?"

"Oh—school. All right, I guess," I said.

"When I get out of here you must come down and see us again," said Philip Haddon. "I won't be able to ride for a while. I'm going to have to wear a big belt."

"I know," I said.

"But we can shoot," he said. "Your father and I were going gunning together when the season opens, but I don't think he'd approve of that now. So you come instead."

"All right," I said.

"As far as that goes, you could ride with me," said Mrs. Haddon. "You could ride the sorrel. That is, if you don't mind riding with a lady."

"Don't let that fool you," said Mr. Haddon. "She rides as well as any man."

Well, the upshot of that conversation was that the Haddons remembered their invitation, and many times in the next couple of years I went to their house and rode with them and shot with him. It did not matter that at first I was aware I was taking the place of their dead son. I would board the morning train and get off at the main line station where Philip Haddon or his wife would meet me and take me to their house for the day. In the mornings I would ride with one of them, and after lunch he and I would shoot. I would arrive dressed in breeches and puttees, and she or he would be in boots or breeches; but nearly always it was she who rode with me. After his operation he had never regained his interest in riding, and if it had not been for me they would have sold the sorrel, and Mrs. Haddon would have had no one to ride with. My visits were fortnightly, seldom oftener than that, and always arranged by the Haddons in advance. I came to look forward to seeing her as much as I did him, and I reached the age where I became more and more conscious of her figure. She got into my dreams.

One day she met me at the train and immediately announced that there would be no shooting that day. Mr. Haddon had been called to Philadelphia on business. He was very sorry—but I was not. She said that instead of shooting that afternoon she would, if I liked, take me to the foundry and I could see the sights, have a ride on the dinkey engine and the traveling crane. Mr. Haddon said I might enjoy that. And so she and I rode the white and the sorrel, and she said she was going to have to change her clothes because Mr. Haddon did not like her to appear before the foundry workmen in riding breeches. "I'll only be a few minutes," she said. "A quick tub and change." I waited downstairs until I heard the water running in the tub, and then I went upstairs and entered the bathroom without knocking. She was standing naked, feeling the water in the tub. "What are you *doing* here?" she said.

"I wanted to look at you," I said.

She reached for a towel to cover herself. "But you mustn't," she said.

"I only wanted to look," I said.

"Well, I should think so, at thirteen," she said. "Now you've seen me, you must go."

"I want to kiss you," I said.

"Yes, well I knew that," she said.

"I love you," I said.

"That's not love, Jimmy. That's something else," she said. "Can't you see that you're embarrassing me. All right, you can kiss me here." She lowered the towel and put back her shoulders so that her breasts stood out. I kissed each of them. "That's enough now," she said. "Go on downstairs and we'll pretend this never happened. Never." But I put my arms around her and was rough with her and she struggled. "Stop it," she said.

"You wanted me to. You did. I could tell."

"Wanted you to what? Thirteen years old, you must be insane."

"What he does, Mr. Haddon," I said.

"Huh. What you think he does," she said. "You could be wrong about that, too. All right, open your trousers." She got down on the floor and I got on top of her, but I could not control myself and she lay there, wanting what I could not give her. "Now let me have my bath, and you go make yourself presentable."

She came downstairs in about half an hour. "We can dispense with the visit to the foundry," she said. "I can take you to the station, there's an earlier train. We can't talk about it any more till after lunch."

"I don't want any lunch," I said.

"Well, you'll damn well sit here while I have mine," she said. "I have the maid to consider." She chattered while the maid came and went.

"He ain't eating," said the maid.

"He lost his appetite," said Mrs. Haddon.

"He always stuffs," said the maid.

"Well, not today," said Mrs. Haddon.

"Maybe because the Mister ain't here," said the maid.

"Very likely," said Mrs. Haddon.

Later, in the sitting-room, I said, "Are you going to tell Mr. Haddon?"

"No. It wasn't all your fault," she said. "I must have been leading you on, without knowing it. I've seen you look at me, so I should have been forewarned. Have I ever looked at you that way?"

"No."

"Have you ever thought I was flirting with you?"

"No."

"Well, if it's any consolation to you, my husband thought I was flirting with you."

"Me?"

"You, and not only you," she said.

"I never thought so," I said.

"I never did either," she said. "But my husband does. There are some women who give that impression."

"Not you, though," I said.

"Do other women flirt with you? Not girls, but women."

"I don't know."

"Oh, you'd know," she said.

"Some, maybe."

"And what do you do?" she said.

"I don't do anything. With girls I do, but not women. You're the only one."

"Failing the opportunity, I suppose," she said. "Well, I'll be more careful in the future. I'll lock my bathroom door."

"You're not cross at me?"

"More with myself than with you. This could have had serious consequences, you know. The maid. My husband. Your father. Nothing like this must ever happen again. If my husband gave you a good beating, your father'd give you one too. Not to mention the fact that I'd also get a good beating from my husband."

"I'd kill him if he did," I said.

"Mm. How chivalrous, and what a mess. Hereafter confine your attentions to girls your own age."

"I don't like girls my own age," I said.

"Well, a little older, when their busts develop. Thirteen is too young for you to *think* of older women. I'm old enough to be your mother, you know. I am, you know. I'm

ashamed of myself. I gave in to you. No matter what happened, I gave in to you. You'll always remember that—and
so will I. I have a husband that I love dearly, and he loves
me. But a thirteen-year-old boy could make me forget
that. Do you realize how much that's going to make me
hate myself? Are you mature enough to understand that?
You could lose all respect for women after today. It could
have a bad effect on the rest of your life. Giving in, that
was the worst thing that happened today. That was a terrible sin."

"Don't think that, Mrs. Haddon," I said.

"Do you deny that it was a sin? I can't. I've heard of
women like that. When I was at school abroad there was a
girl's mother that had a weakness for young boys. It was
such a scandal that the girl was asked to leave school. A
highly respected family. The girl's life was made miserable
by the weakness of the mother, but am I any better?"

The flow of her self-castigation would not stop, and it
began to frighten me. I wanted to comfort her, but I did
not know how without touching her, and an instinct told
me that she wanted to be touched and that that would lead
to what she called giving in. She wanted to weep and would
not weep. My instinct to comfort her was confused with the
sight of the rise and fall of her bosom, and whatever was
going on inside her was happening to the woman on the
bathroom floor. I could not stand it any longer and I kissed
her on the mouth. Her response was complete and eager,
but then as suddenly she pushed me away. "God, what
am I doing?" she said. "What am I *doing?*" She put her
hands to her cheeks. "He's right about me," she said, and I
knew she was talking about her husband.

"Get your cap, and we'll get some fresh air," she said.
She stood up, only barely discernibly unsteady. "I'll drive
you to the station." She had her own car now, a Scripps-

Booth roadster, a three-seater with the driver's seat forward of the other two.

"You don't have to do that," I said.

"You're wrong, I do have to. I want the cold air on my face, to bring me back to my senses. And you need it too, young man."

Because of the odd seating arrangement I had to lean forward in the noisy, windswept, little car, and she had to repeat half of what she said. But our conversation did not touch upon our intimacies. The cool, cold air was having its effect on her—and on me. The newness, the uniqueness of our experience lay for me in the fact that I was learning for the first time in my life that a woman could actively desire a man. I had kissed girls and sometimes found them responsive, but I had never known, never even heard, that a woman was more than submissive to a man. Now I was learning that it was in the nature of a woman to have a hunger for a man or a boy of thirteen who had the functions of a man. This revelation, this discovery was so violent that I needed someone to discuss it with me, but my inexperienced contemporaries were out of the question; already in experience I was so far ahead of them that none of them would believe me. The superlative irony was in the circumstance that the only man, woman, or boy or girl in whom I had the confidence for confiding was Philip Haddon. On my visits to his house I had told him many things about myself and my family and enemies and friends, and he had always listened with more than perfunctory interest. I almost laughed at the thought of telling him what had happened with his wife that day. Well, at least I was sure that she was not going to tell him either.

Just before we reached the station she said, "I'm never going to say any more about today, to you or anyone else. And don't you."

"I won't," I said.

"The next time you go to confession—do you ever go to an Italian priest?"

"No," I said. "Why?"

"Because Italian priests aren't as easily shocked," she said. "I'd always much rather go to an Italian priest. Whenever I have something naughty to confess, I go to the Italian parish in Reading."

"That's not a true confession, if he doesn't understand what you're saying," I said.

"I don't hold anything back. I tell him everything," she said.

"You're not confessing to a man. You're confessing to God."

"I know all that," she said. "All the same, I'd rather say those things to an Italian. And another thing, don't turn pious on me."

I wasn't ready—but is one ever?—for the physical and spiritual revolution that began for me that day. I had yielded to strong impulse, I had seen her naked body and made an incomplete attempt to commit adultery with her, and I was entertaining doubts about the sanctity of the confessional. She became the most fascinating, evil, ignorant, cynical woman the world had ever known. I wanted to escape from her and sin, but I knew that I would have to go back to her and sin and her secret delights and godless thoughts and infinite pleasures.

"I'm not pious," I said.

"No, I know you're not," she said. "In fact, you're very wicked to know as much as you do." With that she won me over to the side of wickedness, completely. I could not say to her that I was ready to abandon the pleasures of wickedness; I could not say it to myself when the opposite attraction was so powerful. As she drove me to the station

I was aware that I was being chastised for improper conduct, the misbehavior of a boy of thirteen with a woman of whatever age she was. It was as much as I could expect, and it was the right thing for her to do. But already I had been matured by the day's experiences to the extent that my childhood was in the past and I knew it. That was all I knew at the moment, but that much was certain.

We sat in the car, waiting for the northbound train, and she seemed fully to have regained her self-possession, her own place in the world, so that she was protected by her dignity and her tweed skirt and her accustomed manner toward me. She offered me a cigarette and I took it, although her husband had never offered me a cigarette because he respected my father's rule against them. In a strange, conspiratorial way she had somehow managed to join with me in an alliance that supported the smoking of cigarettes while, in the time remaining, totally ignoring our sins of thought, word, and deed. The camelback engine came heaving up the track and I got out of the roadster, took off my cap, and looked at her with what must have been apprehension and longing.

"No, don't try to say anything," she said, and smiled reassuringly.

2.

I went away to boarding school that year where I did not know a soul. In the new life I made the new friends and enemies and the associations with the new things that came out of old books. It was impossible for me to risk the scornful disbelief of other boys with the story of my experience with Mrs. Haddon, and I kept it to myself. With girls my reticence was just as strong. They would let me kiss them, but some of them, most of them, would fight or cry if I put my hand on their growing breasts. They would threaten to tell their big brothers, although they never did. During that phase of my adolescence I had dreams about Mrs. Haddon's body, but they were so secret that she as a living person did not exist. When I went home on school vacations I did not see her, and the friendship between my parents and the Haddons was never meant to flourish. Two or three years went by, and Philip Haddon continued to be a patient of my father's; once or twice a year the Haddons and my parents would meet halfway for Sunday lunch at the Lantenengo Country Club; at Christmas they exchanged suitable presents. But Martha Haddon, if it was deliberate, managed to stay out of my sight, and of course I was falling in and out of love with girls closer to my own age. I had guessed her age to be about sixteen or seventeen years older than I, so that by the time I got out of prep school and went to work on a Gibbsville newspaper, she was in her late thirties. My father died, and my mother had a letter from the Haddons, who were traveling abroad and did not hear about his death until a month later. The letter was written by Martha Haddon and Philip Haddon was only formally included in it. "Mr. Haddon must not be well," said my mother. "Otherwise I think he'd had written. He and your father were closer than Mrs. Haddon and I."

"Well, some men hate to write letters," I said.

"Yes, but not Mr. Haddon," said my mother. As was often the case, she was right, for the next time I visited the neighborhood of Batavia I was on an assignment to cover a fatal stabbing, and because I was in the neighborhood I paid a call on the Haddons. From my paper's point of view it was not much of a story. Some Negroes living in a tent and working as day laborers on a highway construction had a drunken brawl in which one man was killed and the others immediately fled. The state police were not even sure of the names, and I was sure that my paper had no interest in the story. But my curiosity about the Haddons was active, and I had the paper's Oakland coupé and time to spare.

It was a hot August day, toward noon. The smoke from the foundry stacks hung thick and low, as though waiting for any light breeze to take it away. At the Haddons' house on the other end of town the awnings and the wire screens seemed to darken the rooms, and there was no sign of life in the yard. But as I got out of the Oakland the porch screendoor opened and Martha Haddon descended. "Are you from the Light Company?" she called.

"No, ma'am," I said. "I'm from the dark company." It was a feeble enough joke, but I would explain it to her later.

"Don't tell me! It isn't who I think it is," she said, and called back to the man on the porch. "Philip, we have a visitor. James Malloy."

"Oh, good," I heard him say. "Dr. Malloy's boy?"

"What on earth are you doing here on this sticky, hot day?" said Martha Haddon. "Come in out of the sun and have a glass of iced tea."

Philip Haddon rose slowly and rested his palm fan and newspaper on a wicker table. He was wearing a pongee suit, striped blue shirt, white canvas oxfords. We shook hands and I explained my presence in the neighborhood and my little joke. "Well, you'll stay to lunch," said Philip Haddon. "You might even have a swim. I think the pool is new since you were here last."

"It is," she said. "This is only our third summer with the pool."

"Has it really been that long since we used to shoot? But then it must be. You're not a boy any more. You're quite a young man. Newspaper work, and watching people carve each other up."

"Yes, I remember when my father carved you up," I said.

"And you came to see me in the hospital," he said. "Well, damn it all, it *is* nice to see you again. Isn't it awful that we can live so near and never see each other? We've never even been to see your mother since your father died."

"Well, *you've* had some excuse," said Martha Haddon. "Mr. Haddon caught some kind of a stomach ailment in Italy."

"Say no more about it," said Philip Haddon. "I think it was nothing more than a recurrence of malaria. Everybody that was ever in the army got *some* malaria. Unfortunately, I've had to retire from the foundry, and we may have to move away."

"We *own* the *house*," said Martha Haddon.

"Yes, but the new superintendent may not like to have me looking over his shoulder," said Philip Haddon.

"As you've probably guessed, this is a frequent topic of conversation," said Martha Haddon. "But we don't really want to leave Batavia. Where to? Good heavens, we came here as bride and groom, and this has been our home, our only one."

"I'm sure Mr. Malloy'd much rather go for a swim than participate in our discussion," said Philip Haddon.

"No, I always liked this house," I said. "I hope you keep it."

"Then that settles it," said Philip Haddon. "You promise to visit us often when they finish the new highway."

For the first time ever I suspected that Philip Haddon was capable of subtlety. "I promise," I said.

"All right, fine, we'll hold you to that," he said. "Now

if you'd like to have a dip before lunch, I'll get you a pair of trunks."

"Aren't you coming?" I said.

"No, if I get a chill I'm through for the day, maybe longer," he said. "But Martha will go with you."

"All right, we haven't much time," said Martha Haddon.

We put on our bathing suits and left him on the porch. The pool was in a corner of the yard, protected on four sides by a tall hedge, and on the way to the pool she and I wore bathrobes. "It's our one concession to Batavia," she said. "They wouldn't approve of a grown woman walking around in a bathing suit."

"Do you really like it in Batavia?" I said.

"I like it better than any place else," she said. "It keeps me on my good behavior—*most of the time.*"

"Oh, you remember," I said.

"Of course I do. It's not something you forget."

"Well, what about him, Mr. Haddon? Did he ever know about me?"

"I didn't tell him," she said.

"That isn't answering my question," I said. "Something a minute ago made me think he knew *something.*"

"You're a young man now," she said. "Yes, he guessed, but he never really wanted to know anything like that."

"Was there a lot to know?"

"You must think I'm very unattractive," she said.

"Far from it," I said.

"You must, if the best I could do was a thirteen-year-old boy," she said. "A twenty-year-old boy is better, but do you think there's been no one in between?"

"Well—*him.*"

"Oh, he's happy now. He likes being an invalid."

"He wasn't always an invalid," I said.

"Most of the time," she said. "Do you know why he liked being a Catholic? It was because he thought it'd make me behave. But it didn't turn out that way. It made him behave, but not me."

"I thought you were deeply in love with him," I said.

"I am. But you have a lot to learn about love."

"I guess I've learned more from you than from anyone else," I said.

"It doesn't really matter who you learn it from, as long as you learn it. I even learned some from you."

I laughed. "From me? A hot-pants kid?"

"An inexperienced kid. You're not that inexperienced any more," she said.

"No," I said.

"You didn't teach me anything, but I learned from you. It was about myself. That I could want someone whether he was thirteen or thirty, provided he wanted me enough, and showed it. You have always been someone who wanted me."

"Today?"

"Of course today," she said. "Look at you. Just look at you."

"Then why don't we?"

"Because you're not thirteen now, and we can wait," she said. "He knows every move we can make, and he's sitting on the porch imagining it. So don't be surprised if he comes down here at just the wrong time."

"What would he do if he caught us?"

"That's a chance we're not going to take," she said.

"What would he *do?*" I said.

"I said we're not going to take the chance, and we're not. Anyway, not today."

"Oh, all right," I said. "He likes to think about it, and you like to talk about it. Which one's worse?"

"Take your swim, and be more respectful to your elders," she said.

I stood on the diving-board and turned my back on her.

"Go ahead, it'll do you good," she said.

I plunged in and the water was a shock but I took a few strokes to get used to the temperature, and when I climbed out Philip Haddon was standing above her at the side of the pool. "You see what I mean about the chill," he said. "It's water that comes from a spring."

"I'll say it does," I said.

"Say, by the way, I brought something to show you," he said. From his jacket pocket he took out an automatic pistol. "Ever seen one like it?"

"No," I said.

"It's a Browning automatic," he said. He handed it to me, and I hefted it.

"It's loaded, isn't it?" I said.

"Oh, yes," he said. "But I know I can trust you with firearms."

"Philip always remembered that he could trust you with firearms," said Martha Haddon.

MALIBU FROM THE SKY

In the hills above Malibu she stopped her car for a look at
the not too distant sea, her first real look at the waters of
the Pacific. And though she had driven out from Hollywood
with no other purpose than to be able to say she had seen
the Pacific, it seemed a waste of time not to stay a few minutes and find out what thoughts came to her on this occasion. The thoughts began to come, and she did not like them
much. She was here, she had come all the way, with too
many stops along the way, and now that she was here, what
the hell of it?

Down there was Malibu Beach, where the big shots
had their beach houses, which they pretended were mere
cottages, nothing at all, really. But she knew enough about
those big shots to know that they had not started life with
anything so grand as those mere cottages. Back where she
had started her own life the biggest house in the whole
town could not hold a candle to most of those beach cottages, in size or luxury. She knew. She had been to the
biggest house in her old home town, and she had been to
a couple of those beach cottages, so-called. In her home
town the biggest house was owned by a rich Irish doctor,
Dr. Kelly, who practically owned the local hospital and was

said to own most of the stock in the larger of the two town banks, and out in the country he owned a farm where he had four or five trotting horses. She had never been to the farm, but she had been invited often to children's parties at the house in town—until, that is, she stopped being a child and started wearing high heels and a brassiere. Then the invitations stopped, although for a while there she was seeing more of Dr. Kelly's eldest son when he was home on vacations from Georgetown Prep. She well knew who had stopped the invitations to the Kelly house—Mrs. Kelly, Kevin's mother. "It's funny I never get invited to your house any more," she said to Kevin one night. She did not think it was very funny, but she wanted to see what Kevin would say. He fooled her. "You want to know why you're not invited any more?" he said. "I can give you two reasons." And he pressed his hand over each of her breasts. He was a wild one, not safe for a decent girl to go out with, everyone said. More money than was good for him, they said. Started drinking too early, others said. Spoiled by both his parents and chased after by everything in skirts, including a couple of married women who had husbands working in the mines. She had had some very anxious moments because of Kevin, especially those first two weeks after he was killed in an auto accident and she thought she might be having a baby. She would never have been able to go to Dr. and Mrs. Kelly for help, help of any kind. But after that narrow escape she left town, with sixty-five dollars her father gave her and thirty-five dollars from her mother. "Get work quick," said her father. "That's the last you can expect from us."

"I'll pay you back, every cent," she said.

"All right, if you can. We'll accept your kind offer," said her father. "But don't send home for any more, because there's none to give you. You only got this much because we won't be supporting you and there'll be that much saved." Her father worked in the mines, made good money in good times, but ever since the big strike, work in the mines was anything but steady. The car went, the washing machine was repossessed, the food on the table was enough to live on but not a pleasure to eat. The only time she saw steak was when Kevin would take her out in his car and they would stop for a sandwich on the way home.

The work she got in Philadelphia was not hard, even if it did not pay well, but with only two years of high school she was lucky to get anything that was easy and in pleasant surroundings and did not take much brains. It was clerking in a candy store near the Reading Terminal, eighteen dollars a week. It did not take her long to figure out why they hired her. Philadelphians eat a lot of candy, and a lot of it is bought by men. The commuters who took the Chestnut Hill local every afternoon liked her looks, as well they might, and pretty soon they were asking her to go out with them. One of them began to get pretty serious. She had no intention of letting him give up his wife and two kids, but she took money from him so that she could dress better and attract men who did not offer matrimony but might help her on her way to Hollywood.

It had always been Hollywood, Hollywood for itself and because it was the great chance for girls like herself. Some of the biggest stars had never had any acting experience, could not sing or dance. The important thing was to get there under contract to some studio, not to go there in the hope of finding a pleasant job in a candy store. A girl would be making a big mistake to go to Hollywood without a contract, and that was one mistake she was not going to make. She had even read about one girl who was *born* in Hollywood and went to school there, but had been smart enough to go to New York to be discovered. They did not think much of you out there unless you had a contract. And so the idea of a contract had always been in her mind.

One of the men she attracted in Philadelphia had a connection with a big movie company. That is, he worked in an office that distributed films. He never got to the Coast, although he often went to the New York office and had met the big stars. He had a lot of inside gossip on the stars and their peculiarities. It was quite a letdown to learn from him that one of her favorites did not like girls at all. How did he mean he did not like girls? "He likes boys," said her friend, Sid. That was her first personal disillusionment about Hollywood, and she did not like Sid for telling her such a thing. However, she went out with Sid and a couple of times she went to New York with him, and through Sid she met the man who persuaded her to come to New York. New York was New York, and she did not feel so strongly that you could not go there without a contract. The new man did not offer her a contract or even a job, but he paid her rent in an apartment just off Fifth Avenue in the West Fifties, and she got work modeling lingerie and hosiery and managed to get along rather well. Arthur, the man who paid her rent, was more important in the film business than Sid. He was in the theater end, with a title that she never could get straight—eastern district something, advertising, publicity, and exploitation. When he took her out to restaurants and speakeasies he was always saying hello to the newspaper fellows, and more or less as a gag one of the fellows that wrote a column put her name in print for the first time: "Model Mary-Lou Lloyd being screen-tested?" The comparatively few people who knew her were very impressed and took the item very seriously. A couple of nights later she was actually introduced as Mary-Lou Lloyd, who was being screen-tested. "Who by?" said the man to whom she was being introduced.

"Oh, there's nothing to that," said Mary-Lou.

"Don't be cagey," said the man. "Give, *give.*"

"No, there isn't anything to it," she said.

"When are they making the test?" said the man.

"That was just something in one of the columns," she said.

"Listen, if you're not signed up, I might be able to arrange a test for you. If you're not signed up. If you already signed, skip it."

"I haven't signed a thing," she said.

"She really hasn't," said Arthur.

"Arthur, I wouldn't believe you under oath," said the man. "Young lady, come to my office eleven o'clock tomorrow morning and we'll have a conversation." The man's name was Lew Linger, and he had a job similar to Arthur's at another studio. "Will you be there? Eleven A.M.?

"Tomorrow I can't, but thanks for the invitation," she said.

"Then when can you?" said Lew Linger. "The next day?"

"All right, the day after tomorrow," she said.

That night Arthur was greatly disturbed. "He means it, Lew Linger."

"Well, that's great," she said.

"Yeah, but where does it put me if *his* company makes a test of my girl? I'm making with the rent and Lew Linger steals her right out from under me. I'll be the laughing-stock. I *could* lose my God damn job. Supposing Lew's company makes a test and they sign you? I heard of guys getting fired for a lot less than that."

"Well, you get me a test with your company."

"I don't have the authority. Those tests cost money, and anyway that's not my department. Who the hell does Lew Linger think he is?"

"I don't know, but he can get me a screen test, and if he's that inarrested . . ."

"Oh, personally he is, all right. Lew Linger is a regular wolf."

"If he can get me a screen test he can take a bite out of me—where it won't show."

"Don't *say* that," said Arthur.

"I will say it. Sixty dollars a month rent doesn't mean you own me. You're getting off pretty light, considering. You don't think I don't get other offers? Listen, there isn't a day goes by without I get some kind of a proposition. And a lot better than sixty a month rent. As far as that goes I could pay my own rent."

"Sixty dollars? You think that's all you cost me? I'm always giving you presents. Who gave you the silver fox, two hundred and seventy-five dollars and worth twice that retail? How much do you think I spent taking you to the cafés?"

"Is it worth it, or isn't it? That's the main question. You're not doing it for charity, Arthur. You make me mad, throwing that up at me how much you spend on me. Big-hearted Otis, sure. Well, listen, Big-hearted Otis, go on back to that dumpy wife of yours in Fort Washington—"

"Port Washington, and I never said she was dumpy," said Arthur. "I said she was zaftig, which doesn't mean the same thing."

"That's your way. You always try to change the subject, but you're not getting away with it this time. I'm mad, see? So either you get me a screen test or don't call me up any more. You can go home right this minute, for all I care."

"At ha' past two in the morning?" said Arthur.

Before the night was over he had agreed to try to get her a screen test, and before the day was over he had persuaded the studio to give her one. His argument was based on the fact that Lew Linger, who was a wolf but a cagey one, had shown so much interest on his very first meeting with her.

The test was made in a studio in Brooklyn, without sound, and consisted largely of Mary-Lou walking around in a silk bathing suit. It was hardly more than some footage of a young girl with an exceptionally good figure, and such tests were as often as not put away and forgotten. But Mary-Lou, who was learning fast, telephoned the fellow who had put her name in his column and thanked him for the mention. He in turn thanked her for thanking him and two days later she was in his column again. "You saw it here," he wrote. "Lovely Model Mary-Lou Lloyd was slated for a screen test, we said. She made the test and execs of the Peerless Studio are readying an all-out campaign for their new discovery."

When the item appeared she telephoned Lew Linger. "Why you double-crossing little bitch," he said.

"Maybe I am," she said. "But it would of been worse to double-cross Arthur. You know how it is with Arthur and I. Almost a year now."

"Don't tell me you're in love with him," said Lew Linger.

"I didn't *say* that, Mr. Linger. But he's been awfully good to me."

"Are you leveling?"

"He has been. If it wasn't for Arthur I never would of got to know all these people."

"If you're leveling—you remind me of an old song. 'I Found a Rose in the Devil's Garden.' All right, no hard feelings. Maybe we have that talk some other time, wuddia say?"

"That's entirely up to you, Mr. Linger," she said.

"I get it. Well, how about this afternoon?"

"What time?" she said.

Lew Linger was a much more interesting man than Arthur, and not only because he was a wolf and Arthur was not. You went out with Lew Linger and people were always coming to *his* table, not a case of him always going to theirs as it was with Arthur. You never saw Arthur's name in the gossip columns, but Lew was in them all the time, either as the escort of some girl or as the originator of some wisecrack. To a certain extent he was a celebrity on his own, not the recognizable kind who was asked for his autograph, but a special kind that got a big hello from a lot of those who were asked for their autographs. More to the point was that when you went out with Lew Linger you often ended up at Reuben's in the company of some very famous people.

Nothing had come of the screen test that Arthur got for her and Arthur naturally stopped speaking to her when he found out that she had dated Lew. It went without saying that Arthur would stop making with the rent money, but Mary-Lou, after an anxious week or two, adopted the habit of borrowing money. She would say to a man, "How would you like to lend me a hundred bucks?"

"What the hell for?" the man would say.

"Well, I might be able to pay you back *some* way," she would say.

"That's a new approach," the man would say. But it was remarkable how often it worked, and putting it on a loan basis made it a different transaction from that of a hustler and a john. She always paid the man back, and not in money, and usually within twenty-four hours. Some of the men were repeaters, and she had a pretty good winter, borrowing from some and going out with Lew Linger, but Lew said no more about a screen test for his company. One movie star invited her to accompany him on the train ride back to the Coast, but she told him she would never go to

Hollywood without a contract. "You're not so dumb," said the movie star.

"Who said I was?" said Mary-Lou.

However, she was beginning to get a bit worried about the summer, when a lot of the men would be going away and things would be slack, as her father always said about work at the mines. Lew Linger was planning a trip to Europe with some company executives. "I wish you'd take me, but it'd be like carrying coals to Newcastle," she said.

"Yeah, or taking a broad to Hollywood," said Lew. "I understand a certain movie star offered you a ride out to the Coast."

"I wouldn't leave *you*, Lew," she said.

"The hell you wouldn't. Don't try to con me, baby. I went for that act once, but not twice."

"Well, you tried to con me, too, you know. That stuff about the screen test."

"You want to know something? That wasn't altogether a con," said Lew.

"Well, you can still get me one," said Mary-Lou.

"You don't want a screen test, you want a term contract."

"All right, so I do. So get me one."

"You want one of those seventy-five a week for the first six months and options up to seven years? You wouldn't want one of those. You're doing better right here in New York City, putting the arm on guys."

"I want to go to Hollywood," she said.

"Baby, you'll be out there six months and they won't take up your first option."

"I don't care, just so I have a contract. Let me worry about the option. Do this for me, Lew, and I'll never ask you for another thing."

"You wouldn't get another thing."

"Listen, I know if I go out there under contract I'll stay. Once I'm in pictures I'm all set. And even if I don't get to be a star, a *big* star, I'll manage all right. There's none of them are better built than I am, and who says you have to act?"

"Nobody," said Lew.

"I just want to be in pictures, Lew. I got a fixation on it, a real fixation. Since I was ten years old, going to the matinees on Saturday afternoon. That was where I wanted to be, up there on that screen."

"Yeah? Who was your favorite movie star?"

"I didn't have any. It was me I wanted to be up there. I didn't go around imitating other people, or wishing I was Clara Bow. I never saw a one of them that I didn't think I was prettier than, and better built."

"I was thinking more of the male stars. Who were your favorites among them?"

"You know the only one I ever sent away for his picture? Eric Von Stroheim. I never got it, either," she said, and paused.

"If I ever got in a picture with him I'd fall away in a dead faint," she went on. "The handsome ones never thrilled me, except one I found out later was queer."

"Who was that?"

"I'd be ashamed to tell you. Everybody knows he's queer, everybody in picture business. You'd laugh at me if I told you. The first time I ever heard it was in Philly, a fellow I knew in the distributing end. I wanted to hit him. But that's me. The only male stars I ever went for, the big heavy and a panseroo. *Get* me a contract, Lew. Even if it's only one of those seventy-five a week ones."

"That's all it would be, too," he said. "All right, I'll speak to Jack Marlborough."

"Who's he?"

"Nobody very big, I assure you. But big enough to get you that kind of a contract. You might say he's vice-president in charge of starlets, only he's not a vice-president. He's assistant to the casting director, and if *he* signs you it's the kiss of death, because everybody'll know he's doing somebody a favor. In this case, me."

They gave her a contract, and it was for seventy-five a week for six months, a hundred a week for the second six months, and so on for five years until she might be earning five hundred a week if all her options were taken up. They paid her fare to Los Angeles, in a lower berth on less famous trains, and she was not at the studio two weeks before she realized that she was never going to be a star in motion pictures. They had her posing for stills—fan magazine art—but the only time she appeared before a movie camera was as a cigarette girl in a gangster film. She was not given lines to read, not even "Cigars, cigarettes." She took a one-room apartment in the Rossmore section and bought a Ford V-8 roadster on the installment plan at a used car lot on Vine Street. She slept with the head cameraman who shot the gangster picture and he put her name in his little black book. Jack Marlborough introduced her to a couple of agents who showed no interest in furthering her professional career, but one of them invited her to a party at Malibu Beach which turned out to be a celebration of the twenty-first birthday of the son of a movie producer. She and the four other girls at the party were required to take off their clothes for the men at the party, who consisted of the birthday boy, the agent, and two college classmates of the birthday boy. It was the messiest party Mary-Lou had ever been to and it lasted two days. It came to an end when the birthday boy's uncle arrived and compelled the agent to take the girls back to Hollywood.

Her next visit to Malibu Beach was hardly more profitable but somewhat less messy. An English novelist, who had been singularly unsuccessful in his efforts to get the big stars to go to bed with him, was the house guest of an aging character actress who had a cottage at Malibu. He complained to her that he simply could not go back to England with his virtue intact, and she told him that he must lower his sights; that he might be a very popular author throughout the United Kingdom, but to the glamor girls of Hollywood he was just another Englishman with ants in his pants and no studio connection. "I'll see what I can do," she said, and Mary-Lou Lloyd got a surprise invitation to dinner from Cecilia Ranleigh, whom she had never met. Jack Marlborough, who had suggested Mary-Lou to the old lady, said that it would be a good chance for her to meet a different class of people.

"What's the gimmick? Why me?" said Mary-Lou.

"You'll find out when you get there. Miss Ranleigh is sending her car for you."

The car, a ten-year-old Rolls-Royce, was reassuring, but when Mary-Lou was greeted by her hostess and introduced to the other guests she knew immediately why she had been invited. The eager smile of the man with the missing molars gave him away. The dinner guests were ten in number, English writers with their husbands or wives, and with the exception of Cecilia Ranleigh, no one Mary-Lou had ever seen before. She had a hard time understanding what they said, but what got through was some juicy gossip about absent members of the British colony. The gossip was not particularly new, but they all enjoyed retelling it. The only man who did not join in was the writer on Mary-Lou's left, and he hung back because he was waiting to be asked to do his spessiality, his collection of Goldwynisms. On Mary-Lou's right was Geoffrey Graves, the man with the missing molars, who was so eager to be pleasing. He emphasized several conversational points with pats on Mary-Lou's knee under the table and she let him get away with it temporarily. Her mood, however, was not jovial. Jack Marlborough had practically ordered her to go to this party, despite the fact that he would not discuss her soon-due option. He was going to get all he could out of her before telling her that the ax was about to fall. In the second place, she was having a lousy time with these people, who managed to make her feel that they all knew she was there to entertain Geoffrey Graves. In the third place, she was not even repelled by Geoffrey Graves. He was a slightly lecherous schoolboy, and neither a Kevin Kelly, a Lew Linger nor an Eric Von Stroheim. In the fourth place, she did not like being made to feel like a foreigner when she was the only person there who was not one. Accordingly, at the dessert, when Mr. Graves let his hand linger on her knee, she looked deep into his eyes and smiled and burnt his hand with her cigarette. All present guessed what had happened, and laughed. But though they were laughing at him, they made it seem that the laugh was on her.

"Could have happened to anyone, you know," said the man who had done the Goldwynisms. "Imeantosay."

It was a great, great joke. "Serves you jolly well right, Geoffrey," one of the woman said, but without in the least being on Mary-Lou's side.

Furious, Mary-Lou got up and said, "If you don't mind, I'm going home."

"Oh, my dear, you've been embarrassed and you mustn't be," said Cecilia Ranleigh. "Really you mustn't."

"Puts old Geoffrey in the spot, I mustsay," said the Goldwynist.

"I'm most dreadfully sorry," said Geoffrey Graves, but he divided his apology between Mary-Lou and Cecilia Ranleigh.

"Skip it," said Mary-Lou. "If you don't want me to take your car, call me a taxi. But I'm getting out of here."

"Well—if you won't change your mind," said Cecilia Ranleigh. She spoke to the butler-chauffeur. "Bring the car around for Miss Lloyd, please."

Mary-Lou left the dining-room and waited in the hall. No one bothered to wait with her, and she could hear a lot of laughter from the dining-room. They were having a lot of fun at the expense of Geoffrey Graves, but at hers too. On the ride back to Hollywood the chauffeur said nothing until they got past Beverly Hills and were in the Sunset Strip with the lights of the Trocadero and other restaurants. It was not yet ten o'clock. "It's early, Miss," said the chauffeur. "Would you care to stop for a drink?"

"With you?"

"That's what I had in mind," he said.

"Don't you have to be back there right away?"

"They could do without me. I could have a flat tire."

"Well, why not?" said Mary-Lou. Without his chauffeur's cap his livery made him look like a middle-aged man in a dark suit. "Not the Troc, though. Let's go to some place quiet."

The place they picked was quiet in that it did not have an orchestra. Otherwise it was lively. The customers were finishing their dinner and settling down to their drinking. It was a youngish crowd, and Mary-Lou recognized some of them. "Strange people," said the chauffeur, when they were seated.

"Who? These?"

"I was thinking of those we left. The dinner party. By the way, my name is Jack."

"You're not a real butler, are you?"

"Not a real butler, but a real chauffeur. I buttle when

I have to but only for the money. There aren't so many jobs for chauffeur only." He was bald and probably close to fifty, but the moment he lit a cigarette he abandoned the servant manner. "Welsh, aren't you? With the name Lloyd."

"My father was Welsh descent. My mother was Irish."

"Quite a combination, isn't it? Produce quite a temper. Well, he deserved it. I've watched him making his passes and getting nowhere, Mr. Geoffrey Graves. He's not a very personable chap, but I suppose at home he trades on his reputation. Here, so few ever heard of him." He talked on and they had two or three drinks until he looked at his watch. "Oh, dear. Time I fixed that flat tire. The bill, waiter, please."

They went back to the car. "I'm going to sit in front," said Mary-Lou.

"Very well," said Jack. "I get Thursdays off and every other Sunday. Could I have your phone number? I'd like to take you to dinner."

"You would?"

"Yes. You like me, don't you?"

"Yes."

"Do you like flying?"

"You mean in an aeroplane? I've never been up in one," she said.

"Never? You must let me take you up. I was in the R.F.C., and I've kept up. Chap out in Glendale lets me fly his Moth. Will you go up with me one day soon?"

"Maybe I might. Not if I think about it, but I might."

"You'd love it. I know you would."

"How do you know?"

"Oh—one knows."

"What else does one know?"

"Well—one knows that you stood up to those hyenas

single-handed. Miss Cecilia Ranleigh is a formidable woman, and the others are not bad individually. But en masse they can be very cruel."

"I hated them," said Mary-Lou.

"Of course you did. Then you'll let me take you up?"

"Yes," she said.

"You might like it enough to learn."

"Let's not rush things," she said.

He never telephoned her, but as it happened he had only two weeks left in which he might have. An item in a chatter column said: "British colony saddened to hear Cecilia Ranleigh's butler, John Motley, killed in plane crash at Glendale." That was all he got in the press, and it was probably too late to send flowers . . .

Down there was Malibu Beach, and now Mary-Lou could honestly say, when she went back to New York, that she had seen the Pacific Ocean. She had almost been able to say she had seen it from the sky.

HARRINGTON AND WHITEHILL

Mary Brown went to the door and opened it. "Hello, Jack," she said.

"Hello, Mary," he said. "How are you?"

"Very well, thank you," she said. "You know where to put your coat. Gretchen just got home a little while ago, so you're going to have to wait."

"I have all the time in the world," said Jack. He hung his coat and hat in the foyer closet.

"Would you like a drink?"

"Sure. What have you got?"

"What you see. Whiskey, and gin," she said.

"Shall I make a cocktail?"

"Not for me, thanks."

"Not for me, either," he said. He helped himself to a strong whiskey and water.

She was uncomfortable, ill at ease under his gaze.

"You don't have to entertain me, Mary. Do whatever you were doing."

"I was washing stockings, and Gretchen's in the tub," she said.

"You staying home tonight?"

"I'm going out later," she said. "There's a dance at the

Squadron, but Billy won't be here till—I don't know—not before ten, I guess."

"You going to marry Billy?"

The question annoyed her. She held out her left hand.

"I didn't ask you if you were engaged to him. If you announced your engagement I'd probably hear about it."

"Then why don't you just wait till you do hear about it?"

"I don't think you want to marry him, but all the same I'll bet you do."

"Jack, why don't you keep your nose out of my affairs? I really don't like those kind of questions."

"It wasn't a question you disliked. It was my analysis of your innermost thoughts. I don't think you want to marry Billy, but I'd bet fifty dollars you're married to him within one year. Would you like to take that bet?"

"Suppose I won? Would you ever pay me?"

"If I happened to have fifty dollars I would. Yes, I'd pay you."

"I'm sorry I said that," she said.

"What the hell? I don't often have fifty dollars, and nobody knows it better than you do. Except Gretchen. And you're a Brown, and the Browns are all very money-conscious. So am I, of course. But you're money-conscious because you have it, and I am because I haven't."

"It *wasn't* a very nice thing to say," she said. "But you always make some remark that just infuriates me, and I say things I don't really mean."

"I do it on purpose," he said.

"Sometimes I think you do," she said.

"I do," he said.

"What pleasure do you get out of it?"

"Oh, come on, Mary. Isn't that obvious? You never fail to rise to the bait. Never."

"Well, I admit I'm not as clever as you are."

"Who said anything about clever? You're so used to having the same things said to you, and saying the same things yourself, that anything out of the ordinary throws you off."

"I'm not used to clever people. My friends aren't clever people."

"If you're talking about Billy, I'll agree with that. No one will ever accuse Billy Walton of being clever. He's safe there."

"He has a very *fine* mind."

"Maybe he has. *Mens sana in corpore sano.* A sound mind in a sound body, that's Billy Walton. You ought to have very healthy children. Although I'm only going on what I see. There may be all sorts of loathsome diseases in the Walton family history. The Browns, too, for that matter. But just from looking at the present generation, you and Billy, I'd say you had a pretty good chance of producing fine specimens. Reproducing, I should say. Because that's what you'll do. You'll reproduce. The offspring will bear some resemblances to you and some to Billy, but they'll be essentially the same. You perpetuate the line, without incurring the risk of bringing forth genuine idiots, as you would if you married your brother or a first cousin."

"When I was working with the Junior League I saw children that had mixed ancestry, and believe me some of those were far from perfect."

"I know," he said. "I've seen them too. It makes you realize what a big chance you're taking when you bring *any* children into the world."

"Therefore, why not pick someone you know something about?"

"Like Billy Walton," he said.

"Yes. He was the twelfth highest man in his class, and he rowed on the varsity crew for *three years*."

"I see what you mean, all right. It was a winning crew, too. I never rowed, myself. Not that I was big enough for the varsity, but I never went out for the jayvees or the hundred-and-fifty pounders. I know it's very good discipline and teaches you teamwork and all that, but I didn't have the real spirit. Besides, I heard that oarsmen all got boils on their asses. I had a boil on my ass once, and it's no fun. Did you ever have a boil on your ass, Mary?"

"Another of those remarks. But this time I know you said it on purpose."

"I always do. I told you," he said. "Did you ever have a boil there, Mary?"

"No."

"Where?"

"On my ass. You wanted to make me say it, so now I have."

"I'm glad you escaped that," he said. "Not only because of the pain, the discomfort. But for aesthetic reasons. A boil just doesn't belong on your ass. Or anywhere else on you. Or on Billy Walton either, except in line of duty for good old Yale."

"Harvard, and you know it," she said.

"Yes, I did know it. But the Yale varsity and the Harvard varsity, except for all those Saltonstalls on the Harvard crews, they're both just a continuation of Groton and St. Mark's. Hard to tell them apart."

"Billy didn't go to Groton *or* to St. Mark's," she said.

"*Why* didn't he? Maybe you ought to do a little digging on that, Mary. You might learn something before it's too late. Where *did* he go to school?"

"He went to Pomfret, where all his family went."

"Oh. Well, I guess you're safe. If there were family reasons for going to Pomfret, you'll have to make allowances."

"Is that supposed to get a rise out of me, too?"

"Nothing will, tonight," he said. "You're on your guard. Do you mind if I cadge another drink off you?"

"Gretchen pays half, it's not all mine," she said.

"Well, do you mind if I cadge another drink off you and Gretchen?"

"Go right ahead," she said.

"After all, you're first cousins. And I guess Billy Walton takes a drink here now and then. So, in a sense, you might say half of his drinks are practically mine, inasmuch as I'm the one that comes to see Gretchen. And Gretchen pays half the liquor bill. Do you follow me?"

"Oh, yes," she said.

"I wasn't sure. I had a little trouble with it myself."

"Don't make the next one so strong," she said.

"Oh, my present state of mind wasn't produced by the drink I just finished."

"I didn't think so," she said.

"You're so observant, Mary. Did it show, that I stopped off at Dan Moriarty's on the way here?"

"I could tell you'd stopped off somewhere."

"It's payday, and I wanted to reestablish credit. Today it was Dan's turn. I'm all clear with Dan now, which means that Gretchen and I will dine at Giuliano's, on the cuff. The week after next, not next week, but the week after next, I shall reestablish credit at Giuliano's."

"How can you *live* that way?" she said.

"Huh. You might better ask, how could I live any other way? Were it not, were it not for the liberal policy of certain speakeasy proprietors, I would often go without food or drink. Not only what I charge to my account, but I can cash cheques. They don't bother to try and put the cheques through. They just hold them for a while, and tear them up when I come in with the cash. But don't you tell Gretchen."

"Don't you think she knows?"

"Not positively."

"You'll never be able to get married if you don't start saving *some* money."

"Wrong," he said. "If I were to save ten dollars a week —a very unlikely prospect—but say I saved ten dollars every week, in one year I'd have five hundred and twenty dollars. Right?"

"Yes."

"In *two* years, *two years*, I'd have one thousand and forty dollars. In *ten* years of this fantastic scheme, I'd have amassed the sum of five thousand, two hundred dollars. Fifty-two hundred bucks. Do you know what that is?"

"Well—"

"Don't bother to think about it. It's exactly, I happen to know, exactly the allowance Gretchen gets from her mother in one year. Not what she gets from both parents, but from one parent. Her father gives her the same amount plus birthday and Christmas presents."

"I know. But still—"

"Wait a minute, I haven't finished. Do you know how much I get paid?"

"Seventy-five dollars a week."

"Oh, she told you. Well, that's right. Seventy-five a week. I pay sixty dollars a month rent. That's one I have to pay. If I don't pay the rent, out I go. No place to rest my weary head. So I do pay my rent. Not right on the dot, but somewhere in the first two or maybe three weeks of every month. Sixty bucks, cash. And I pay a woman six dollars a week to clean up my apartment. She doesn't come in Sunday, and a damn good thing she doesn't, some Sundays. But that's twenty-four dollars a month. Sixty and twenty-four, eighty-four. More than a week's pay and so far I haven't even bought a pound of coffee. I make my own coffee and have a couple of doughnuts every morning, but so far we haven't come to that. I haven't paid the phone company yet. The rent, the maid, the phone company, and the laundry bill. You can't wear a shirt two days in New York City, not if you have a white-collar job. The light company. They'll turn off the light. Gas. No hot water for my coffee. The dry cleaners. When you have two suits and a Tuck, there's always one or the other at the dry cleaners'. And so far, no food, no coffee, and no cigarettes, not a damn thing to drink. I haven't even left my apartment."

"But people live on a lot less than that. When I was with the Junior League—"

"I know that, too. When you were with the Junior League you saw families getting by on twenty-five or thirty dollars a week. But did they want to? *I* don't want to. I can't get by on *three times* that much. I can't save four dollars a month, and live the way I have to. It's no use arguing that I could stop going to Dan Moriarty's and places like that. Why should I? To save fifty-two hundred dollars in ten years? Ten God damn miserable, joyless years? And be thirty-six years old at the end of it?"

"Well, I don't know," she said.

"Mary, your grandfather, or maybe it was your great-grandfather—"

"My grandfather, if you're going to say what I think you are."

"Opened a little store in Cleveland, Ohio, on probably a great deal less than fifty-two hundred bucks capital. And now your family are worth God knows how many millions. Well, your grandpa worked very hard, raised a large family, made a big pile of dough, and now I'm drinking his liquor. And whenever she's ready, I'm going to take his granddaughter out for dinner."

"Yes?"

"Well, why should I sweat and strain to save five thousand dollars when I can go out with Gretchen tonight and have a better time than old J. J. Brown ever had or ever gave anyone?"

"If a good time is all you want to get out of life," she said.

"I sure as hell don't want to have a bad time."

"But you are having a bad time. You worry about money, you can't marry Gretchen. You're not having a very good time, Jack."

"No?"

"No."

"Well, are you? Are you having a good time? Washing your stockings and waiting for a stuffed shirt to take you to a dance at Squadron A?"

"Of course I am," she said.

"And wondering if this is going to be the night Mr. Billy Walton will propose honorable marriage? And you can go back to Cleveland, Ohio, and get ready for the big wedding. Got yourself a real, genuine, old Knickerbocker family specimen."

"I think you're horrible! And I mean that," she said. "You're detestable."

"Sure. But you're all right. The one life you have to live, and what are you doing with it? Saving your virginity for him. You may be a peasant, but you're a virgin peasant."

"Horrible, horrible," she said, and began to cry as she left the room, her face covered with her hands.

He sat silent for a moment, took a sip of his drink, then got up and threw the glass in the fireplace. He was staring at it when Gretchen came in.

She went to him without a word, and they embraced.

"Sorry I'm late," she said.

"Why do you let them get away with it?"

"With what?"

"I'm sure everybody else goes home at five, but they don't seem to care how long they make you stay. God knows they don't pay you enough."

She smiled. "The last two weeks they didn't pay me at all," she said.

"The next thing will be when they try to get you to put money in the business."

"They've already asked me to," she said.

"Are you going to?"

"I don't know. I might. It wouldn't be a lot. Where are we going?"

"Giuliano's," he said. "Shall we go?"

"Could we wait a few minutes? Mother phoned and I wasn't here, and I think she may call back. I'd like to find out how Father is."

"Is he home from the hospital?"

"He got home yesterday, but they're keeping two trained nurses."

"He must be a lot better or they wouldn't have let him go home from the hospital."

"That's what I'm hoping," she said. "We can have a cocktail here. Will you mix me a Martini? And what are you having? No drink?"

"Don't pretend, Gretchen. You know I've had a lot to drink."

"I wasn't going to say anything. How did you happen to break the glass in the fireplace?"

"I was drinking a silent toast to Mary and Billy Walton."

"Oh, she told you? How can you worm those things out of her? She hasn't even told her family."

"She hasn't told me, either. I just guessed."

"She must have told you something," said Gretchen. "What did she tell you?"

"She told me I ought to start saving money."

"Well, I'm sure you had a good answer for that. She worries about you, you know. She really likes you."

"Am I supposed to jump for joy because Mary Brown likes me?"

"You could be more agreeable. Whenever you have any conversation with her you always manage to somehow hurt her feelings. You say things."

"Yes, damn near every conversation I have with anybody, I say things."

"Oh, don't start picking on me. It doesn't get you anywhere. I know your ways. But Mary *isn't* used to having people make her feel like an absolute dumbbell. And she's not, either. She's very bright. But you're always so condescending with her, trying to trip her up on everything she says."

"How long are we going to have to wait for your mother's call?"

"Why? Are you in any particular hurry?"

"I don't want to go an hour without a drink."

"Well, have one. It's there. And I told you, I asked you to fix me a Martini. What's got into you tonight?"

He started the business of making her cocktail. "Money."

"Money?"

"The whole damn subject of money. Your cousin got me started on it, and before I knew it I was telling her all about my finances."

"Well, she understands."

"Understands? Who gives a damn whether she understands? I wasn't trying to make her understand anything.

But it made *me* realize what a hell of a state my finances are in. I hadn't stopped to think about it lately."

"Then maybe it's time you did. You have a good job—"

"A good job—and I make less than you get for spending money. You have a job that's supposed to pay you twenty-five dollars a week, and when they don't pay you, you can laugh it off as a joke."

"It's not a joke, and I don't laugh it off. Neither do they. These two boys are trying to publish good things, not just mystery stories and trashy novels. But all the good authors are signed up by the big publishers. These boys are trying to keep their heads above water until they discover someone that hasn't been published before, and that's not easy, because the literary agents, if they find somebody good but without an established reputation, they take their discovery to one of the big publishers like Scribner's. Doubleday. I'm in favor of what we're doing, and I wish I could help."

"They'll give you your chance to help."

"Well, I'd rather put my money in that than in a lot of other things I could think of."

"Such as?"

"What other things? Well, museums, for instance. Grandfather put a lot of money into the Museum, and we're all expected to contribute once a year. But I'm not going to this year. I'm going to put my money into Whitehill and Grimes."

"The boys."

"Well, they're not boys any more. Both over thirty. But they're young in the publishing business. What I can give them, or lend them, is only a drop in the bucket, but they need all the help they can get. And I'd get much more satisfaction out of helping them than just writing a cheque to the Museum and then forgetting about it. Wouldn't you?"

"I'm not faced with any such dilemma."

"Oh, come on. Don't you agree with me? Isn't it better to do what you can to help develop new writers than—excuse me. I'm sure that's Mother's call." She went to the telephone.

"Hello . . . It's all right, Mary, I've got it . . . Mother? How are you, dear? . . . How did it go? . . . Oh, they did? . . . Well, how is he now? . . . Oh, dear. That's not very good, is it? . . . Oh, you poor dear . . . Who else is there with you? . . . That's good . . . What does Dr. Brady say? . . . Uh-huh. Uh-huh. Yes . . . Then I'll tell you what I'll do, Mother. I'll take the midnight . . . Well, I'll sit up in the day coach if I have to. But I think I ought to be there, knowing Dr. Brady. He isn't prone to exaggerate . . . I hope *you're* getting some rest, but I suppose you're not . . . Well, I'll take the midnight, and don't have anyone meet me. I'll get a taxi . . . I know, dear, and all we can do now is hope . . . Goodnight, Mother."

She hung up and sighed. She lit a cigarette. "Not so good. Not so damn good. He had a hemorrhage this afternoon and he's been in a coma ever since. Wonderful Dr. Brady, I adore that man. He said we'll know tonight, but I think he knows already. He's trying to spare Mother. Poor Daddy. Strange. Calling him Daddy. We stopped calling him Daddy when my brother was born. He didn't want his son calling him Daddy, so we all changed to Father. I hope he is in a coma, a real one. He couldn't stand to have people fuss over him."

"What can I do, darling?"

"Oh—sit with me. Put your arms around me, and if I cry, let me, a little. I don't think I'm going to, but yes I am." She began to weep quietly and he sat with her. "I want to see him once more," she said.

Mary Brown stood in the doorway, unseen by Gretchen and Jack, and she quickly vanished.

2.

It is two years later. A Sunday at lunch time, the apartment of Jack and Gretchen on Park Avenue. Jack was reading the Sunday paper when the doorbell rang, and he went to admit Billy and Mary Walton. He kisses Mary on the cheek, shakes hands with Billy.

"Look at you two," said Jack. "You look as if you were all set to pose for the rotogravure." He inspects Bill Walton, who is attired in short black coat and striped trousers and has a bowler in his hand.

"I've always been meaning to get one of these outfits," said Jack.

"Adore them," said Mary. "They make any man look distinguished."

"Well, I'd put that to a severe test, but damn it, I'm going to order one tomorrow," said Jack. "You two been to church?"

"Not only to church, but you made a good guess," said Billy. "About the rotogravure."

"I was going to wait and tell Gretchen," said Mary.

"You've been posing for the roto section?" said Jack.

"For the *Herald Tribune*," said Mary. "It's linked up with some charity. Mr. and Mrs. Williamson Walton, and I think Borden's Milk."

"I don't think we *are* Borden's Milk, Mary. Didn't the man say that that had been a mistake? I know he did, as a matter of fact. He said we were Hellman's Mayonnaise. The Borden's Milk people have the Schermerhorn twins."

"Oh, I didn't hear that part of your conversation."

Gretchen came in. "Hello, my dears," she said. "Did you have your picture taken?"

"In front of St. Bartholomew's," said Mary.

"And I happen to be a member of St. Thomas's. *We* are," said Billy.

"Was it bad? Mary was dreading it," said Gretchen.

"It wasn't really so bad," said Mary.

"Except having people stop and stare at us. I felt like a model," said Billy.

"And you look like one—I mean that as a compliment. Do you want to see the baby, Mary?"

"Of course," said Mary.

"Billy, I won't subject you to that," said Gretchen.

"Oh, why I'd love to—"

"No, you stay and talk to Jack," said Gretchen. She and Mary left the room.

"You're a coward," said Jack. "I don't know how many times I've had to say goo-goo to your kid. And frankly, she isn't half as good-looking as my young man."

"That's a matter of opinion," said Billy. "What's new at Harrington, Whitehill and Grimes?"

"Can you keep a secret?"

"I think so," said Billy.

"I'm buying out Grimes. We're going to keep his name for a year, but only a year. Next year it'll be Harrington and Whitehill."

"Congratulations," said Billy.

"Thank you."

"Did you have to pay Grimes a lot of money?"

"Quite a lot. Or at least let's put it this way. It wasn't a very large sum, but it had to be cash. He wouldn't agree to any other terms. But it worked out all right. When he insisted on cash, that made it just that much easier to tell him that we weren't going to carry his name. And therefore, if we were not going to carry his name, he wasn't entitled to very much money for good will. He outsmarted himself."

"I think you probably *let* him outsmart himself," said Billy. "Frankly, Jack, I have more and more respect for you as a business man. There was a time when I didn't think you had it in you, but I was good and wrong about that. I used to think you were one of those Greenwich Village Bohemian types, but I take it all back now."

"I thought I was, too."

"By the way, I spoke to Harry Judson. Your name comes up on the fifteenth, I think it is, and according to Harry you can start wearing the hatband as soon as you send them your cheque. In other words, you're in."

"Well, thank you for that, too, Billy. I wouldn't have made it without you."

"You're damn right you wouldn't. Because three years ago if your name had come up, and anyone asked me about you, I'd have said no. Shows how wrong you can be."

"No, three years ago you'd have been right. But three years ago I wouldn't have been up for any club."

"I suppose a lot of fellows go through that phase. I never did. I know it sounds stuffy, but I never felt that I had to rebel against my mother and father. I don't know of two finer people in the world. I liked Harvard and my friends there. I didn't like everybody in prep school, and I got into a few scrapes there, but nothing very serious. So I never went through that phase. As a matter of fact, the rebellious ones always struck me as a bunch of soreheads. I don't mean you necessarily, but yes, I do. You were sore at something."

"I was sore at everything."

"Well, you have the courage to admit it, and it takes courage. What were you sore at, if it's any of my business?"

"I was adopted. My father and mother both died in the flu epidemic in 1918, and my aunt and uncle adopted me."

"Were they nasty to you?"

"Not a bit. But I was sixteen years old when my parents died, and at that age you don't grow a new set of parents. They're not the same as your own father and mother, and no matter how much they did for me, and it was as much as they could afford, I resented it because I felt they were doing it out of a sense of duty."

"Well, if you don't mind my saying so, you sound as though you were already a bit of a sorehead when you were sixteen."

"Maybe I was. But let's not go into this too deeply or I may find out that I'm still a sorehead."

"No, I don't think you are any more. You've had a change of heart, and Gretchen's responsible for that. That's a girl I think the world of, and so does everybody else. Mary feels much closer to her than if she were her own sister. She's often said so to me."

"Well," said Jack. "How about a drink?"

"Can't. We have to go to Mother's this afternoon, and she just hates it when Father or I have a drink in the middle of the day. Her brother, my Uncle Phil Williamson, was a notorious rumpot. Died of it in his early thirties. I don't know if you've ever noticed, but when you've been to Mother's for lunch, you're offered one sherry. One sherry, and that's all."

"I've never been to your mother's for lunch."

"Yes you have, haven't you? Well, anyway, now you're forewarned. Don't ever go there with a hangover and expect the hair of the dog. My father wasn't very much of a drinker, either."

"Mine was. Periodic benders. And I guess that's why we never had very much money. But my uncle didn't drink at all, and he wasn't exactly rolling in wealth."

"Your father was a lawyer. Why do so many lawyers like the booze? I should think you'd have to have a pretty

clear head to be a lawyer. But some of the hardest drinkers
I know are lawyers, and yet it doesn't seem to affect their
work. One of the most brilliant lawyers I know makes absolutely no bones about it. I'm not telling tales out of school.
It's George Wingman, partner in Mortimer and Miller. I've
seen him in his own office, put the bottle right up on the
desk, and slug away at it. But when you know the tax laws
as well as he does, you don't have to worry about where
your next job is coming from."

"I know George Wingman," said Jack. "Some day you're
going in his office and it won't be a bottle on the desk. It'll
be a dame."

"So I've heard. A tail hound. That's something I never
could see. I don't say I was a purity boy, but this thing of
chasing one woman after another—I just don't see it. Do
you?"

"I suppose I've done my share of it."

"Well, maybe in your Greenwich Village days. But
George Wingman, for instance, he's married."

"Yes, I know his wife. She's from my home town, or one
of my home towns."

"How does she put up with it? She must *know*."

"She knows, all right," said Jack.

"Oh. Meaning that what's sauce for the goose and so
forth?"

"They seem to have some kind of an arrangement."

"What a way to live. What a way to live. Why be married if that's all it means? Whenever I hear of friends of
mine considering getting a divorce—I think you can solve
any problem except that one. Unfaithfulness. Infidelity. I'd
never try to help out two friends of mine if I knew for sure
that one of them had been unfaithful. I have helped one or
two, when there were financial problems. And one guy that
let his wife sit at home while he went to the hockey matches

or the ball game. You know, sometimes just a word will do the trick. But not when—" he interrupted himself as Gretchen and Mary returned to the room "—you have that other problem."

"Problem? Problem? What other problem?" said Gretchen.

"Oh, we were discussing a legal problem," said Billy. He looked at Jack, rather proud of his half-truth and quick thinking.

"Oh, yes," said Gretchen. "Jack's been spending a lot of time with lawyers lately. Did you tell him, dear?"

"Yes, I did," said Jack.

"Everybody's in on this but me," said Mary.

"You tell her, Jack," said Gretchen.

"Simply that I've bought out Grimes."

"Grimes?" said Mary. "Oh, your partner, Grimes. Why, that's wonderful, isn't it?"

"We think so," said Gretchen. "Next year the firm will be known as Harrington and Whitehill, without the Grimes."

"Well, didn't you tell me that Grimes was more or less of a weak sister?" said Mary to Gretchen.

"She shouldn't have said that, if she did," said Jack. "He after all was one of the original founders of the firm."

"Well, heavens, I don't go around repeating everything Gretchen tells me."

"I'm sure you don't, Mary. But—"

"Wait, wait, wait, wait," said Gretchen. "*I* was the one that *originally* said Stanley Grimes was a weak sister. Long ago. When I was still working for Whitehill and Grimes. Stanley was a nice, ineffectual boy. He was supposed to be the one that would discover new authors, and Ray White-hill would manage the business end. But Stanley would take the authors to lunch and make all sorts of promises, then Ray would have to repudiate the promises. If Stanley

Grimes had had his way, the firm would have gone bank-rupt. Five-hundred-dollar advances for little slim volumes by unknown poets. Nobody has to feel sorry for Stanley. When Jack decided to buy him out, Stanley suddenly de-veloped a very keen sense of the value of money. He in-sisted on cash. Thirty-five thousand dollars cash."

"Wow!" said Billy.

"I should say so," said Gretchen.

"But we got rid of him," said Jack.

"And it was Jack, not Stanley, that discovered the only two authors on our list that have made money, so far. Jack discovered Julian Joplin and Serena Von Zetwitz."

"Hot stuff, that Von Zetwitz woman," said Billy. "Is that her real name?"

"Yes, why?" said Jack. "Doesn't it sound real?"

"It sounds real, but I'll bet she never goes back to that town in Iowa, not after that book."

"Nebraska," said Jack. "No, I guess she won't be going back there for a while. Anyway, she's living in Italy."

"What's she like, to meet, I mean?" said Mary.

"Rather plain," said Gretchen. "Soft-spoken."

"How old?"

"Early thirties. Maybe thirty-three or four," said Gretchen. "This was her third novel—"

"Fourth," said Jack.

"That's right. Three unpublished, and then she wrote *Harvest Time*. Jack read the manuscript of one of her earlier novels and encouraged her to try again. And guess where he discovered that manuscript? In a pile of manu-scripts that Stanley Grimes had rejected but hadn't got around to returning. *Harvest Time* is entirely due to Jack. I'm very proud of my husband."

"Well, she didn't pull any punches," said Billy. "Some of it was pretty raw. Pretty raw."

"And I don't think it's a true picture," said Mary. "You can go to any small town in America and find *some* queer birds, but why doesn't she write about some of the decent people?"

"Wouldn't sell," said Billy.

"Oh, I don't know, Billy," said Jack. "*Laughing Boy* is selling. Edna Ferber has a new book out, and that's selling. Naturally we'd like to have Edna Ferber and Oliver La-Farge on our list, but we haven't got them. But we also want to publish new people, like Serena Von Zetwitz and Julian Joplin."

"And how exciting it is when they sell," said Gretchen. "A year ago nobody'd ever heard of either one of them, and today they're both famous."

"Well, they've all heard of the Von Zetwitz dame, all right," said Billy. "Especially in Boston. Did you plan that, Jack? Getting her book banned in Boston?"

"Naturally," said Jack.

"Oh, you did not," said Mary.

"Of course I didn't, but Billy likes to think I did," said Jack.

"I was only kidding. Can't you take a joke?" said Billy.

"Not very well, I guess. Not where our books are concerned."

"The one I'm dying to meet is Julian Joplin," said Gretchen.

"Oh, haven't you met him? I thought you met all your authors," said Mary.

"Most of them, but he hasn't been to New York."

"Not even when you published his book?" said Mary.

"Won't come," said Gretchen. "He won't budge out of Kentucky."

"He's one I'd be afraid to meet," said Mary.

"Why? I didn't read *his* book," said Billy. "Does he write like the Von Zetwitz dame?"

"Yes, and no," said Mary. "He describes worse things than she does, but you have to read it over again to make sure. Isn't that right, Gretchen?"

"Yes. He has such a complicated style that you *can* read and reread long passages in his books, and then it begins to dawn on you that he's been describing something perfectly awful."

"Like what?" said Billy.

"Well—it's sex, but not just ordinary sex. Jack, you explain," said Gretchen.

"Perversion."

"You mean like a couple of fairies?" said Billy.

"No. A man and a woman, but having an extremely unconventional affair. Read the book. Maybe you won't even notice it."

"I'll sure as hell notice it if Mary did."

"Well, I had to go back and reread it, to make sure. Even so I'm not altogether sure," said Mary. "Did you get it first time you reread it, Gretchen?"

"The scene in the churchyard? Yes, I think I did."

"You didn't have to ask Jack?"

"I did ask him, but I'd guessed right," said Gretchen.

"Well, you're a lot more sophisticated than Mary," said Billy.

"Don't ever say that about any woman, Billy, that she's less sophisticated than another woman," said Jack.

"I suppose I'm less sophisticated than Gretchen, but I'm getting there," said Mary. "You make me sound not quite bright, Billy, but I know a lot of things I don't necessarily talk about."

"Well, don't talk about them, because I think it's very unbecoming. Gretchen *is* more sophisticated than you are, but still she doesn't talk about such things the way some girls do nowadays. Have you got anyone else coming for lunch besides us?"

"Yes, are you getting hungry?" said Gretchen.

"A little, but no great hurry. I had breakfast at ha' past eight."

"What on earth for, on Sunday morning?" said Gretchen.

"I didn't say I got up at ha' past eight. I only said I had breakfast. We didn't actually get up till about an hour later. Mary got up early, but then she came back to bed."

"You might as well describe our whole morning," said Mary.

Billy was baffled, then realized the inferences that could be taken. "Oh," he said. "Well, we're married."

"Oh, hush up, Billy. You're only making it worse," said Mary.

"I'm not, but you are. To change the subject, who *is* coming for lunch. Or *are?*"

"You've never met them. Michael and Josephine Landers. Jack just hired him a few weeks ago, as a sort of general assistant in the editorial department. And she writes for *Harper's Bazaar.* She's had some light verse published in *The New Yorker,* you may have seen. He's written a novel that we're going to publish, but he needed a job and Jack hired him."

"He got the novel out of his system. Pretty terrible. But I think he's going to make a very good assistant. Anyway, we agreed to let him try it for a year," said Jack.

"And they needed the money. Michael spent over a

year writing his novel, and they apparently had to live on her salary, which wasn't much. Michael was really quite desperate for a job, and he's very grateful to Jack."

"Well, we don't have to go into that," said Jack. "We're not paying him much, but I think he has a hell of a future in the office. I just hope he doesn't decide to go back to writing novels. The one I read was really quite bad, and I think I know."

"You certainly do," said Gretchen. "There! There they are."

"What's their name again?" said Billy.

"Landers. Michael and Josephine Landers," said Gretchen.

Michael and Josephine Landers came in and were introduced. They were slightly younger than the others. Josephine was smartly dressed in a good but not new suit. Michael in Brooks clothes from tie to shoe, all new and stiffish. It could be guessed that his new outfit had coincided with his new job. She was smallish and pretty, with light brown hair and bright blue eyes. He was tallish and thin, under six foot, loose-limbed and not quite awkward in his movements and his manners, saved from awkwardness by an integral self-confidence that came near to being arrogance, but was not.

Immediately after the introductions Michael Landers addressed Billy Walton. "Didn't you row on the Harvard crew?"

"Yes, I did. How did you know?" said Billy. "Did you row in college?"

Michael looked quickly at Mary Walton, then back at Billy. "No—I just recognized your name."

"Were you at Harvard?"

"No, I went to Brown." He spoke with a finality that

indicated his unwillingness to continue past the identification of Billy. But then he had a change of mind. "You
don't remember me at all?"

"That's kind of putting me on the spot, but no, I'm
afraid I don't."

"I don't mean that you'd recognize me, but doesn't my
name mean anything to you? Michael Landers?"

"You've got to help me out," said Billy. The others were
taking a keen interest in their conversation.

"All right," said Michael. "My father was the gardener
on your family's place in Mount Kisco. Now do you remember?"

"Of course. Now I remember. But you have to admit,
that was a long time ago," said Billy.

"How interesting," said Gretchen. "Your father worked
for Mr. Walton's father?"

"For about twenty years," said Michael Landers. "Do
you want to tell her, Walton?"

"I don't particularly want to, but I will, if you insist,"
said Billy. "Mr. Landers's father, David Landers, was the
head gardener at our place in Mount Kisco. And when
I was about thirteen or fourteen, at Pomfret at the time,
there was a robbery at our house. A lot of my mother's
jewelry was stolen, and the police were convinced it was
an inside job. They questioned Mr. Landers's father."

"They didn't only question him. They arrested him."

"Yes, I guess they did actually place him under arrest,
on suspicion. But they released him. It was an inside job,
but the guilty party was my mother's maid. She confessed,
and they recovered all the jewelry. But Mr. Landers's
father quit his job, although my father and mother wanted
him to stay. Is that a fair statement of what happened?"

"Oh, very fair. You never knew what happened to my
father, did you?"

"No. I was away at school, and about all I knew was that he quit his job, and he and his family, which would include you, left Mount Kisco."

"Under a cloud, would you say?" said Michael.

"Not as far as we were concerned. I know my father wanted him to stay."

"But didn't keep the police from arresting him."

"I don't know anything about that part of it."

"But that's the important part, as far as my father was concerned. And as far as *I'm* concerned. My father was incapable of stealing anything. He'd worked for your father and your grandfather, for twenty years. But they allowed the police to put him in jail."

"No necessity to bring my grandfather into it. My father couldn't have prevented the police from—"

"Your father, in Mount Kisco, could have prevented anything. If he hadn't suspected my father, they never would have arrested him." He turned to Gretchen. "I'm sorry, Mrs. Harrington, but you'll have to excuse us."

"Well, under the circumstances, I suppose there's nothing else to do," said Gretchen.

"Yes there is," said Billy. "You can excuse us. Mr. and Mrs. Landers can stay. We were going to have to leave early anyhow, to go to Mother's. So I really insist, Gretchen."

"I don't know," said Jack. "Why don't you all stay?"

"Ridiculous," said Mary Walton.

"No more ridiculous than reopening an old wound and then not trying to do something to heal it," said Jack.

"Sorry, Jack, but I didn't reopen it, and I don't think it can be healed. Mr. Landers could have postponed this little scene till some other time, but as soon as he heard my name . . . No, we'll leave, and you can get the rest of the story from Mr. Landers."

"I'll see you Tuesday, Gretchen," said Mary.

The Waltons left.

"There's no use trying to talk about something else," said Gretchen. "What happened to your father, Michael?"

"Do you know what gardeners are like, Mrs. Harrington?"

"In what way?" said Gretchen.

"They're generally very quiet men, really more interested in what they're doing than they are in people. Most of the time they're working with dirt, the soil. And all they produce is beauty, and often the most beautiful things don't last very long. A few days, maybe a few weeks. But it's worth it to them, to bring that beauty up out of the ground. My father knew every flower in the Walton's garden, and every petal on every flower. He was up at five o'clock every morning, seven days a week most of the year, and in all kinds of weather. He was no more capable of stealing Mrs. Walton's diamonds and pearls than he could have taken one of her prize roses and crushed it in his fist. My father didn't even carry a watch. He had a watch. This one. It was given to him on his twenty-first birthday, but he never carried it. He only owned one necktie, to wear to church on Sunday. But as soon as he came home from church, right after Sunday dinner, he put on his work clothes and was back in the garden. He had two helpers, two Italians, but they wouldn't work on Sunday, and some things had to be done while the weather was right. He was paid twenty dollars a week and we got the cottage rent-free and all our fresh vegetables, that he grew, although one of the Italians did do most of the work in the truck garden. He wouldn't have known a diamond from a piece of cut glass.

"Well, that was the man that J. W. Walton suspected of stealing his wife's jewelry. Locking him up in jail, even just for one night, was the most heartless, most senseless, cruelest thing I ever knew of. He didn't understand it at the time, and the more he tried to understand it later, the worse he got. I mean—well, it affected his mind. He wasn't very bright anyway. He hardly ever read the newspaper. Seed catalogs and books on gardening were all he ever read. I'll tell you something else about my father. When they released him from jail, he was actually going back to work in the garden. He'd missed a whole day. It was my mother that stopped him. I was about seven years old, but I can remember coming home from school and my sister telling me that Pop had been arrested and was in jail. She and I and my younger brother cried all night, and the next day we stayed home from school. Then when my father got home we packed our suitcases and cardboard boxes and went and stayed with my uncle and aunt in New Rochelle.

"My father got a job in a greenhouse in New Rochelle, but two years later he got t.b., and the next year he died.

"Maybe no one else would call it murder, but I do."

3.

The editorial and business offices were on the second and third stories of an old brick-and-plaster house in East 38th Street. Jack Harrington's private office was on the second story rear, and except for the furniture the room remained as it had always been, with an open fireplace, two long windows, residential wallpaper. Jack, in shirtsleeves, was at his desk, with his back to the window at an angle, so that he could look out by swiveling his chair. It was evening.

Michael Landers came in, likewise in shirtsleeves, and carrying some papers. "I finished it," he said.

"What's that?" said Jack.

"The Julian Joplin novel."

"And the answer is?"

"No," said Michael. "At least as far as I'm concerned."

"Well, that's pretty far, Michael. I haven't overruled you yet. What's the matter with it?'

"You haven't read any of it, at all?"

"No, you're the only one that's seen it. I *will* read it, of course, but you don't think we ought to publish it?"

"It's absolutely filthy, for one thing. It would never get through the mail. But it isn't worth fighting for. It's all shock. Four-letter words, five-letter words, one shocking scene after another, and without a single redeeming feature. In other words, I don't see that it has any literary value, none whatsoever."

"You liked his first novel."

"This one makes me doubt that it was written by the same man. In the other one he had scenes of depravity and degeneration, but he was subtle about it. Artistic. Poetic. In this one he writes like a dirty little boy, putting down all the dirty thoughts he ever had. I may be wrong, but I'd be willing to bet that he wrote this one a long time ago, and now he wants to cash in on his reputation."

"That often happens, of course, but Julian Joplin, he didn't strike me as that kind of a guy. I don't think this *is* out of the trunk, but I guess we'll never know."

"It's not out of the trunk, it's out of the cesspool."

"You realize, of course, if we don't publish this, we lose Joplin. And he's one of the two authors that kept this firm going. He and Serena Von Zetwitz."

"You can't publish this, Jack. It'll be banned all over the country, and rightly. And it's not going to help the reputation of Harrington and Whitehill. Here, let me show you one page," said Michael. He laid the typescript on Jack's desk, and Jack read it in silence that lasted a full ten seconds. When he finished he looked up.

"Yeah," he said. "That could get us into a lot of trouble. Is there more like that?"

"As bad, and worse," said Michael. "And it isn't a question of cutting. I couldn't edit this, and I don't think you could either."

"Not if there's more like this," said Jack. "Horace Liveright and Alfred Knopf both think Joplin is great. I do too, for that matter. But Joplin isn't a guy you can reason with. He owes us first look at this book, and if we reject it, he's free to go where he pleases. That's the contract. Well, I'll read it tonight and let you know in the morning."

"Don't show it to Gretchen," said Michael.

"Oh? Why not? She's seen worse than this. You're still pretty new in this business, Michael. This is bad because it was written by Julian Joplin, but I've seen worse and so has Gretchen."

"*Gretchen* has seen worse than this?"

"We got a manuscript two years ago, maybe three. A translation from the Portuguese, written by a Brazilian millionaire. Gertrude Gelsey, the literary agent, was handling it, and it finally came down to us after everybody else had had a look at it. The English title was something like *Forgive Us Our Sins,* and it was this millionaire's memoirs. It was like reading all the Havelock Ellis case histories, but all happening to one man. I asked Gelsey why the fellow would want to publish it under his own name, and she laughed. She said he wouldn't let it be published *unless* it was under his name. That was going to be his greatest thrill, to be famous as the most depraved man of our time. Yes, Gretchen read it."

"She must be awfully well balanced to read that kind of stuff and be as normal as she is."

"That's what well balanced means, doesn't it?" said

Jack. "Anyway, I wouldn't dare reject Joplin's novel without letting her read it. You know where the money comes from in this firm. Everybody does."

"Yes, but I know who's doing most of the work, too," said Michael. "Are you going to buy out Ray Whitehill?"

"I could say that that's none of your business. But unfortunately Ray gets a few drinks in him and tells the whole Yale Club bar that I am."

"He wasn't in today," said Michael.

"I know. Why do you think I'm working this late? I'm not going to let Whitehill or anyone else wreck this business. The book business generally is taking an awful beating, just at the time we were beginning to get somewhere. But it'll come back. Statistics show that more people are finishing high school, and that means more people will be going to college. They won't all read books, but education is going to have a good effect on the book business. Things may not look so good now, but if we can survive this depression, we'll be all right. Meanwhile, I'm working my ass off because I want to. We have to stay a while longer in this old firetrap, instead of having office space in the Graybar Building, but we're a young firm. We can put up with inconveniences. You don't happen to have forty thousand dollars on you, do you?"

"Not just now," said Michael. "Do you need forty thousand?"

"To buy out Whitehill. Grimes got thirty-five. The only thing that's going up in price these days is a partnership in this firm."

"I wish I had forty thousand dollars, and I'd buy in."

"I wish you had, too, Michael. You better get home to your wife. I'll see you in the morning," said Jack.

"Goodnight, Jack," said Michael, and left.

Jack telephoned home. "Speak to Mrs. Harrington,

please. Dear? I'm stuck here. I'll send around to the deli-catessen. I like liverwurst sandwiches. I used to like them when I *had* to like them. It's a delicatessen down on Lexing-ton Avenue. We often patronize them. I promise, I'll phone them right away. Not before ten-thirty or eleven. Kiss him goodnight for me, and tell him I'll have a story for him *tomorrow* night. I'll be home when I get there, and I'll have a manuscript for you to read. You can read the first half while I read the second. Goo'bye." He hung up, got to his feet and stretched, then returned to his desk and tele-phoned the delicatessen. "Mr. Kleinhans? This is Mr. Har-rington. Harrington and Whitehill? Very well thank you. Have you got one of your boys there that can bring me a liverwurst sandwich on rye bread? No mustard. Your liver-wurst doesn't need mustard, that's right. A quart of coffee, sugar and cream separate. One quart. No, no thank you. No strudel. Tell the boy to ring the doorbell, on the right hand side of the door, and my office is on the second floor. All the way back. No, I won't let him in. The superintendent will let him in, but I'll be here in my office. And as soon you can, huh? Thank you, Mr. Kleinhans. Auf wiedersehen. Ja. Ja."

He looked at the work he had been doing, dismissed it for the moment and picked up the Joplin manuscript and went to an easy chair with the idea of putting in a few minutes on the novel. He thought he heard the front door-bell, frowned, but decided he must be wrong. Too soon for the liverwurst.

His door opened, and it was a cleaning-woman, with bucket, floor brush, and rags. "Oh, *you're* still here?"

"Still here."

"When can I do this room?"

"Maybe you'd better skip it tonight. I'll be here quite late."

"That's all right with me, if it's all right with you. You don't want me to just dust around a little?"

Now the doorbell could be heard distinctly.

"No thank you. Wasn't that the doorbell?"

"The super'll get it. That ain't my job, answering the door."

"I'm expecting some sandwiches from the delicatessen."

At that moment Mary Walton appeared in the doorway. The cleaning-woman looked at Mary, smartly dressed, and then at Jack. "Here's your sandwiches," said the woman, and went out.

"What did she call me?" said Mary. "A witch?"

"Not exactly," said Jack.

NOBLESSE OBLIGE

The uniformed guard, an exceedingly white-faced, white-haired Irishman, recognized Frances Treadway, greeted her politely and acted as escort as she walked the familiar course to the office of Mr. Knox. The guard's single comment on the weather lasted them conversationally until they reached the office, and there was no need for more than a good-morning exchange between Mrs. Treadway and Miss Ahearn, private secretary to Walter Knox. Mrs. Treadway was expected; Mrs. Treadway was to go right in.

Walter Knox got up from behind his massive desk and came around to shake Frances Treadway's hand. "Good morning, Frances," he said.

"Hello, Walter," said Frances Treadway. "You're looking very well."

"Well, I lost thirty pounds while I was in the hospital."

"Really?"

"I've put some back on again, unfortunately."

"Oh, I don't think *unfortunately*. I think you're just about right. You wouldn't want to look scrawny."

"My doctor wouldn't mind if I looked scrawny, as long as I kept my weight down. Thank you for the flowers."

"You're very welcome. I almost went up to see you, but then I decided I didn't know you well enough."

"Isn't that strange? While I was there I suddenly wished you would come and see me, and then I realized that we *don't* really know each other that well, do we?"

"Considering that you know more about me than anyone else, except possibly my doctor, it is strange."

"And yet not so strange," said Walter Knox. "Sometimes when I read about you in the paper—"

"You read about *me* in the paper?"

"Yes. I often see your name on the society page."

"Oh," said Frances Treadway. "Patroness. Do you read that stuff?"

"Always."

"Do you really? What for?"

"Habit. When I was younger, much younger, I used to get asked to the deb parties, and I admit it, I always looked for my name. They don't print those lists any more. 'Among the young men present.' Those lists used to be watched pretty carefully. A young man that got asked to a lot of parties, the *good* parties, he might make a good customer's man. It didn't help me, or at least I don't think it did. I had to finish law school first, and by that time I wasn't on the lists any more."

"Well, I hope you don't regret it. You sound as though you did."

"Do I? No, I don't regret getting off the lists. I guess that was just nostalgia creeping into my voice. Dan Moriarty. Matt Winkle."

"They don't sound like society friends."

"They weren't. They ran speakeasies. Twenty-One. When I went to what you call Twenty-One it was Forty-two, and it was on Forty-ninth Street."

"That was before I came to New York."

"Oh, yes. Years before. Speaking of which, would you like a cocktail before lunch?"

"Are we having lunch here? In the office?"

"I thought that would be more convenient."

"Then no thanks, but you go ahead."

"Oh, not me," said Walter Knox. "When have you ever seen me drink a cocktail down here?"

"Never, I guess."

"Never is right. I've ordered a consommé, lamb chops, black on the outside and pink on the inside, hashed-in-cream potatoes, and a salad for you."

"Fine, thanks. What about you?"

"The same, except for the salad."

"What about those hashed-in-cream potatoes. I thought you were weight-conscious."

"I am, but I'm taking a bisque."

"Good God. Taking a bisque on hashed-in-cream potatoes! What do you do when you go on a tear? Sneak down to Schrafft's and have a nut-fudge sundae?"

He smiled at her and murmured, "Hmm," then pressed a button on his desk, and a man in short black coat and striped trousers wheeled in a cart with the covered dishes. He went out and came in again with a folding table and the table linen.

Frances Treadway and Knox kept silent during the preparations. Once again she had become impatient with the man, and as always, shown her impatience with his smugness and snobbishness by picking on some unimportant and unrelated speech or act or mannerism. On another occasion it had been on his habit of wearing the same necktie every day: always a blue bow tie with white polka dots, with a knot that was noticeably larger than most men make. He always wore the same gray suit, always with the vest, even on the warm days of spring and autumn, and always with a watch-chain of long, heavy gold links. He had been wearing the same uniform in all the fifteen years she had been his client, and it was just right for Walter Knox, but predictably there would come a point in his conversation when his stuffiness would have on her the effect of a deliberate attack, and at such times she would fight back with a sarcastic comment of some sort.

They moved to the luncheon table and Walter Knox used the move to proceed into a new, second phase of their interview. The servant departed, and they were alone again. "I have a small batch of papers for you to sign, and then I'd like to talk to you about going out to Ohio for the dedication." He did not wait for the papers to be signed, but continued: "I think you ought to be there, Frances. I think it would mean a lot to them."

"Who is them?"

"Who is them? Well, the college. The board of trustees. The faculty. The undergraduates. The townsfolk. Alumni."

"Why me, though?"

"As the widow of Orville Treadway, donor of the Treadway Observatory. And don't forget, Frances, they know, those people know that you yourself gave an extra fifty thousand dollars to complete the installation. And therefore I think they ought to have the opportunity to thank you in person."

"The Observatory was Bud's idea, not mine."

"All the more reason why you should get your share of the credit. You didn't *have* to give them the extra fifty thousand. There was nothing in the will—"

"I know all that, Walter. But everything I have Bud left me."

"True. But you didn't have to give them a cent. That was a free-will gift on your part. Your own money. They could have gone out and collected the rest from—"

"Then it wouldn't have been Bud's gift. I have Bud's money, but it's still Bud's money."

Knox shook his head. "By Jove, you are a remarkable woman, Frances. You really are."

"I don't think so," said Frances Treadway.

"Well, I do, and I wish you'd seriously consider going out for the dedication."

"You mean to take some bows."

"All right, yes. Take some bows. You're entitled to them."

"And that's the way you feel about it?"

"That's the way."

"Then let me tell you something. I wouldn't be found dead at the God damn place. Do you want to know why Bud left them so much money?"

"Well, naturally I'd say because he went there, loyal alumnus. But I guess there must be some other reason."

"Well, you can say that again. The real reason was because Bud had a sense of humor. Orville Treadway, loyal member of the Class of 1927. But did you ever see any initials after his name? Any degree? No. Because Bud never got a degree. He wasn't there long enough. He was kicked out for having a girl in his room, and if you want to know who the girl was, you're sitting across the table from her. I was a townie, worked for the telephone company, toll operator. When we got caught, Bud was expelled, and of course I had to leave town, too. So Bud and I went up to Chicago and got married."

"I must admit I knew some of that."

"Yes, I'm sure you did. But there's a lot you didn't know. For instance, when Bud would try to get a job I'll bet you didn't know the kind of a recommendation the college gave him. Expelled for conduct unbecoming a gentleman and in flagrant violation of the college regula-

tions and rules of decency. You can imagine how General
Motors and Standard Oil and the rest of them pleaded with
Bud to take a job with them. And I was no help. If Bud
hadn't married me it might have been a different story.
Bud used to get invited to those debutante parties. Cleve-
land. Columbus. Pittsburgh. Bud was a Psi U."

"That's a coincidence. So was I."

"Yes, it is a coincidence. It's too bad you never met
him, you could have exchanged the grip."

"Didn't his father help him?"

"His father? His father wanted to have me arrested
and Bud arrested with me. Did you ever know any of
those rich Ohio farmers?"

"But old Mr. Treadway left him quite a considerable
sum."

"That was later, after Bud started getting somewhere
on his own. But not while I was a waitress at Thompson's
in Chicago, and Bud was driving a taxi. Or selling Fuller
brushes in South Chicago. Or trying to sell insurance on
straight commission, no drawing account. Oh, sure, the old
man came through after Bud began making money. Oh,
my, they even had a dance for us at the hunt club, no less.
They even found out I was distantly related to them."

"Now that I never did know."

"I'm sure you didn't, Walter. They didn't either till
they found out what my mother's name was before she was
married."

"What *was* your mother's maiden name?"

"Treadway. Anna Treadway. Oh, there're lots of Tread-
ways in Ohio and Indiana, but they nearly all originated
with the same one. In Massachusetts, around Sixteen Something."

"Oh, really? How close were you, you and your husband?"

"Not close enough for any, wuddia call it, incest. I guess about fourth cousin, maybe third."

"Didn't you ever look it up?"

"What for? To find out who was trying to have us arrested?"

"No, but later it might have been interesting, after you and your husband's family came to terms."

"No, I don't think they would have liked it," said Frances. "I think my mother's people had a better claim on old What's His Name, the Massachusetts fellow, than Bud's father did. I'm not positive, but that's my impression. Bud's father, when he found out what my mother's name was, he said, oh, yes, he knew that branch of the family. That's as far into it as he wanted to go."

"It just occurred to me, Frances. Your own maiden name. Pulaski. You're probably some connection with Count Pulaski."

"Oh, sure. Didn't I ever mention that to you? The one they named the Skyway—sure. My father was—well, to be honest with you, that was in the Old Country, as my father used to call it. But it's the same family. Home we had a picture of my grandfather, my father's father, all dressed up in a general's uniform. When my father used to get his load on he'd cry and carry on, all the land and stuff he gave up to come to America. But when he was sober, never a word. I think he ran away from Poland to stay *out* of the army."

"Not to change the subject, but I've often noticed your hands."

"Oh, yes. They used to give us these tests, when I worked for the telephone company. I was the fastest girl on the toll position."

"I didn't mean that, exactly. I was thinking of how —well, aristocratic-looking they are."

"Oh, then you should have seen my sister's hands. Mary. The other night on TV I happened to see this commercial, supposed to be beautiful hands. Compared with my sister's they were truck-driver's. And teeth. People compliment me on *my* teeth, but Mary, it was a pleasure to watch her talk."

"Was?"

"Well, she's not dead, but she took the veil. A nun. And I don't see her but once every two years. She's in a convent over in Cleveland, how very different from me."

"You started to say something about Bud's sense of humor."

"Oh, the money. Well, Bud said he was going to leave them so much money that they couldn't refuse it, they'd have to take it, and then they'd just quietly change all the records. Instead of being a bum, kicked out for a woman in his room, they'd have him down as a loyal member of the Class of 1927. And he said to me, 'Wherever I am, Frannie, I'm gonna laugh like hell.' He said, 'I'll never give them anything while I'm alive. I'll never ask them for anything. I'll just let them suck around, hoping, and then when I die, they'll have to do it all themselves.' And don't you think I got fifty thousand dollars' worth of pleasure out of it, too?"

"Yes," said Walter Knox. "Yes, at least. A form of noblesse oblige."

She looked at him quickly, almost ready to say something about his necktie, his breast-pocket handkerchief. But she checked herself in time. A person shouldn't lose their temper twice inside of an hour.

HEATHER HILL

In the Litchfield County hills, hidden by man and nature, was the deceptively large estate of John W. Heatherton, whose money had come from so many sources that he was sometimes described as a financier, sometimes as a capitalist. Seeing his place from the air, people would say, "All that belongs to John W. Heatherton? I had no idea." The winding roads that formed the extremely irregular boundaries of the estate were misleading to the traveler by motor, since there was no straight stretch of highway to call attention to a dimension, and the casual passerby would assume that he had been driving through a woodland that was cut up into numerous properties. He would have noticed that there were breaks in the woodland, side roads, perhaps, or entrances to the separate properties, and there was no sign to indicate that these breaks were all driveways to the main house or anywhere else.

The main house could not be seen from any point on the public highway, and as so few people had occasion to see it from the air, the vastness of the house was known only to visitors who had come there on business or social invitation. Even those who came with the tools of their trades saw little more than was necessary. The superintendent, Ethan Putnam, discouraged wandering and lingering, and visitors who were not guests of the Heatherton family were restricted to Putnam's cottage, where he had his office, and the particular area requiring the craftsmen's attention. If a craftsman made so bold as to suggest that he would like to have a look around, Putnam would say, "What would you like to see?"

"Well, I heard tell you've got a good-sized machine shop," the man might say.

"A machine shop?" Putnam would say. "A lathe, a small drill press, a forge from when we used to shoe our own horses. That's your machine shop. These rumors get exaggerated."

The persistently curious would be shown what they asked to see, but they were never let out of Putnam's sight and were reminded that they had come there to work. Putnam was one of them, and knew how to handle Yankee workmen. He was a shade less understanding with the Irish who asked if John W. Heatherton was on the property. "Mr. Heatherton minds his own business, a good suggestion for all to follow," Putnam would say. Heatherton paid him well and supported his decisions, with the result that Heatherton could relax on the property, comfortable in the knowledge that Ethan Putnam would make no decisions that would be radically different from Heatherton's own. Considerable sums of money were spent or withheld on Putnam's advice, and locally his prestige was a replica of Heatherton's in the world of finance. Happily, the two men were of a size, and Ethan Putnam went about in the tweeds and moleskins of the best bespoke tailors in all England. He was easily the most elegantly turned out superintendent in Connecticut, and probably the only one who wore Newmarkets instead of ordinary gumboots. John W. Heatherton adhered to the philosophy that it was a responsibility of the rich man to buy only the very best of everything, not only because the best was always good value, but because the man of means owed it to himself and his successors to ensure the survival of superior crafts and craftsmen. John W. Heatherton believed that the rich man who paid large sums for paintings by artists dead a hundred years was shirking his responsibility in much the same way as the rich man who bought his suits off the rack and his shoes from W. L. Douglas. The immediate beneficiaries of John W. Heatherton's principle were, of course, Ethan Putnam and the tailors and bootmakers who made Heatherton's clothes, but his influence was wide and his habits were emulated by men who needed a good excuse to justify extravagance. John W. Heatherton, a fine figure of a man anyway, inspired imitation. A man who could be so right about investments must have the right ideas about other things as well.

He had twelve motor cars in the garage on his Litchfield County estate, and while it was not feasible for his younger admirers to purchase the Rolls-Royces with which John W. Heatherton headed his fleet, they could start with a Dodge station-wagon like Heatherton's. The younger and less affluent men in the neighborhood, by imitating Heatherton, maintained Heatherton's standards, and the neighborhood had style. The fact that the vastness of the estate was inconspicuous, that no one was ever likely to see John W. Heatherton's twelve motor cars at one time, that only his valet knew that Mr. Heatherton owned seventy-one pairs of leather shoes for his personal use (apart from such items as tennis shoes for guests), that all this and more was secluded behind a barrier of woodland made John W. Heatherton immune to invasion by the curious and critical. Nobody, at any hour of day or night, got close to the main house unasked or undiscovered. The watchmen were entitled to carry constables' badges, and their dogs were well trained. The accidental trespasser would suddenly find that he had company—a man in corduroy breeches and high laced boots holding a German shepherd on leash. "You get a little lost?" the man would say. "I'll show you back to the road. You just come along with us, and watch out for the snakes. The rattlers don't always rattle, you know, and the copperheads can't. The blacksnakes are harmless, though." Sometimes they would see a reptile on their way back to the road, and sometimes the German shepherd dog would growl in a way that conveyed to the woodsman the presence of a bobcat. "Now they can be pretty mean, bobcats," the woodsman would say. "But the worst is the snakes." The idly curious trespasser and the potential housebreaker were likely to stay away from the John W. Heatherton estate thereafter. It was all done so efficiently that the watchmen seldom had to invoke their police powers, and no one had ever been attacked by the German shepherds.

Heather Hill was the name of the estate, and the small patch of heather that gave verisimilitude to the name was kept alive by the head gardener, Kenneth Sprague, a former city florist who had been a discovery of Mrs. John W. Heatherton's. "I want you to give Kenneth a try," she had said to her husband. "I don't know how good he'll be with some things, but he knows flowers and he has great taste, and he knows what I like. The other man, Macdonald, not only didn't know what I like but didn't care." Macdonald, who had been on the estate when John W. Heatherton bought the original property, had not cared much what Heatherton liked either, and his retirement was mutually satisfactory.

"Macdonald was never our boy," said John W. Heatherton. "Nobody has to put up with a surly servant because he was able to bully the previous owner. We'll try Sprague."

Sprague was anything but surly, but he was better in the greenhouse than in the gardens, and he frequently had to be reminded that Mr. Heatherton wanted the heather to stay alive. "I don't consider the heather a flower," Sprague would say.

"Let's do it to please Mr. Heatherton," said Mrs. Heatherton.

"Of course we will," Sprague would say. "I'm so pleased to have this job, I'd grow cactus if he wanted me to." The Heather Hill roses grew moderately famous under Sprague's thumb, and Janet Heatherton gave him most of the credit.

"Kenneth Sprague is there a lot of the time when I can't be, and I'm not going to steal his thunder," said Janet Heatherton. "I want him to have the write-ups." He embarrassed her by bursting into tears. So many of his old friends had seen the write-up in the New York *Sun* and written him about it. "Those are the kind of thing that can really please a person," he said. "I had letters from friends of mine that thought I was dead, literally. Me dead! If they could see me with this coat of tan I've got." Kenneth Sprague was devoted to Janet Heatherton, and there was nothing he would not do to please her. She did not ask the unreasonable.

Joseph Kemble, the butler, had been with the Heathertons longer than anyone else on the staff, and he too was one of Janet's selections. The private joke between John and Janet Heatherton was that Joseph had been with them since John's second million, as John Heatherton would not retain a butler until he could call himself a millionaire. The house the Heathertons lived in while John was making his first million was adequately staffed with women servants, and on occasions where the entertainment called for a butler, one was hired for the evening. Joseph Kemble, one of those hired butlers, asked the employment agency to be placed on the Heatherton's list of repeaters. He soon knew where everything was—the silverware, the napery, the wines, the cigars—and he convinced Janet Heatherton that he was indispensable. He was rather young for a butler—thirty, he said, although he looked younger. But his pale complexion and thin lips and imposing nose gave him a butlerian mien, and his comparative youth stood him in good stead for the demands of the steep stairs in the house in East Thirty-eighth Street. He had been in service all his life, the son of a butler who had never come to America and refused to believe Joseph's favorable reports of life among the upper classes of Murray Hill. "I should never mistake one for an Englishman," wrote Joseph's father, and in this judgment Joseph concurred, while still maintaining that an American could be a gentleman. In that class he placed John W. Heatherton and several of Heatherton's friends, notably the yachtsman, the fox hunter, the amateur archeologist, and the sportsman whose father had been a friend of the 8th Marquess of Queensberry. Such men were already visitors to the Heatherton house when Joseph Kemble was a temporary, and it did not escape his notice—nothing did—that they paid respectful attention whenever Mr. Heatherton joined in discussions of the financial situation. Dinner parties at the Thirty-eighth Street house were apt to be built around Mr. Heatherton's business acquaintances in those early days. It was not until the Heathertons opened their Seventy-first Street house that Mrs. Heatherton's artistic interest were reflected in their guest lists. Mme. Schumann-Heink, Mr. and Mrs. Enrico Caruso, James K. Hackett, John Drew, Robert Chanler, Mary Cassatt, Winthrop Ames, William Lyon Phelps, Mark Twain, Ignacy Paderewski, Anna Pavlova, Richard Le Gallienne, Booth Tarkington, and Amelita Galli-Curci wrote their names in the Heathertons' guest book during the period of John Heatherton's fifth to his twentieth million, which preceded the assassination at Serajevo. Thereafter the Heatherton fortune could not be estimated with any degree of accuracy from week to week or million to million, inasmuch as his investments were so sensitive to fluctuations completely beyond his control. Iron and coal, lubricants, things to eat and things to wear, methods of moving things and people from one place to another, ways of transmitting the written and spoken word, could make money one day and lose money the next, and money itself was not always worth as much as it was supposed to be. "Mr. Heatherton has never put me on to a good thing," wrote Joseph Kemble to his father in England. "However, I have kept my ears open so that if certain shares are mentioned, I have my little flutter in them. Consequently, I can afford to invite you and Mum to visit the U.S. at my expense, should you change your mind about working here." But Kemble père and Mum preferred to stop where they were, thank you. America might seem grand to the young, but England was good enough for them, and Mr. and Mrs. Albert Kemble passed on without seeing Joseph again or their grandson ever. "No, she didn't last very long after m' Dad passed on," said Joseph. "They were very devoted. Straight on from childhood. More like a single individual than two separate entities, they were, ma'am."

"I had always hoped they'd come and stay with you," said Janet Heatherton.

"A visit would have been all, ma'am," said Joseph. "My missus being an American girl, and part French-Canadian into the bargain, I wasn't foreseeing a long visit. I'd have sent them up to the Niagara Falls and various places of interest. My Dad would have enjoyed an excursion to Pittsburgh, being interested in the steel industry. But as for a prolonged visit with us, that was out of the question, ma'am.

You didn't know my Mum. She'd have been telling my
missus how our young one ought to be brought up, and I'd
give that one week."

"Yes, I see," said Janet Heatherton. "Well, perhaps it
all worked out for the best."

"I'm inclined to believe so, ma'am," said Joseph.
"Though my Dad would have enjoyed Heather Hill. Winderleigh, where he spent forty years, was some five thousand acres, but none of the modern improvements we have
here. He'd have enjoyed talking with Mr. Putnam. Winderleigh didn't have the electricity laid on while I was growing
up there. We went to bed by candlelight. A servant's room
with electric lighting was simply unheard of, and here Mr.
Putnam has his power plant for any emergency. I can hear
my Dad say it was downright socialism."

"But not to Mr. Putnam."

"No, ma'am, I know Mr. Putnam's views on the subject.
Socialism and the Roman Catholic religion will be our
downfall, he says."

"I thought they were against each other."

"Not according to Mr. Putnam, ma'am. The Democratic party is controlled by the Catholic religion and it's
the Democratic party that has all the socialistic ideas."

"Well, put that way, Mr. Putnam has an interesting
point," said Janet Heatherton. "Mr. Putnam is a very serious
thinker."

"Indeed he is, ma'am, and very convincing. He reads a
good many books, as well as periodicals. Him and my Dad
would have seen eye to eye on many problems. Though I
daresay not on American history. My Dad considered Washington—begging your pardon, ma'am—a traitor."

"I don't imagine Mr. Putnam would agree with him
there," she said. "As a matter of fact, I never think of Mr.

Putnam as a reader. He's always so occupied with things to do."

"An omnivorous reader, ma'am. Omnivorous. Stays up till midnight sometimes, reading a book. It's the electricity, ma'am. If you grew up with the electricity, reading came natural to you. Having only candlelight, my people didn't take naturally to reading."

"You can make up for it now, Joseph," she said.

"As soon as my boy is ready to start his schooling, I'm going to form the habit, ma'am. Indeed I am. Young Putnam is at the head of his class in high school because his father hears his lessons every night."

"Yes, I know. At least I know he's a very good student. His father wants him to study law. And who knows? He might go into politics and be elected governor of Connecticut. Wouldn't that be nice? Some relation of theirs was a governor of Connecticut one time."

"I want my boy to enter the world of business. University, then business. Politics is too unstable unless a man has a private fortune. But no doubt Mr. Putnam would like his son to drive the undesirables out of politics, and he could count on my vote."

"Mine too," said Janet. "Well, Joseph, it's been very interesting."

"Thank you, ma'am," said Joseph. "And we're expecting three couples for the weekend as you said?"

"General and Mrs. Snowden in the corner room. Mr. and Mrs. Harrison in the room next door. And the Bishop and Mrs. Overton in the room next to the Harrisons. The bishop is a very early riser, remember?"

"I do, ma'am. And the general is not," said Joseph.

"No, the general must have had his fill of early rising in the army."

"Mr. and Mrs. Harrison, ma'am? They've never been here."

"Mr. Harrison is recovering from an operation, but if he's feeling well enough he may want to play golf with Mr. Heatherton. They're golfing friends from Georgia, and she's a very good golfer too. Dinner Saturday will be for twenty-eight. Sunday there will be as many as forty for lunch, possibly thirty-six. Tea Sunday will depend on the weather, and Sunday supper not more than ten, if that. I just remembered that Mrs. Snowden is a Catholic and doesn't eat meat on Friday. Well, all right. We'll have fish."

"Cook does a nice sole Marguery, ma'am."

"I know, but the general's not a Catholic and neither are our other guests. I wish I hadn't remembered. But she's always so *touched* when I remember, as if I'd been in communication with the Pope. I must say our Italian friends will eat spaghetti with meat sauce on a Friday, but I suppose it's usually Saturday by the time our opera friends get to our house. Jews have peculiarities too. Something about oysters or crabs. I pay no attention. It's there, and if they don't want to eat it, too bad. They can have some wine and a sandwich."

"But not a ham sandwich, ma'am."

"No, and no wine, if they're Mohammedans. Are Jews ever Mohammedans? They'd starve to death in our house."

"Very unlikely in your house, if I may say so, ma'am," said Joseph.

"Next week is my niece and probably her fiancé and four other young people. Steak, steak, steak. But we'll discuss that later. The sleeping arrangements will be the problem then. An extremely attractive young woman, as you know."

"Extremely attractive, ma'am."

"And a darling girl. And I'm going to require all your

tact and diplomacy, Joseph. House parties for young people never turn out as badly as I'm afraid they will, but I don't care what happens to the older people, and about the young I do. So I'm going to count on you, Joseph."

"Thank you, ma'am. It's been my experience that situations are usually created by one young man."

"Yes, and he grows up to be a middle-aged man who goes on creating situations."

"Quite so, ma'am. He's the one to keep an eye on. Unfortunately he isn't always the obvious one. The seemingly well behaved, in other words, on a yacht or at a country house make their own rules."

"How well I know," said Janet Heatherton. "Well, that's next week. And the next week we sail for England and you'll have a few weeks' rest. The painters will be here while we're gone. All the windows on the upper stories. Ethan says it's not a good time for painting, but we want it done while we're away. Then work will begin on the new tennis court. There's always something, isn't there?"

"That's lawn tennis, ma'am?"

"Oh, heavens, yes. The other kind would be ridiculously expensive and nobody'd ever use it. That was a rumor, but Mr. Heatherton decided the money would be better spent elsewhere."

"And so it would, ma'am. I'm heartily in accord. They had real tennis at Winderleigh when I was a boy, and they got very little use out of it. Always having to have a man down from London to make repairs." He shook his head. "A man with a speciality, he can name his own price."

"I suppose that's only fair," said Janet Heatherton.

"And they know it. He'd come down from London, take as long as he liked, and leave when he was ready. My Dad had a very low opinion of him, but he had his speciality. For less money they could have had the electricity laid on, but that was the way they ran Winderleigh. The horses foundered for lack of exercise, candles and a tennis court nobody ever set foot in from one year's end to another. Mr. Heatherton would never put up with that kind of waste."

"No, Mr. Heatherton knows where every cent goes," said Janet Heatherton.

"The way it should be, ma'am, when you're footing the bills. At Winderleigh the penny was pinched, and don't think it wasn't. But at Heather Hill, no."

"A nice balance, wouldn't you say?" she said.

"My very words, ma'am," said Joseph Kemble.

A few hours later he dropped in on George Stowe, the owner of the grocery-meat market in the town. "Sit you down, Mr. Kemble. Have a cigar," said Stowe.

"Thank you, I'll smoke it this evening," said Joseph.

"What's the problem, Mr. Kemble?"

"Nothing what you might call an emergency, Mr. Stowe," said Joseph. "However, the lady of the house and yours truly had one of our conversations that we have now and then. Merely one of those conversations, all in good spirit and all. But I like to see how the wind is blowing."

"And how is it blowing, Mr. Kemble?"

Joseph wet his finger and held it up in the air. "A slight squall from the direction of Heather Hill. Any time madam and I get on the subject of economy, it's a good plan to keep the next month's bills down, Mr. Stowe."

"Yes, that is a good plan, Mr. Kemble."

"These squalls always blow over. But if this month's bill is lower than last month's, it's better for all concerned. They're going abroad soon, and there won't be any entertaining. But if this month's bill is lower than last month's, we won't have to cut down quite so much while they're away. Do you see what I mean?"

"We can spread it," said Stowe.

"As the French so aptly put it, *vous avez raison*, Mr. Stowe. They will be having quite a few large parties in the year to come. A niece will be announcing her engagement, and whenever they go abroad they entertain for the people who entertained them in England. It's going to be a big year, Mr. Stowe. But let's make this month a moderate one, shall we?"

"I'm agreeable, Mr. Kemble. This is a third generation business, you know, and the fourth and fifth generation are coming along, twenty-six years old and two years old. Where shall we effect these economies?"

"Here in your office, Mr. Stowe. You're a third generation provisioner, while I'm only a second generation butler. I shouldn't undertake to tell you your business, should I?"

"You can leave it to me, Mr. Kemble. Just as long as we understand each other."

"I was sure you'd see it that way, Mr. Stowe."

"Take along this box of candy for Mrs. Kemble. A sample the salesman left today. I know she likes sweets."

"Too much for her own good, but they don't seem to do her teeth any harm. Thank you, Mr. Stowe, and thank you for the cigar," said Joseph.

"And good day to you, sir," said Stowe. "Oh, do you happen to know if Mr. Heatherton is still thinking of buying that land on Ox Pasture Road?"

"You own that land, don't you, Mr. Stowe?"

"My brother. Ethan Putnam is a cousin of ours, but he won't give us a yes or no answer, and we've had another offer. You tell Ethan they're getting close to our price."

"Mr. Putnam and yours truly don't get any closer to one another. Mr. Putnam hasn't got much use of a man that works indoors, Mr. Stowe. He likes to act the squire in the squire's tweeds, if you know what I mean. Was an ancestor of his actually governor of Connecticut, Mr. Stowe?"

"Yes. Our great-grandfather, Ethan Stowe."

"Ah, so it was a Stowe, not a Putnam?" said Joseph.

"Well, there was a Putnam in there too somewhere, but I know more about the Stowes. We're all cousins around here, if you leave out the Irish and the Poles. But give them time. Putnam O'Brien that has the undertaking parlor, his mother was a cousin, his father was a barge captain till he deserted her. Never another word heard from him, and that taught us Yankees what to expect from the Irish. A fine woman, Ann Putnam O'Brien. One of the few women a licensed undertaker in the entire state, so I'm told. Makes piles of money."

"I daresay I'd as soon a woman as a man prepare me for burial, although I don't know if my missus would approve."

"At that point what difference does it make? Women have men undertakers, and we don't complain," said Stowe. He chuckled. "I remember Ann when she was a young woman. I'd have played dead to have her—well, you know."

"Speaking of matters along those lines, Mr. Stowe, a friend of mine from New York asked me to recommend some feminine company next time he visits me. Have you any suggestions?"

"A friend from New York, you say. If he made his home in this neighborhood, well, I don't think I could be much help. But a stranger that was willing to drive to Danbury could be accommodated. The same salesman that gave me that box of candy knows a party in Danbury. She charges ten dollars, but you have to be known. She doesn't run a regular house. I'll give you the name, in case your friend asks you again."

"And could I mention your name as a reference?"

"It might be better if I made the telephone call myself. When your friend comes up from New York, you let me know. You wouldn't mind if I told the party she should expect a visitor named Kemble?"

"I suppose there'd be no harm done if he used my name," said Joseph. "I don't often get to Danbury."

"No, and even if you did, this party has too much sense to go around telling everything she knows."

"I admire discretion in a woman," said Joseph. "In a man, too, for that matter."

"Me too," said Stowe. "What is it they say—discretion is the better part of valor? It's the better part of a lot of other things too."

"I quite agree, Mr. Stowe," said Joseph. "I'll take these chocolates home to my missus with your compliments. And my friend will appreciate your assistance in the other matter."

"And I appreciate your suggestion regarding the Heather Hill account. Cooperation is what I believe in."

Joseph waited a day or two before calling upon Stowe for cooperation in the Danbury matter, but Stowe had not forgotten. The party in Danbury turned out to be a woman in her early thirties who lived in a cottage near the fair grounds. "Mr. Kimball?" she said.

"Kemble," said Joseph.

"I been expecting you," she said. "Would you care for a glass of wine? I don't have anything stronger. I don't like my company leaving here with a half a jag on. Or coming here with one on either. I don't cater to drunks. But a glass of wine to be sociable." Her scrutiny was thorough while they drank a glass of wine, and when the wine was gone she said, "Well, we had a good look at one another and now I'll let you have a better look," she said. She unbuttoned her gingham dress and looked down at herself with a certain pride. "No complaints so far, eh, Mr. Kemble? You want to come upstairs with me and we'll get informal." She helped him undress, button by button, and lay on the bed for him to explore her body. "You got something here you can be proud of," she said. "They say it isn't the size of it, but all the same a man ought to have something else besides hair on his chest. I'm going to show you my appreciation, Mr. Kemble, that's what I'm gonna do. I'm gonna show you my appreciation." She kept looking up at him and rolling her eyes, and then she lay on her back and spread her legs for him.

Downstairs he gave her a ten-dollar bill. "You knew how much without asking," she said. "What if I said twenty?"

"I'd have given you twenty," said Joseph.

"I can tell you're a married man," she said.

"Most men are, aren't they?" said Joseph.

"Yes, but some are more married than others, if you know what I mean," she said. "You don't cheat much. But the next time you're in the neighborhood, let me hear from you. We ought to get better acquainted. There's some things you don't get at home, but if you and I got better acquainted, you know what I mean? I have a little friend she'll have a drink of wine with us too. She's extra, but twenty dollars won't break you. She's only a couple minutes' walk from here, and pretty as a picture. She has a steady job or I'd send for her. I took an interest in her, and she'll come any evening I want her to. They're a poor family and the father's out of work, but I want to tell you, this kid is why men leave home. You interested?"

"Yes, quite," said Joseph.

"Think about it, Mr. Kemble. You only live once, you know."

"I didn't know you had any other, uh, associates."

"Our friend Mr. Stowe doesn't know everything, and

this kid is somebody I took an interest in her. You're a more sophisticated man anyway. Think about it."

Joseph thought about it, and in a month or so he paid his second call at the cottage in Danbury, and there he met the kid who had been so highly touted. She was sixteen or seventeen and her name was Rita Marco. She had almost no hips, but her bust was fully developed. Joseph had acquired an impression that the kid was ignorant and innocent, but she was neither, and before he went home that night he was infatuated by her. Her obedience to Mary Jones' fantastic suggestions was in a spirit of youth and gaiety, as though she were eager to catch up with the erotic experience she had been deprived of by her youth.

"You see?" said Mary Jones. "This kid'll do anything. Anything I say the word, she'll do. You. Me. Is she worth her ten dollars? I'll say she is. I'd like to take her where the big money is, the only trouble being I'd get arrested. They got this Mann Act, taking a kid out of the state for immoral purposes, and I was never arrested working independent. If the kid could sing or dance or anything like that, I could get around it. But all she can do is what she did tonight. If she ran away on her own, she'd be a two-dollar hooker inside of a month. This way she has a steady job and I make her a few extra bucks, and she'll get knocked up and marry somebody and be all washed up by the time she's twenty-one."

"Yes, I believe you've made an accurate prediction," said Joseph. "But she's delightful, no denying that."

"She liked you, too," said Mary Jones.

"She did rather, didn't she?" said Joseph. "She doesn't know our friend Stowe, does she?"

"He wouldn't appreciate her, not saying why. But he isn't as sophisticated," said Mary Jones.

"No, I shouldn't think he would be, Stowe," said Joseph. "A down-to-earth man. No real subtlety, wouldn't you say?"

"I guess that's what I *would* say," said Mary Jones. "Uh-huh."

"I'll be back again in a week or two," said Joseph.

"I'll have the kid here whenever you say," said Mary Jones. "Any time you want her without me, just say the word. I'll have to charge you, but I have the rent to pay, you know."

"Of course you have," said Joseph. This Mary Jones did have real subtlety; at least she knew her business.

His visits to the cottage in Danbury began to be burdensome financially, and when Mary Jones told him that the kid had quit her job—or was fired—Joseph was confronted with a crisis. The obvious and indeed possibly the only solution was through some rearrangement of his transactions with George Stowe. "I don't wish to kill the goose that laid the golden egg, Mr. Stowe. But my expenses have increased, and I was wondering whether you had any suggestions."

"Several, Mr. Kemble. These expenses, they wouldn't be over toward the direction of Danbury, would they?"

"Oh, I see," said Joseph. "Well, all right, yes they are."

"You gave Mary Jones the idea that you were a big spender," said Stowe.

"What else has she told you?"

"Well, you took a fancy to a young neighbor of hers. I can see why, too."

"You've, ah, met the young neighbor?" said Joseph.

"Uh-huh. But I don't think she's over fifteen or sixteen. That age a man can get into all kinds of trouble. Mary Jones is one thing. Over thirty, I'd say, and I took her for a woman with more sense. But she could get into trouble too, you know. What do you want me to do, Mr. Kemble?

I got a going concern here, a third-generation business. I don't want to see it all go down the drain because you got a case of hot nuts for a sixteen-year-old girl."

"It's more than hot nuts, Mr. Stowe," said Joseph.

"Yes, but they're your hot nuts, Mr. Kemble, not mine. A little piece of nooky with Mary Jones, that wasn't going to give me any trouble. But you could get me into a lot of trouble. John W. Heatherton is just the kind of a man that could drive me out of business. All he'd have to do would be to open up another store here and go into competition with me. The cash-and-carry I don't worry about. My customers are the better-off ones that don't mind paying a little extra for credit and delivery. But John W. Heatherton is a man I don't want to antagonize."

"You and I have always had our understanding, Mr. Stowe."

"But I never let it go too far. These rich people, when they don't have anything better to do, they start comparing household expenses."

"I'm a butler, Mr. Stowe. I know that. Any butler, any chauffeur knows that much," said Joseph.

"Well, how much more do you think you could get away with?"

"Two hundred a month."

"*What?* You mean for yourself? That would mean four or five hundred I'd have to tack on to my monthly statements. Oh, you must be touched in the head as well as somewhere else. A hundred a month is as much as I'll do, and there you're cutting into *my* profits."

"Mr. Stowe, I'm already dipping into my own savings."

"If you want my advice you'll dip a little more and get rid of both Mary Jones and that sixteen-year-old kid."

"It isn't only a question of the money, Mr. Stowe," said Joseph. "The girl is some kind of a drug with me. I have a nice wife and a fine youngster, but all I keep thinking of is when I can be with that girl again."

"Then the only other thing I can think of is if you quit your job and go away somewhere."

"I'd be back here in a week," said Joseph. "That's as long as I can stay away from her."

"Mr. Kemble, I don't see how I can help you. A few hundred dollars I could lend you isn't going to solve your problem. Only make it worse if you gave it to this kid."

"That's apt to be what I'd do with it," said Joseph. "Well, Mr. Stowe, at least you didn't take a high moral tone, and for that I thank you."

"I'm not a high moral man, Mr. Kemble. I'm as human as the next fellow, and I always liked my pussy since I was fifteen years of age. Right here in this store, when we still had the dry goods counter. She wasn't pretty, but she'd always let me have a little feel. If my father ever knew that, he would have given me a lambasting. He *was* a high moral man. Your old-fashioned Connecticut Yankee. Oh, my. 'Stop getting in Mrs. Corby's way, she has her work to do back there.' As soon as school was out I used to make a beeline for the dry goods counter. Mrs. Corby's pussy. So I understand your predicament, Mr. Kemble."

"Perhaps you do, though mine is prettier," said Joseph.

As a desperate measure he considered confiding in Mrs. Heatherton. She was generous, pleasant, and in the manner of the unembittered childless, likely to be sympathetic to unconventional appeals. She gave money to passé sopranos and forgotten actors, and made more substantial contributions to Indian schools and distant orphanages for illegitimate children. Some of her philanthropies disillusioned her, still new ones came along. But the sopranos and the actors, the Navajos and the bastards had one advantage and one virtue: they were absent. Janet Heatherton's largesse was directed toward institutions a couple of thousand miles away and individuals who, in their Broadway hotels, might as well have been. She might not, Joseph reckoned, respond so satisfactorily to an appeal by a man who day after day served her breakfast, lunch, tea, and dinner. Indeed, her response might be to dismiss him from a job that was practically a butler's dream. The less Mrs. Heatherton knew about that side of his life, the better.

And yet he had no one else to turn to, and by eliminating the possibility of Mrs. Heatherton he was down to the hardest facts, dollars that he did not have. Very soon his wife would want to know what had happened to his savings. He had been supporting Mary Jones and Rita Marco, who had retired from what Mary Jones called circulation at his request. Mary Jones no longer was receiving such visitors as George Stowe, and Rita Marco had taken up residence in the Danbury cottage. A second-hand Chevrolet, which Rita was learning to drive, and a brand-new Victrola, which Rita played all day, had taken a thousand dollars out of Joseph's savings, and when Joseph bought a wristwatch for Rita he was compelled to buy something for Mary Jones. He had gone from the twenty-dollar visit to the support of an establishment. Already Mary Jones, being of a practical turn of mind, was making tours of the countryside in the hope of finding a tea room for sale. If not a tea room, a roadhouse, but she was sure Joseph would rather have Rita in a tea room.

It was Mary's new venture that brought about a showdown. "I found a place," said Mary. "It's about ten miles from here. Two old maids own it, only one of them croaked and the other wants to sell."

"Oddly enough, Mary, I was going to have a talk with

you about that. The happy, spendthrift days are over. I'm strapped. Broke. I'm afraid you and Rita are going to have to count on someone else from now on."

"I could get this place for twelve thousand dollars," said Mary.

"If you could get it for twelve dollars I couldn't manage it. Here, all I have in my pocket is eight dollars."

"Cut the shit, Joseph," said Mary. "Rita's gonna need three hundred and fifty right away. She's knocked up. She can get rid of it with a darning needle for a half a buck, but they die that way. If you're honestly broke, I can go back to hustling, but Rita's gonna start getting big. I thought you had plenty."

"Whatever I had, it's all gone."

"Well, I guess I always knew it couldn't last. You still have your job with the Heathertons, don't you?"

"It's all I have, but I do have that, yes," said Joseph.

"This is your kid that Rita's carrying. You gotta do something about that."

"Sell the car. You ought to get five hundred for it."

"No, you got screwed on that, too, Joseph. I didn't pay any six hundred for it. You gave me six hundred, but I only paid four hundred for it. I could get Rita a few dates and maybe make a hundred or two for her, but it'll have to be soon. She's starting to throw up in the morning. I love this kid. I'm queer for her. That was on the level, not just an act for you. And you're stuck on her too. God damn it, in this life everything always boils down to money."

"And money boils away," said Joseph.

"Well, the tea room boiled away fast," said Mary. "What do we do next? She won't want to hock her wristwatch you gave her, but she don't need a watch, she needs a calendar. I can stall off the landlord, and I got credit at the grocery, and I can get the word around that I'm back in circulation."

"Looking on the bright side, eh, Mary?"

"Listen, if I couldn't do that I'd of cut my throat years ago. Very few I got as much enjoyment out of as you and the kid. You were always a gentleman. The English are. The kid, though, I don't know what to do about her. I can run up a bill at the grocery, but the abortion doctor has to have cash on the line. They won't even lift your skirt without the cash. You couldn't put the touch on old Heatherton?"

"I thought of Mrs. Heatherton."

"Oh, you gave her a little sample of that thing of yours?"

"No. I wish I had."

"Maybe it's not too late. With some women it never is. Go wave it at her and see what happens."

"Afraid I passed up that opportunity years ago."

"If he was queer, but I guess you'd know that by now."

"He's not," said Joseph.

"Listen, pal, everybody's queer and don't try to tell me any different."

"Well, for our purposes, he's not," said Joseph. "He's an extremely dull and extremely rich man, and I'd like to go on working for him. Which I shan't be doing if the breath of scandal touches me."

"Ah, the good old days when a trick would cost you twenty dollars."

"Lasted about a week, as I recall," said Joseph.

"Didn't your wife ever catch on?"

"Oh, the hell with her. She's bored me for years. And me her, I venture to say. Why didn't yours ever get droopy, up here."

"Maybe because they never had any milk in them," said Mary. "Rita's'll get enormous."

"Where is she now?"

"Out driving the Chevvy. She'll miss that, all right."

"Too bad. But not as much as I'll miss her."

"You don't have to give her up, Joseph. You're for free."

"Am I indeed? I hadn't noticed."

"Any time. When you get back on your feet again, you can always leave a ten or twenty where I can find it, but we can write it on the ice till then."

"'Write it on the ice.' I must say, Mary, you use expressions I seldom hear at Heather Hill."

"There's the kid. Don't say anything. You're not supposed to know she's knocked up."

"The father's the last to know?"

"She doesn't want anybody to know. But I do, and pretty soon everybody will. The whole God damn world," said Mary Jones.

Among the earliest to know was Sebastian Marco, unemployed section hand, whose attention was called by his wife. "You, Rita, you momma say you look kinda big," said Sebastian. "Who da man?"

"Nobody," said Rita.

"You no tell me a big lie, Rita. I beat you. Who da man?"

"Oh, mind your own business. Go get a job," said Rita.

"Minda my business. Issa my business my daughter have a bastard in her belly. You tell me who da man or I beat you. You disgrace."

"Don't you touch me, you old bum."

"Issa bum, eh, your owna father issa bum. Issa better a bum or a hoor. I find out. I aska that hoor, Mary Jones, that hoor."

In the half-ton Ford that Sebastian's son drove for a

fish market Sebastian was taken to Mary Jones' cottage. "You, Missa Mary Jones, you tell me who knock up my Rita. You hoor, I count ten. A one, a two, a three, a four, a five—"

"Ask Rita, you dumb bastard, don't ask me."

"You hoor, I beat you up, then I beat Rita. A six, a seven, eight, a nine, a ten." He slapped her face with his laborer's hand, and made a fist. "See my fist? Now I hit you tits, you hoor. A one, a two, a three—who knock up my Rita?"

"Don't hit my tits, you dirty bastard. I'll tell you."

"You tell me quick or I punch you tits," said Sebastian. "What his name? Where he work?"

"He's an Englishman, and he works for John W. Heatherton," said Mary Jones.

"Oh ho ho, John W. Heatherton," said Sebastian. "He work for that bastard, eh? That bastard put me out of work. Wall Street bastard."

"I didn't say it was John W. Heatherton. I said he worked for him. His name is Joseph Kemble."

"He work for John W. Heatherton in Litchfield? That big Wall Street castle. I fix him," said Sebastian. He shoved Mary Jones hard and she fell back on the sofa. He left the cottage and got in the half-ton. "You take me to Litchfield. You know where John W. Heatherton live. Wall Street bastard."

"Sure, I know, Pop, but John W. Heatherton wasn't monking around Rita," said Arthur Marco.

"Did I say Heatherton is monking around Rita? Is an Englishman work for Heatherton."

"Oh, that's different," said Arthur. "What's his name?"

"Kimball, Kemble. Some English name like that," said Sebastian.

"Pop, have you got your gun?"

"What do you think I got my gun? You bet I got my gun," Sebastian patted his hip pocket.

"That Heatherton place is pretty well guarded. No trespassing," said Arthur.

"No trespassing, eh? Wall Street bastards trespass on you sister. Now she get a Wall Street bastard."

"Pop, you and your God damn socialism, you better go easy," said Arthur.

"Shut up or I hit you," said Sebastian.

They drove to Heather Hill, and Arthur took the half-ton slowly through one of the driveways until he came to the area of the garage and smaller buildings. "There he is, your Englishman," said Arthur. He pointed to a tall man in a plaid suit with plus fours.

"How you know?" said Sebastian.

"Oh, look at that suit. Look at that cap. That's English, Pop."

"You wait here," said Sebastian, and got out of the truck.

Ethan Putnam, in a splendid outfit that had been made for John W. Heatherton in Savile Row, turned and faced Sebastian. "You looking for somebody?"

"Maybe I looking for you," said Sebastian. "You know my little girl Rita?"

"Go on, get out of here or I'll throw you out," said Ethan Putnam.

"Uh-huh, *you* the English bastard. You put a baby in my girl's belly."

"Get off this property, you crazy ginny. I never heard of your daughter. And put that gun in your pocket or I'll take it away from you. I can put you under arrest."

"You so brave, you rape my little girl. You disgrace," said Sebastian. He stepped back and raised the .38 auto-

matic, and as Ethan Putnam came toward him Sebastian
fired four shots before stopping. Two shots hit Ethan Putnam in the chest and a third in the neck. He seemed to be
stopped in the midst of an argument, and then he fell and
he was dead. Sebastian looked down at him.

"Come on, Pop, let's get out of here," Arthur called.

Sebastian looked about him at the evidences of John
W. Heatherton's prosperity. "Bastards," he said, and got in
the half-ton.

"Maybe you got the wrong man," said Arthur. "He
looked English, them clothes. Now where do we go?"

"My brother Pete, take me there," said Sebastian.

"New Haven? Uncle Pete's?" said Arthur. "That's a
long way."

"I got plenty time," said Sebastian.

The police did not come to Peter Marco's house until
the next morning. It is a rather common name, Marco, and
Peter Marco was a law-abiding citizen who sold a little
wine in the rear of his grocery store, but was firmly opposed
to his brother's socialistic ideas. "My brother hates Wall
Street," Peter Marco told the arresting officers.

"Yeah. Well, he got even with *them* all right," said
Sergeant Terence Mullaly.

"He fixed *them*," said Patrolman John J. Redmond. "I
bet they go out of business tomorrow, eh Terry?"

"Yes *sir*. Sebastian L. Marco knew just what to do,"
said Mullaly. "Well, Sebastian, come along and tell us all
about it."

TUESDAY'S
AS GOOD AS ANY

Saturday afternoon, along about three o'clock, was George Davies's time for his regular visit to the establishment conducted by Nan Brown. The bank closed at noon and George could be finished up with his work by one o'clock. He would eat lunch at the Olympia—alone, and at the same table against the wall where he had lunch six days a week —and at the cashier's desk he would buy a cigar, light it, and smoke it on his leisurely stroll to Dewey Heiler's poolroom. Dewey's was the respectable poolroom, patronized by men who for one reason or another had not joined the Gibbsville Club and by a few who had. Dewey did a brisk trade among the ten-two-and-four customers, whose jobs permitted them to drop in for a dope, as they called it. A dope was only a Coca-Cola, but nearly all the men under the age of seventy called it a dope. Dewey did not bother with anything but dopes and chocolate milks. No ice cream. Nothing to eat but butter pretzels. And anyone who wanted to sit down had to go to the rear of the shop where there were benches for the pool players and spectators. But there were some customers who never set foot in the rear of the shop, and George Davies was one of them. You never saw a judge or a doctor in the rear part of the shop. They played their pool at the Gibbsville Club or at the Elks'. On the other hand, the younger element seldom lingered in the front of the shop. They would make their way to the pool tables and the benches. It took a bit of nerve for a young fellow to hang around in the front of the shop and try to join in the conversation with the business and professional men who were having their dopes.

Banking hours being what they were, George Davies was not one of the ten-two-and-four customers, but he was a Saturday afternoon regular, and he was welcome in the front of the shop. He had been a customer of Dewey's ever since the shop first opened, good for a box of cigars once a month and for boxes of the fine candies that Dewey put in for the Christmas trade. By and large, George was probably as good a customer as any Dewey had, and in any case he was respectable, clean, never loud, and no one disliked him. At Gibbsville High he had been salutatorian and manager of the basketball team, and in the class prophecy it was predicted that he would one day be Secretary of the Treasury, a not entirely wild guess in view of the fact that it was known that he was going to go from high school to a job at the Gibbsville Trust Company. If his father had not died in junior year, George most likely would have gone to the Wharton School at Penn, but his mother was alone in the world and needed George at home. She was a fragile woman and terrified by the fear that she might fall down the cellar stairs and lie there while her cries for help went unheard, as had happened to old Mrs. Tuckerman on North Fourth Street. And so George went from high school to the bank, while his mother kept house for him on North Third Street.

"Seven o'clock, George," she would call to him in the morning, and he never had to be called twice. He would shave and dress, and breakfast would be on the table when he came down; ham and eggs or scrapple on the mornings between Hallowe'en and Decoration Day, corn flakes with a sliced banana or berries during the warmer months. It was a six-block walk from the house to the bank, and unless he had to leave a pair of shoes to be resoled or to do some other errand, George would follow the same route every day: a block and a half to Market Street, three blocks on Market, and a block and a half on Main. It was not a long walk, but at the pace George set for himself it was enough exercise to get the circulation going and the mind alerted for the bank's arithmetic, and, after his first three years, for the intercourse with the bank's customers.

As an assistant teller he enjoyed the contacts with the customers. He well understood that the customers he was likely to deal with were neither rich nor important, and that to them he represented the substance and prestige of the bank. Nobody knew that better than George. He could put himself in the place of a customer and imagine the customer's thoughts, see himself as the customers would be seeing him, a trusted custodian of their hard-earned cash and in certain ways the controller of their credit. Actually George was not called upon to make decisions on their credit; it was not part of his job to give his advice on loans. Nevertheless he encouraged customers to believe that behind his dignified friendliness was a shrewd judge of character who had a good deal more to say in the bank's affairs than his modest title indicated. He would smile knowingly when friends casually asked him how things were at the bank. He was close-mouthed to such a degree that he conveyed the impression that discretion was demanded of him by the confidential nature of his duties. In due course his superiors and his fellow-workers at the bank began to accept his performance as generally desirable. Although his dealings were with small depositors on a small scale, it certainly did no harm if he could make people feel important.

It was not really so strange that George's Saturday visits to Nan Brown's establishment passed unnoticed. Without telling anyone where he was going, he would say so-long to the men in Dewey Heiler's poolroom and walk the half block to Main Street, making sure that he was not compelled to linger with anyone he encountered in the shopping district. Nan Brown's place was on Railroad Avenue, but in the immediate neighborhood there were warehouses and commercial enterprises such as tinsmiths and wholesale grocers, a non-residential area usually frequented by men who would not know George by sight, and all, at that time of day, on business bent. The traffic in the area was nearly all trucks, large and small. George's only risk was if some friend happened to see him actually enter Nan's establishment; but the risk was not great, and it was one that George had carefully calculated. Three o'clock on a Saturday afternoon gave him a margin of several hours before the Saturday night customers would begin to arrive and all the time he needed before the late-afternoon drinkers. He would walk purposefully up Railroad Avenue at a steady pace that would be taken as that of a man who had a long way to go; then as he reached Nan's place he would abruptly turn left and enter the house, go to the room between the front parlor and the kitchen, and sit down and wait for Nan.

"Hello, George," she would say. "How's the world using you?"

"Oh, about the same. How are things with you?"

"Can't complain. Who do you want this afternoon?"

"I was thinking of Dottie," he would say.

"All right, she's awake. You want to go on up? Save me a trip. I got this God damn rheumatism and I can't seem to get rid of it. I decided it must be the climate. As soon as I get enough put away I'm moving out to the West Coast, California."

"You've been saying that as long as I've known you."

"Well, one of these days I'll do it. I got it all figured out. I could probably open up inside of a month or so, as soon as I got the name of a good lawyer. There'd be no trouble getting girls, all those kids that go out there looking for jobs in the movies. You never been out there, have you, George?"

"I've never been west of Pittsburgh, and then only once. I like it right here in town."

"Well, I wouldn't mind it if I didn't get this rheumatism. I hate to tell you how long I been here."

"I know how long you've been here."

"Then you can pretty nearly guess my age," said Nan. "I was twenty-two years old when I came here."

"You must be pretty well fixed, Nan."

"I didn't come here as the owner of the place. I was only one of the girls, working for Millie Harris then."

"I remember."

"You didn't used to come in as often then. I remember who you came in with, the first time. Fred Raymond, Lord rest his soul. He was one of my regulars. Millie didn't used to like it when a customer got attached to a girl, but I said to her, in this business the customer's always right. Give them what they want was my motto. Well, you want Dottie. Who'd you have last Saturday?"

"Arline."

"Next Monday I got a new girl arriving from Philly. I had good reports on her from different parties. I'll show you a picture of her."

"All right."

"Here, have a look. You can't tell if you're gonna like her by her picture, but you can't complain about that shape.

She says the picture was taken last month. I'm putting her to work as soon as she sees the doctor. That always takes a couple days."

"Well, maybe next Saturday, Nan."

"Okay, George. Enjoy yourself in case I don't see you," said Nan.

He would be out of the house by five o'clock, at peace with the world and with himself, and ready for a shave and a facial at Lou Yoker's barber shop, where he would fall asleep in the chair. Sometimes he snored, and the other customers would laugh, but when he awoke from his nap, his face under the hot towels, they would stop laughing because they were to that degree respectful toward a man whose word meant something at the bank. Lou Yoker's barber shop was in the basement of the Y.M.C.A., and when he was finished with his shave and facial, George, carrying his coat and vest and hat and collar and tie, would go to the Y.M. locker room and take off the rest of his clothes and go for a swim in the deserted pool. Although he had been a member of the "Y" since its beginning, the only use he made of its facilities was his weekly dips in the pool. He liked to swim. There was a rule that forbade the wearing of bathing trunks in the pool, based on the theory that the dyes were not fast and contaminated the water. All swimmers therefore were naked. George would leave his glasses on a shelf in the lavatory, lower himself into the pool, and for half an hour (or fifteen minutes, if the hour was later than usual) he would luxuriate in his solitary possession of the pool.

"Did you have a nice swim?" his mother would say when he got home.

"Fine," he would say.

"Who did you see?"

"Oh, a few fellows," he would say. She was aware, he

knew, of the Y.M.C.A. rule that required nude bathing, and for a few minutes in her imagination she could picture the friends of her son, splashing about in innocent nakedness. Once, a long time ago, she had expressed the thought that after a certain age the swimmers ought to be required to wear bathing suits. Senior members, eighteen and over, ought to wear *something*, she had said. But he had convinced her that a rule was a rule and must be obeyed by one and all. Besides, no ladies were ever permitted in the basement. "I should hope not," said his mother. "I should certainly hope *not*." She would give him his supper, and after the dishes were washed and dried she would join him in the sitting-room while he read the paper and smoked his cigar. It was their time for conversation that concerned the house and housekeeping, their relatives and neighbors and friends. Mrs. Davies did not like to bother George during the week, when he would have his mind on bank business. Saturday after supper was the best time, and really the only time, for conversation. At nine o'clock she would retire and he would hear the water running in the bathtub. Sometimes he would wonder why it took her so long to finish her bath, but she was entitled to take as long as she liked. After all, Saturday was his time for his visit to Nan Brown's and his shave-and-facial and his dip in the pool, which constituted his preparation for the best night's sleep of the week. Once she had retired to the bathroom he did not see her again until Sunday breakfast, but he knew that after her bath she took her tonic and went to bed and apparently slept as well as he did.

She kept one bottle of her tonic in the bathroom and another bottle in the kitchen closet so that she did not have to climb upstairs every time she felt the need of it. The label said "Dr. Fegley's Reliable Compound" and the tonic was manufactured in a little town in Ohio. George's mother had relied on it ever since he could remember, long before his father passed away. The label recommended it for the treatment of run-down and nervous conditions, thin blood, rheumatism, and organic disorders. The picture of Dr. Fegley on the label inspired confidence. He was a bearded man with half-spectacles and a shock of white hair, and his tonic had first been recommended to George's mother by old Mrs. Tuckerman, who but for her unfortunate fall down the cellar stairs might still be taking it. George had never inquired into Dr. Fegley's tonic. He had always assumed that certain women needed tonics for certain ailments at certain times, and his mother had been taking Dr. Fegley's as naturally as she wore a skirt. As long as he could remember, it had been delivered by the case, two dozen bottles at a time, with a discount on orders in case lots, and no danger that she would ever be without it. She spent so little money on herself that the last thing he would ever question her on was the cost of her tonic. She, of course, had no way of knowing that part of the money he said he spent on cigars was in fact a cover-up for the money he spent at Nan Brown's.

His mother, but no one else, was aware that George's forty-third birthday and the twenty-fifth anniversary of his going to work at the bank fell in the same week in June. His bank anniversary happened to be on a Tuesday, and he had hoped that the directors, who regularly met on Monday, would call him in and congratulate him. Monday passed, however, and it was not until closing time Tuesday that the president and the cashier, marching together and grinning, came to George's cage and Charles C. Williams, the president, said: "George, we have a little surprise for you."

"For me, Mr. Williams?"

"For you. Maybe it escaped your attention," said Williams, "but twenty-five years ago on this very day you joined our staff. Today is your twenty-fifth anniversary with the Gibbsville Trust Company. Don't tell me you didn't know it."

"Well, I won't say it never crossed my mind."

"Well, we didn't forget," said Williams. "And to commemorate the occasion I have here this token of our esteem. Open it, George." He handed George a parcel wrapped in tissue paper and secured with the seal of Lowery & Klinger's jewelry store. Other members of the bank staff had slowly gathered around to watch the ceremony.

"You want me to open it now, in front of everybody?" said George.

"Sure, go ahead. It won't explode in your face," said Williams. His laugh was jovial.

George undid the wrapping, tossed the tissue paper in a wastebasket, and looked at the black velvet box. "I wonder what's in it?" he said.

"You'll never find out if you don't open it," said Walter Strohmyer, the cashier.

George pushed up the velvet lid and saw the matching silver pen-and-pencil set. "Well, say, isn't that nice," he said. "A pen-and-pencil set."

"Sterling silver," muttered Strohmyer.

"Yes, it ought to last forever," said George. "Well, say, thanks. Thanks very much."

"Read the engraving," said Williams.

" 'To George W. Davies, twenty-five years' service, Gibbsville Trust Company, June 1924.' Well, say." There was a light flutter of handclapping by the staff and handshakes by Williams and Strohmyer.

"There is also the usual cash bonus at the end of the year," said Strohmyer. "Being a twenty-five-year man yours'll be larger this year."

They were interrupted by a stenographer who told Williams he was wanted on the telephone.

"Did they say who it is?" said Williams.

"They said if you couldn't come to the phone to give you a message. It's Mr. Choate. He said they were starting without you and you could meet them on the third tee."

"All right," said Williams. "Tell him you gave me his message. I damn near forgot I had a golf date. Well, George, I hope we're all around when you make it fifty."

"Oh, I doubt that, Mr. Williams. I'll be sixty-eight then."

"What the hell, pardon my French, ladies, but wouldn't you say George looks good for another twenty-five years?" said Williams.

"Oh, at least," said one of the women.

"Well, give my regards to your mother, George," said Williams.

"Thank you. That will please her very much."

"I'm sorry I have to go now," said Williams. "But I always like to be around when we honor one of our faithful employees. George came here straight out of Gibbsville High and's been with us ever since. One of our old reliables, you might say. Very highly thought of. Well, George."

"The proudest day of my life," said George. "Thank you, everybody."

"And we'll see to it there's a little article in the paper," said Strohmyer.

On that note the ceremonies were concluded, and the bank employees, a little late, headed for home. The last to leave was George. It was a day to celebrate, and the usual way to celebrate was to drink some liquor. But George had no taste for strong drink and he had always stayed away from saloons and speakeasies. He thought of dropping in somewhere for a glass of beer, but it was not like George

to drop in anywhere, and there was no one at the bank
whom he might invite to join him. They were not beer
drinkers at the bank. Walter Strohmyer was a Sunday
School superintendent, and another of George's colleagues
was prominent in Christian Endeavor Society activities.
Even Murphy, the retired policeman who was the bank
guard, practiced total abstinence and had not touched beer
or whiskey since his thirtieth birthday, although he had a
brother who ran a saloon near the steel mill. "Well, goodnight, Murph," said George.

"Goodnight, George," said Murphy. "See you in the
morning."

"See you in the morning, bright and early," said
George.

He had his pen-and-pencil set in his pocket, and he
would have liked to show it to the men at Dewey Heiler's,
but he was unequal to that kind of ostentation. He could
not casually pull the box out of his pocket and say, "Look
what the bank gave me." The men at Dewey's would all
be polite and show an interest, but one of the regulars at
Dewey's was a director of the bank, who just might not
like the idea of that kind of showing off.

He walked along Main Street among the late shoppers
and the homeward bound, the men and women waiting at
every corner to take the trolley to the neighboring towns.
It was one of the busiest times of day in Gibbsville, with
the automobiles blowing their horns and the trolleys clang-
ing their bells and the newsboys peddling the afternoon
papers. "Get your late scores! Phillies win! Getcha paper!"
He came to Market and Main, but he did not turn to the
left. He knew where he was going, without knowing why.
He turned right and irresistibly was drawn to Nan Brown's.
She was standing in the downstairs hallway, talking to one
of her girls.

"George, what are you doing here? It's *Tuesday*," said Nan Brown.

"It's all right if I come in, isn't it? Are you open?" said George.

"Oh, sure. Any time," said Nan. "Any old time, and Tuesday's as good as any. We were just starting supper."

GEORGE MUNSON

Not too much should be read into this brief biographical sketch of George Munson. He was, after all, a man of no exceptional talent or remarkable ability. It is true that he made several million dollars—the estimates went from as low as three to as high as ten—but he had not begun life as a poor boy. His father, Theodore L. Munson, was the principal stockholder of the Wesleyville, Ohio, Bank & Trust Company, and sole owner of the T. L. Munson Building Supplies Company, which dealt in brick, lumber, roofing materials, and cement. The Munsons lived on a practical (as distinguished from a "gentleman's") farm on the outskirts of Wesleyville, near enough to town for George to walk to school most days, but far enough removed from the borough limits to come under the township tax assessor, who was Mrs. T. L. Munson's brother. As a director of the Wesleyville Power & Light Company, T. L. Munson was able to have electricity on the farm without having to pay pole and wiring charges, although other farmers on the line were required to pay their pro rata share of such charges. T. L. Munson paid nothing at all for the installation of the telephone at the farm, and he enjoyed free local and long

distance service until the Wesleyville Telephone Company
became part of the Bell System.

The Munson farm was often described as a showplace
by the comparatively few visitors to the owner's residence.
The main house was only partially visible from the county
highway, obscured by willow trees in its immediate vicinity
and by the apple orchard that stood along both sides of
the highway. A stranger proceeding on the highway might
not turn his head to look for the main house; a neighborhood farmer might look, but he would know that he would
never see the inside of the Munson house. His children
might, if they were friends of George Munson or his sister
Althea; but the only grownups who were invited to the
main house by T. L. Munson and his wife were Wesleyville
business men, a lawyer, a doctor and, once a year, a
clergyman, and their wives. Even those on the approved
list were seldom entertained in the evening. T. L. Munson
and his wife had guests nearly every Sunday dinner, but
from Monday through Saturday they would have their
supper with the children, play cribbage while the children
did their homework, and retire at ten o'clock at the latest.
T. L. Munson was an early riser. He would eat a big breakfast and put on his gumboots and go out to the barnyard
and have his talk with Albert Moyer, his farmer, who had
to have Munson's approval of every decision, from servicing
a cow to painting a silo. People who were not well acquainted with T. L. Munson thought of him as an amateur
farmer, but he knew everything that was going on and
where every nickel went. In a daily half hour's chat with
Albert Moyer he kept up to date on farm activities, and
moreover he kept Albert Moyer from getting into any bad
habits. There were some farmers in the valley who said
that Albert Moyer had the best job in the county, and

others who said he had the worst. Albert Moyer knew the truth of both statements, but he was planning for his son as well as for himself, since he guessed that George Munson had no real interest in farming, and some day Harold Moyer would be in charge of the Munson farm. At least so long as the farm stayed in the Munson family, and Althea continued to love the farm.

T. L. Munson sent George off to Culver Military Academy, over in Indiana, and George would come home on vacations, wearing his uniforms and smoking cigarettes with the boys in front of Gordon's drug store. There was nothing much to do in Wesleyville, for the boys home from school and college, and some of them got into trouble. Wesleyville was a town of slightly more than 4000 population, not all of them law-abiding citizens. There was no whorehouse as such, but there was a cheap hotel down near the railroad station where anyone who had the price could drink whiskey and have a woman. The woman could be old or young, white or black, and the bartender sold contraceptives and prophylactics. For young men who did not wish to smell of liquor when they went home, there were Sen-Sens. For the more fastidious young men, who did not like the surroundings in the hotel, there were the girls who worked in the stocking factory—"charity girls," they were called, because they would do it for nothing. And in another class were the young women and the not so young who liked to have men visitors in their homes. They were widows or divorcees, who worked for a living and whose homes were in respectable neighborhoods. The men would bring a bottle of wine or two, and with the shades lowered and the children sent off to bed, the woman and her visitor would drink the wine until the moment came when the talk ran out and the man would try a kiss. The kiss was never resisted, but in the next phase the woman was sure to say, "Is that the kind of a girl you think I am?" If the man replied, "What do you think I'm here for?" he would be asked to leave; but if he observed the ritual and politely protested that he thought she *liked* him, he was on his way to satisfaction in one form or another.

Melba Dixon was one of those women, and George Munson visited her for the first time when he came down from Ann Arbor on Christmas vacation of sophomore year. He had gone through the other phases—the railroad hotel and the charity girls—without catching a disease or being held accountable for bastardy. He had often seen Melba Dixon on the street, as she walked past the drug store on her way home from her job at the Wesleyville *Evening Republican*, where she was an ad-taker, switchboard operator, proofreader, and timekeeper, earning $25 a week. She wore rimless bifocals and she dressed quietly, and on the way home she was usually carrying a paper bag filled with her purchases from the grocery store. As she passed the young men in front of the drug store she pretended to be unaware of them until, as sometimes happened, one of the young men would break away from the group and speak to her. The conversation would be brief, and the young man would return to the group and smugly say nothing.

Melba was about thirty, ten years older than George, and though he had often seen her, he did not know her name. She belonged among the anonymous women of all ages whom he saw only on Main Street, women who clerked in the stores, wives and daughters of farmers in town for market day. Unless they had some noteworthy feature of face or form they retained their anonymity as far as George was concerned, and he had had no curiosity about Melba Dixon during the years in which he was at Culver and Michigan and a member of the regular group who had their headquarters in front of Gordon's pharmacy. But during that sophomore year Christmas vacation he was standing with Boyd Williams, a friend who was a senior at Denison, when Melba went by. Seeing her, Boyd suddenly left George and caught up with Melba and had a few minutes' conversation with her. She then resumed her homeward progress and Boyd rejoined George. "What's her name, anyway?" said George.

"The one I was just talking to? Don't you know Melba Dixon?" said Boyd Williams.

"Not to speak to. Watched her go by here a hundred times, but I never knew her name. What does she do?"

"Darn near anything, if you ask her in the right tone of voice," said Boyd. "You want a date with her? Not tonight. I just got fixed up for tonight, but I'll tell her you're interested."

"Oh, I don't know," said George. "Where does she live?"

"Down on School Street. She has some kind of a job with the *Republican.* Didn't you ever remember Ray Dixon, the fellow that was killed in France? He was in Company E. She gets some kind of a pension from the government. She has a kid about five or six years old, a boy."

"I wouldn't say she was very pretty," said George.

"No, and she's dumb as hell," said Boyd. "But she likes it."

"She does?"

"And don't judge a book by its cover. If you could see her without any clothes on you'd change your mind about her."

"Where do you go with her?" said George.

"You don't have to go anywhere with her. Her house. She sends the kid to bed around ha' past eight, and I show up a little after nine. In the summer it has to be later, because it doesn't get dark early. But I never took her any place. I offered to take her out to Starlight last summer, but she said she didn't have anybody to mind the kid. That was just an excuse, though. She doesn't want to go out, not with anybody our age. She's looking for a husband, and she knows damn well *I* wouldn't have the slightest intention of marrying her. But she likes her nooky."

"Tell her I was asking about her and see what she says," said George.

"Oh, I know what she'll say," said Boyd. "She'll say you're T. L. Munson's stuck-up son. You'd be surprised how many people she knows that don't know her."

"She doesn't know me," said George.

"Yes she does. You can get a date with her, but you have to ask her for it yourself."

"Then why do you have to tell her I was interested?" said George.

"That's all I'd tell her. The rest'll be up to you."

"Don't you care if I get a date with her?" said George.

"No skin off my elbow," said Boyd. "I'll have a date with her, and one or two with Josie Spitzer, and then I'm going up to Columbus for the rest of vacation. There's nothing to do around here."

"I know. I'll be in Columbus, too, part of the time," said George.

"Be here tomorrow this time, when Melba's on her way home from work. Just go up and introduce yourself. She'll know you, all right," said Boyd.

The next afternoon George did not wait until Melba had reached the drug store. He stationed himself nearer to the *Evening Republican* office and saw her leave. He had no desire to risk being rebuffed in front of the drug store group.

"Hello, Melba," he said, blocking her path but tipping his hat.

"My, aren't we forward in our raccoon coat?" she said.

"Do you have anything against raccoon coats?"

"Why, were you thinking of giving me one? I'd sooner have squirrel, if you want to be big-hearted," said Melba.

"I'm not as big-hearted as all that," he said. "What are you doing tonight?"

"I have a date. Why?"

"What about tomorrow night?"

"I have one tomorrow night, too," she said.

"How about some night next week?" said George.

"You're very persistent," she said.

"I have to be, with you."

"Why?"

"Because I want to see you," said George.

"Why?"

"Because I want to."

"You mustn't believe everything Boyd Williams tells you," she said.

"I don't. That's why I want to find out for myself."

"Aren't we clever?" she said. "All right. Do you know where I live? Did he tell you that, too?"

"School Street, but not the number."

"Two-eleven, the third house from the corner of Maple. But not before ha' past nine."

"Tonight?" said George.

"Yes. Now get out of my way because I have to go home and make supper. And I don't want T. L. Munson seeing me talking to you."

Without her rimless bifocals and without one of her ill-chosen hats, with her waved brown hair and a simple green dress, she was barely recognizable as the woman he had seen so many times on Main Street. She was still not pretty, but she was wearing more, or a darker, lipstick, and in her own house she was noticeably more sure of herself. She let him in and quickly closed the door behind him, and pointed to the sitting-room, now lighted by the single bulbs in each of two table lamps. The furniture was a dismal collection of bad pieces from several American periods, but it filled the room. There was a table model oak-finish Victrola on a Pooley cabinet in one corner. "Got any good records," he said.

" 'Cohen on the Telephone,' " she said. " 'Waiting for the Robert E. Lee.' But we couldn't play the Vic anyway. Wake up my son."

"What do you do with him in the daytime?"

"My son? He goes to school. He's in third grade. He goes to my sister's from school, till I stop and get him after work. Why do you want to know about him for?"

"I just wondered. No particular reason," said George.

"Why, do you like children?"

"Do I like children? To tell you the truth, I was never asked that question before. I guess I do, yes."

"I've been thinking of getting a radio. It's quieter than the Vic, you can turn it down. Or listen to it with one of those headsets. But I have to wear a headset when I'm on the switchboard, and I get pretty tired of it. Do you have a radio? I suppose you do, out at your place."

"Yes, they just finished putting an aerial on our house. I haven't seen the set yet, but I know what it is. A Stromberg-Carlson. My old gent was against having one, but my mother wanted one for Christmas. Do you smoke? Care for an Omar?"

"Yes, I'll take one," she said. "At the office nobody smokes when the boss is around. The building's a regular fire-trap. Maybe I shouldn't say that, considering who owns the building."

"Who owns it?"

"A man by the name of T. L. Munson."

"He does? My father?"

"Well, he might as well. He holds the mortgage, I understand. At least that's what I've been told. He owns that whole block."

"Oh, yes. I did know that," said George.

"And some day you'll own it. When you do I hope you won't be as strict about a few cigarettes. Would you care for a drink of rye? It's supposed to be all right. A friend of mine gave it to me. That is, he had a couple and I had a couple and the rest he left here."

"Who? Boyd Williams?"

"None of your business who," she said. "But it wasn't Boyd. He brings a bottle of Dago Red."

"That's what I brought."

"I'd rather have that, but if you'd rather have the rye? Which would you rather have?"

"The wine. It's in my coat pocket."

"You didn't wear your raccoon," she said. "I'm glad you didn't. I almost called you up and told you. You don't see many raccoon coats on School Street. As far as that goes, you don't see many in Wesleyville. I guess you could count them on the fingers of one hand. You and your father, that's two. Teddy Church. Three. Morris Gitlow. Four. Old Doc Eltringham. Five."

"There are more than that, but not many more. Henry Vail. Buddy Proctor. Roland Kelly. Under ten, I guess. That's not counting the black bearskins. Just the raccoons." He placed two bottles of wine on the table. "I'll need a corkscrew."

"And two glasses," she said.

They finished a quart of wine in about an hour. "You're a slow drinker," said George.

"And you're a fast one," she said. "I like it to slowly creep up on me. If you drink it slowly you get the full effect, gradually."

"You didn't even drink half of that bottle," said George.

"A half a bottle is all I need to feel just right."

"Just right for what?"

"Not *for* something. Just right."

"Well, have another glass and maybe you'll feel just right."

"Okay," she said.

He opened the second bottle and poured a full glass. "Drink that, and you'll be feeling just right," he said.

"And you finish the rest of the bottle and *you'll* be feeling just right."

"Such is my intention," he said.

She took a sip of her wine and looked at him across the top of her glass. "This isn't the regular Dago Red," she said.

"No, it isn't," said George. "This is Burgundy. It came from the family's private stock. They have enough to last them the rest of their lives."

"I didn't know T. L. Munson ever drank," said Melba.

"Wine and beer. Very seldom drinks anything stronger. He gets good beer sent from Cincinnati. A friend of his there."

"It must be wonderful to be rich," she said.

"If you think my old gent's rich you ought to see some of the guys in my fraternity, the places where they live. I have one fraternity brother, he lives in Grosse Pointe. They have a garage for eight cars. Three Pierce-Arrows. No, four. Two chauffeurs. A yacht. A speedboat. A couple of small sailboats. You go there to spend a weekend and you have your own personal valet, presses all your clothes, shaves you in the morning. They have an indoor swimming pool so they can swim all winter in heated water."

"Where did they *get* all that money?"

"Well, this boy's father owns some patents that they use in manufacturing spark plugs. Half the money they took in cash, and the other half in stock. The stock went from something like five dollars a share to four or five hundred. You talk about gold mines, or oil wells. These people will be getting big money as long as people buy automobiles. Bigger every year. No limit to it."

"Are the women happy?"

"Happy? God, they have everything a woman could wish for."

"Your friend's mother. Is her husband nice to her?" said Melba.

"Well, he gives her everything she asks for. But just between you and me, she doesn't know what to do with herself. He keeps busy, taking care of the money and working on some new invention. But she likes the bottle. I was there one night when the butler had to carry her upstairs. As soon as the husband goes away she starts hitting the booze. She can't stand prosperity."

"That's the trouble with too much money. But how much is too much? If I got paid a hundred dollars a week, that would be a lot of money to me, because I'm not used to it. But I could keep my head. On the other hand, if I got *two* hundred dollars a week—but there aren't many *men* in this town that make that much. If I can ever get to fifty a week, I think I'll be satisfied. Or maybe seventy-five. That's three hundred a month. I'd get a nicer house, and all new furniture. And I could put Tommy through college. I'd like to live out toward your end of town, on West McKinley. You know that house where the Proctors live?"

"Sure."

"That'd be about right for me. Not too big a house, but plenty of ground around it. I wouldn't want too big a house."

"Well, maybe your husband would have something to say about that."

"My husband. If I had a husband that earned a hundred

dollars a week, and I earned seventy-five or had that much coming in. But what's the use of talking about that? It isn't going to happen. I'll be lucky to be working on the *Evening Republican* the rest of my life, if my eyesight doesn't get worse. I can't read the large type on that label without my glasses."

"Well, that's what glasses are for. Most people wear glasses," said George.

"Trying to make me feel better?" she said.

"Not necessarily. Just a statement of fact."

"You're nice and you don't even know it," she said.

"Am I?"

"That's my opinion," she said. She stood up. "I'm going up and see if Tommy's all right. I'll be right down."

She was gone about five minutes, and when she returned she was wearing a wrapper.

"You've got too many clothes on," she said. "Coat and vest and all. I made *my*self comfortable. Why don't you?"

"Well, that's a happy thought," said George.

"Men are so modest. They're much more modest than women. I don't know why, either. Most women are nothing to brag about stripped."

"Neither are most men."

"Young men are," she said. "Till they start getting fat."

"Then you have a treat in store for you. I'm practically skinny."

"You have a treat in store for you. I'm not. Put your clothes over on that chair, in case the doorbell rings they'll all be in one pile and you can go back to the kitchen. Do you have a rubber?"

"Yes."

"How long is it since you had a piece?"

"October. About two months. Why?"

"Well, we'll see. Maybe you won't need the rubber

right away. Now come here and let me have a look at you. You know I'm nearsighted."

"I'm glad I'm not."

"You like, huh?"

"Of course I like."

"Just remember now, you don't have to go home till four o'clock."

"Why four o'clock?"

"That's when the railroad crews start getting up, and I don't want them to see you leave." He touched her and she stopped talking. She watched every move he made with a calmly critical, almost blank expression. Nothing was new to her, but it was all new because he was new to her. He had expected her to be helplessly wild, and instead she was controlled and studious and quiet, very quiet, and her quiet took command of him. She knew immediately, as though he had announced it, that the initial curiosity had left his fingers, and at that moment she switched from her passive to her active role. It soon became too much for him, and she compelled him to lose all control.

"I'm sorry," he said.

"Why? That's what I wanted," she said.

"Oh," he said.

"That's not all I wanted, but I wanted that," she said.

The fierce tautness was gone from his nervous system, while his brain worked so fast, so crowdedly, that a thought would be displaced by another thought before he could find speech for it. A thought would be overwhelmed by a question, and the question by a new thought, and the confusion was too great for utterance.

"Are you awake?" he heard her say.

"Was I asleep? I must have been," he said.

"Nearly an hour," she said.

He was lying beside her on the davenport, but now he

saw that she was in her wrapper again and that she had covered him with his overcoat. "Boy, I was asleep, wasn't I?"

"Out like a light," she said.

"Did I snore?"

"A little," she said.

"Did you sleep?"

"No. I wouldn't let myself fall asleep down here. Tommy might wake up and come down."

"You take a big chance on that, don't you?"

"You mean if he should walk in? Yes. He sleeps pretty sound, but the day will come, I guess."

"Then what will you do?"

"I don't know," she said. "I'd have to stop this, or let my sister raise him. I couldn't rent a room in Wesleyville. If I did that I might as well turn into a whore and make some money out of it. But I could never be a whore. I have to like the man, and whores can't be choosy. You're probably thinking what's the difference between me and a whore, but I often go six-seven months without a man. I don't get to be very good company, I'll tell you. But I can do it. I dream about bananas and pickles and big bugs crawling all over me. What I do for that kid!"

"Could you ever settle down to one man?"

"Could, and did. And not my husband. This was three years ago. One fellow, very prominent in town."

"Not my father, by any chance?" said George.

"No, but a friend of his. He helped out with money, too. But one night he came here and like you and me an hour ago, that's what he walked in on. The first time I cheated on him I got caught."

"Was it the first time?"

"Yes, it really was," she said.

"Who was it? Was it Mr. Proctor?"

"Yes."

"What did he say?"

"What could he say? He never said a word to me, then or since. I guess I could make as much trouble for him as he could for me. How did you know it was him?"

"There are only three or four it could have been, and he was the logical one."

"He was all right, most ways. But he wasn't entitled to my whole life. He went with other women. Fair exchange is no robbery. I went with another man. Much younger."

"Boyd Williams?"

"Uh-huh. I'm surprised at Boyd," she said.

"Why?"

"I thought he could keep his mouth shut, but he told you about me. The next time he asks me for a date, I'm going to be busy. He ought to learn to keep his mouth shut."

"It isn't all his fault. I asked him about you."

"He told me," she said. "But he didn't have to tell you all he did. Once those boys at Gordon's drugstore start talking about a person, you won't have any reputation left. No, I'm through with Boyd."

"How do you know I'll keep *my* mouth shut?" said George.

"I *don't* know, unless you tell me. Boyd'll ask you questions and want to know all about tonight. But if you tell him, I won't think much of you either."

"I've seen you stop and talk to other fellows besides Boyd," said George.

"Yes, but they don't all get dates. You can't hang a man for trying, but most of them don't get anywhere. A few kisses. Most of them are rank amateurs. They come here and bring a bottle and get spifflicated, but they're rank amateurs. Boyd's the only one ever got anywhere with me. You can't name any other."

"No, I guess I can't," said George. He was beginning to get bored with her conversation, but he was revived and strong after his nap, and he knew without her telling him that she had taken away Boyd's privileges and given them to him. It did not matter why, and he was not convinced that it was because Boyd had talked too much. She wanted him, George Munson, and he knew even if she did not that it was because he was superior to Boyd Williams. He had always *felt* superior to Boyd, but it was fascinating to have this evidence of his superiority. He put his hand under her wrapper and dry-milked her breast and she smiled.

He left her house shortly before four o'clock and walked through the tree-lined streets of the neighborhood in the invigorating, bitter cold. He stopped in at the Acme, sat at the counter, and ordered a cup of coffee and a piece of cocoanut custard pie. He was joined by Stan Kovy, the policeman on night duty. "You're out pretty late," said Stan. "Getting your ashes hauled?"

"Wouldn't you like to know? I'll buy you a cup of coffee," said George.

"I get it free."

"Coffee, or your ashes hauled?" said George.

"Both. I'm a married man. The coffee I get free, here, the ashes I get hauled at home. I didn't see your car nowhere."

"It's in the garage, with the company trucks. I didn't want it to freeze up."

"You mean you didn't want to park it outside of somebody's house, on School Street," said Stan.

"Is that what I mean?"

"She's all right," said Stan. "One of these days she's gonna get knocked up, but I guess you can afford it. The only trouble is, can she afford it?"

"Do you worry about her?"

"I do, yes. I guess you didn't know that. She's my wife's sister. That makes me her brother-in-law. She got this kid, the same age as one of our kids. He's at our house near every day after school. If it wasn't for that kid I wouldn't worry about her, but she worships that kid. She can't do enough for him. He eats better than some kid that his father owned a butcher shop. No hand-me-downs for that kid. He ought to be living out on West McKinley somewhere. But Melba gotta have her ashes hauled, too, and there's where the trouble is. So far, she's lucky. Maybe too lucky. She don't stop to think how lucky she is. Luck, luck. Six years a cop and I never had to pull my gun. That's luck. Your old man had some luck, to make all that dough. You had plenty of luck, those tramps I seen you with."

"Not very often."

"It only takes once, and those bimbos are all clapped up. You were lucky, George, and don't deny it. I been lucky. T. L. Munson. Everybody. But it runs out on you when you need it. And that's what'll happen to Melba."

"I don't happen to think it will," said George. "A friend of mine told me how dumb she was, but I think she's pretty smart."

"You're both right. She's smart, and she's dumb," said Stan. "All of us are. Every single one of us."

"You're a regular philosopher tonight," said George.

"That's the only subject that interested me at State. Philosophy. You had to do too much reading to keep up, but I used to enjoy the lectures. Do you take philosophy?"

"Not yet. I get that next year."

"Yeah. What I got was a course they called Introduction to Philosophy. It wasn't as deep as the regular philosophy."

"A pipe course," said George.

"Everything I took was a pipe course. I didn't have

time to study even if I wanted to. But I enjoyed some of that philosophy. There was about half the guys on the squad took that course, but you know I was the only guy on the team that got a C-plus in it. That was because I used to ask the professor questions, and he only gave me the C-plus because I showed him I was staying awake. I wasn't sucking up to him. I was inarrested. But not inarrested enough to do all that extra reading. How could I? I had a schedule that I could be on the practice field by ha' past three, and we were out there till it was too dark to see the ball. Then supper, and after supper we had skull drill. It'd be ten o'clock or later by the time I got back to the fraternity house, too tired to shoot a game of pool. I broke my leg in the Purdue game and I could of studied then, but that was senior year, and I didn't take Introduction to Philosophy that year. I only had that sophomore year. Well, what the hell? For a Polish boy that both parents couldn't hardly speak any English. I was born in Wheeling, but I only lived there till I was ten years of age, and then my old man moved us to Youngstown. That's where State heard about me, and I got my scholarship."

"Did you get your degree at State?" said George.

"Oh, sure. I got a B.A. My kids can say their old man's a college graduate. And I came out of the army a first lieutenant. I was offered a job with the company police in Youngstown, but if you ever heard my old man on the subject of company police. He would of disowned me. I heard about this job here, and I took it because it was the first thing open. I never even heard of Wesleyville when I took the job, but the pay was good and they gave me to understand that it was cheaper to live. You know who hired me was your father, T. L. Munson."

"How did that happen?"

"Through him being president of the bank. They never had a night watchman at the bank, but the night-duty policeman was supposed to do that. Check it every hour."

"But you were paid by the borough. The bank got a night watchman free," said George.

"Uh-huh. But I guess they were entitled to it. The bank is where all the taxpayers keep their money."

"My old gent always knows how to save a dollar," said George.

"Well, yes, but every town has somebody like T. L. Munson. The leader. The one that they all look up to. He votes in the township, but everybody knows he runs Wesleyville. And those that vote in the borough, they know how T. L. Munson wants them to vote, so his one vote don't make any difference. Anyway, he had the say when I applied for my job, and he put through a raise when I got married and twice since."

"With borough money," said George.

"Yes, but he only charges me fifteen a month rent for my house, and the other houses in the row pay twenty-five. That's a hundred and twenty a year I save right there. He goes on my note at the bank if I have to borrow for something. And I'm allowed to fill up my tank at the company garage whenever I want to. He does a lot of things like that that all add up."

"I guess there are other things, too," said George.

"You hinting that I take graft? Tell me something. If you young guys, not to mention the older guys, if you didn't have someplace to go and get your ashes hauled and get soused, what would happen in this town? I'll tell you what'd happen. The same thing happened when I was in the army. Rape. A woman wouldn't be safe on the streets at night, just going home from the movies. Maple Street. School Street. All these streets with trees, as dark as the inside of your hat. That's nature. Human nature. You got to have a place where a man can go when he has to have a piece of tail, or pretty soon you have rape, or buggery, or molesting young children, and I don't care if it's a college campus or an army cantonment. They can't all get a date with Melba Dixon. You ought to know. You tried it both ways. I never took a nickel off the people that run the joint you went to. But I'll tell you this much, George. If certain respectable citizens didn't agree with me, that joint would be shut down tonight. So you just draw your own conclusions."

"In other words, my old gent approves of legal prostitution," said George.

"You got it wrong. That isn't legal prostitution. It's illegal. They're breaking the law all the time they're open. But there's such a thing as looking the other way."

"You didn't seem to be looking the other way tonight, when I was down on School Street."

"I wasn't looking the other way, or this way, or that way. I didn't have to. She told my wife she had a date with you."

"That's good, that is. She was complaining about somebody that can't keep his mouth shut."

"I guarantee you she can't keep hers shut," said Stan. "She never takes it into consideration that her sister is married to a cop. So I guess I know the name of every guy she ever humped. And believe me, some of them would wish I didn't. One of the high muckymucks out on West McKinley was humping her for a year or more, till he accidentally walked in on her one night and caught her frenching a younger guy. That was rich. Because the older guy voted against giving me a raise, and I was pretty sore. But I didn't say anything. It'd only of got Melba in trouble at the paper."

"A policeman's lot is not a happy one," said George. "Gilbert and Sullivan."

"I don't know about that," said Stan. "As long as my luck holds out. That's what they call fatalistic. Fatalistic. If it's gonna happen, you might just as well sit back and wait for it to happen. Some Saturday night I'll go by Gitlow's store the same way I do every Saturday night, because he keeps money in the safe till the bank opens Monday morning. All the receipts for Saturday, when the hayseeds do their shopping. Up to a thousand dollars he has there some Saturdays. And I'll try the door. First the front door, and then the side door in the alley, and then the back door. And there'll be some son of a bitch in there working on the safe, and either I'll kill him or he'll kill me."

"You have it all figured out," said George.

"I do. The years I been a cop, on night duty and very seldom a conversation like tonight, I figured out every store in town, what I'd do if I's a crook instead of a cop. You take now, there's only Gitlow's, Gordon's drug store, Wilcox' furniture store, and Doc Eltringham that have any sizable amount of cash Saturday night. By sizable I mean five hundred or over. They're the ones the hayseeds pay on Saturday after the bank closes."

"The movie theater," said George.

"Two hundred at the most. He don't take in two hundred dollars on a Saturday. Fifteen cents for kids, two bits for adults. The kids and the adults won't go to the same picture, unless it's Tom Mix. That's what Goldstein told me. If he has a Tom Mix picture, the kids'll go to the matinee and the adults to the evening. But the kids won't go to a love story. I know all about it, from Goldstein, and he wouldn't lie to me about that."

"What about this place, the Acme?" said George.

"Gus'll have two or three hundred in the till, but there's too many customers to make it worthwhile. And he keeps all the lights on all night. You take as big a chance as if you were robbing a bank in broad daylight here. And for small money. That's not saying the bank wouldn't be easy. Two guys that knew how to shoot, and one guy in the car outside. They could stick up that bank any day and get away with a young fortune. Twenty, thirty, forty thousand dollars, cash. The Wesleyville bank around Christmas-time is just sitting there like a big fat turkey. But that would have to be a daylight job. If anybody ever tries to open that safe at night they'll never leave the bank alive."

"You'll stop them singlehanded?"

"Not singlehanded. I worked out a plan. Twenty fellows from the Legion, all with rifles or shotguns and know how to use them. If I see anything the least bit wrong, I go to the nearest phone, give the night operator a certain message, and she notifies all twenty guys. They all know what to do, every one of them. I worked that out myself."

"Why wouldn't the same idea work in the daytime?"

"Too many innocent people could get killed. But God help anybody tries to rob the bank at night. They'll be dead by the time they get the safe open, if they ever do get it open. No, I'm not worried about the bank. It's Gitlow's, or one of those others. The worst, and the easiest, would be Doc Eltringham. Sometimes he forgets, and I know him to walk around with over a thousand dollars in his pocket. I see him on night calls, around town, or sometimes he comes in here for a cup of coffee. 'Doc, how much money you got on you?' I'll say to him. And he'll say, 'Now Stan, you're not going to relieve me of it.' But he'll hand over five, six, seven hundred dollars for me to take care of. Tonight, earlier, I saw him coming out of Gordon's and he just laughed and said he only had twenty dollars on him. He was with his missus and they both laughed. She's a nice little woman. I always liked her. You going home now?"

"Why? Are you trying to gently persuade me?" said George.

"Well, there's not much else for you to do, is there?" said Stan. "And it's after five. I'll walk you over to the garage."

"Okay," said George. He put a quarter on the counter, and he and Stan got into their overcoats. "Goodnight, Gus," said George.

"Uh-huh," said the proprietor, eyes heavy with weariness.

"He gets less sleep than I do," said Stan. "He'll be here at ten o'clock in the morning. I think he sleeps in the afternoon."

"I think it's gotten colder, or maybe because we were sitting in that overheated restaurant," said George, as they walked up Main Street.

"I don't mind it being overheated," said Stan.

"No, I guess it comes in handy these nights. When do you go off duty?"

"Oh, the day fellows come on around ha' past seven."

"And then can you go right to sleep?" said George.

"After the kids go off to school. I'll be seeing Melba around a quarter to six. She stops for her kid."

"There's something you want to tell me about Melba, Stan. What is it?"

"Why do you think that?"

"Am I right, or am I right?" said George.

"Yes, you're right," said Stan.

"It's obvious that you're a little stuck on her yourself," said George.

"You can like a person, and worry about her, without

being stuck on her. And I'm a Catholic. I got her sister to become a Catholic when we got married. She often talks to Melba about taking instructions, and there was a while there when it looked like Melba was ready to. But some new fellow came along. She told my wife she was getting ready to ditch young Williams, but now she's got you. I don't hold it against you, George. Don't get me wrong. But Melba doesn't know what she's doing to herself, and she better start thinking about her future. She's thirty years old and she's gonna end up behind the eight-ball."

"You *are* stuck on her," said George. "But what do you want me to do? It's up to her, isn't it?"

"I guess it is. I often get the temptation to stop in there when I'm down around School Street. And it wouldn't mean anything to her. Another piece of tail. Like stopping in at Gus's for a cup of coffee. She likes me, I know that. She walks in the house sometimes and I'm in my underwear and my wife is out, and it wouldn't take much for the two of us to go at it. She even kids me about it. 'What have you got down there? There must be something there,' she says. She knows damn well what's there. She can give me a hard-on just by looking at me. But I never touched her, never. Because if I did I might as well give up my home and my job and my religion. Everything. That's the way she'd affect me. And for what? My wife is twice as pretty as she is. I wish to hell she'd get married, that's what I wish. But she never will as long as she goes from one guy to another. I wish she'd get married and go away, and stay. I stay away from School Street as much as I can, but it's like some magnet that draws me down there. I was there tonight when you got there. I didn't hardly recognize you without your fur coat, but I knew she had a date with you. I could have plenty of gash in this town if I wanted to, but the only one that bothers me is Melba."

"Well, I can't tell you what to do, Stan. It sounds to me as if sooner or later if you don't start something, she will."

"That's it."

"You were talking earlier about fatalism."

"Oh, to hell with that," said Stan. "Well, here we are." He took out his flashlight and trained the beam on the garage-door lock.

"Thanks," said George. He put his key in the lock, and pushed the doors open. "Can I give you a lift anywhere?"

"I see you got the top down. Are you a fresh-air fiend?" said Stan. "No thanks. I'll close the garage doors after you. And don't say anything, what I told you tonight."

"You can rely on my discretion," said George. He started the motor, warmed it, and backed out of the garage. "Goodnight, Stan," he said.

Stan waved the flashlight, and the last George saw of him he was closing the garage doors. It was the last, the very last he ever saw of him. The *Evening Republican,* on the street at four o'clock in the afternoon, confirmed the rumors that had been all over Wesleyville since the late hours of the morning. Assistant Chief of Police Stanley W. Kovy had indeed gone to the home of his sister-in-law, Mrs. Raymond F. Dixon, 311 School Street, town. He had indeed proceeded to the second-story bedroom of Mrs. Dixon and killed her with a single shot to the heart, and then turned his revolver on himself and committed suicide by firing a shot in his right temple. No motive for the double tragedy could be determined, according to Assistant District Attorney Peter G. MacNeill. Kovy had had an excellent record as a member of the Wesleyville police force, and Mrs. Dixon was the popular member of the business staff of the *Evening Republican.* A coroner's inquest would be held. Private funeral services for Mrs. Dixon would take place

Saturday. Word had not yet been received from the chancellor of the Roman Catholic diocese in Columbus as to the nature of the funeral services for Kovy. Under Roman Catholic rules, requiem Mass and burial in consecrated ground are denied to persons who take their own lives.

At about the time the *Evening Republican* was selling an extra six hundred copies in the business district, George Munson was having his breakfast. Amy Coles, the Munson cook, served him a second batch of flannelcakes before remembering what she was trying to remember. "I know," she said. "You was wanted on the telephone. I told him you's asleep and he should call again. He did, too."

"Who is *he*?"

"Boy Williams," she said, and laughed. "Not Girl Williams. *Boy* Williams. As if he had to tell me *that*. He made me write down some number, for you to call when you woke up. Here 'tis. Two, two, four."

George recognized the number of the pay station in Gordon's drugstore. Undoubtedly Boyd had an itch to know the details of the date with Melba Dixon, to find out what she had done with George that she had not done with Boyd. Or vice versa. Such conversations were not so much a pooling of information as a competitive comparing of notes, but they were sometimes useful. George was deciding how much to tell Boyd when he was called to the telephone.

"It's Boyd. You just get up?"

"Just finishing my breakfast. Why?" said George.

"Would it be all right if I drove out to your place?"

"Sure, come on out. If I'm not in my room I'll be in the can."

George was cleaning his razor as Boyd appeared in the bedroom.

"You didn't hear about Melba?" said Boyd.

"No, what'd *she* do?" The imperativeness of Boyd's interrogation warned George that this was serious.

"She was murdered by Stan Kovy, and then he shot himself in the head."

"Where did you hear that?" said George.

"It's all over town. It's in the *Republican.* I brought one to show you. I didn't *think* you knew about it."

George read the *Republican* account. "It says shortly before dawn this morning."

"Yes. When did you leave her?"

"About twenty of four," said George.

"I'm the only one knows you had a date with her," said Boyd.

"No you're not."

"Who else did you tell?" said Boyd.

"Nobody. But she told her sister."

"Then you're going to get mixed up in it."

"I sure am," said George. "As soon as they start tracing Stan's movements. I was probably the last one to see both of them alive." He related the factual details of his encounter with Stan Kovy.

"As soon as they ask Gus what he knows, you're in for some questioning," said Boyd. "What surprises me is they haven't been here already."

"They'd have been here, but Gus sleeps in the afternoon."

"Do you think it might be a good idea to leave town?" said Boyd. "I'll lend you my car."

"Thanks, Boyd. But I don't think that would be such a good idea. I'm not really in this damn thing, but if I blew town—"

"Yeah."

"How to tell the old gent," said George. "And I'm going to have to tell him."

"Yeah, lucky for you he's no angel himself."

"How do you mean?" said George.

"Mrs. Tatnall," said Boyd.

"Mrs. Tatnall that has the gift shop? She and the old gent don't even speak to each other."

"Not any more, but they used to. On account of your old man, her husband left Wesleyville. You and I were too young to know about that, but it's true. All the older people know about it."

"My father and Mrs. Tatnall? How come I never heard about it?"

"Who would tell you? Not your parents, and the people in town wouldn't."

"My father—and Mrs. Tatnall. That fidgety little woman, and Theodore Lorenzo Munson," said George. "You're sure?"

"Ask anybody over forty," said Boyd.

"Well, it's a good thing to know, to have in reserve," said George. "Now the question is, do I go to my father or wait till he hears about me?"

"I say wait," said Boyd.

"And I say the opposite, knowing my father. He'll be home in a little while, or I'd go down to his office. Anyway, this'd be a better place to talk than there. Boyd, would you mind going back to town? I'll phone you at Gordon's or your house."

"Yes, I better not be here when your father gets home," said Boyd. "Do you feel funny? I mean about Melba?"

"Not yet, but I will," said George. "Afraid?"

"Afraid? Yes, that's part of it. He shot her in the heart, and the first thing I thought of was her teats. Only the night before last I was feeling her teats, my hand feeling all around where the bullet went in."

"Only about twelve hours ago I was doing the same thing," said George.

"I don't have any thoughts at all about Stan Kovy," said Boyd.

"You know, neither do I. He should be some kind of a villain and instead of that he's nothing at all. I'll tell you more about that sometime. He confided in me. I don't mean he said anything to make me suspicious. But I know why he killed her."

"Because she wouldn't screw him," said Boyd.

George shook his head. "Not because she wouldn't, and not because she did. I'll have to tell you some other time, Boyd."

"Phone me after you talked to your father," said Boyd.

George Munson had not long to wait, and when he heard the front door close he called to his father. "Dad? I'm in the den."

Theodore Munson hung his hat and overcoat in the clothes closet, went to the den and closed the door behind him. He took a cigar out of the walnut humidor and clipped it with the cutter on his watch chain. "Cigar?" he said.

"No thanks," said George.

"To save words, I found out you were with her last night. How long has it been going on? Now I want the truth, son."

"It was the first time."

"You did have relations with her, though?"

"Yes, I did."

"You would have been better off with her than with some of those others," said Theodore Munson. "Tell me about your conversation with Stan Kovy. You and he were

at the Acme, and you left there together. Did he say anything to indicate he might be going to do anything drastic?"

George recounted the conversation as fully as he could.
His father listened in silence, turning the cigar in his fingers.
At the end of George's story his father nodded, paused, and
said, "You see what can happen, even to a decent man. This
didn't only happen last night. It's been eating Stan for God
knows how long. In a couple of hours he would have been
home with his family. But that would only have postponed it, I think. Under a different set of circumstances
he might have gone there some night when *you* were there,
and he'd have shot you, too. As it is, he's brought disgrace
on his wife and children and the Dixon woman's boy. The
son of a war hero that gave his life for his country. And the
disgrace is something *they'll* feel, the widow and all those
different children. But there's something just as bad, if not
worse. It's what it does to a town like Wesleyville. A good,
decent town. With its faults, but fewer faults than the average town. You know where I stand in this community. You
couldn't help but know. We came here about a hundred
years ago, the Munsons, before it was called Wesleyville.
Before the railroad. We've always been hard-working and
prosperous, and we always had a good deal to say about
what went on in the community. For the most part, although
we made our mistakes, I honestly believe we've acted in
the best interests of the community. That's what makes me
sorry you got anywhere near this present terrible thing.
You're not in any trouble. I can reassure you on that score,
son. This is a clear case of a murder and suicide, both
people dead, and therefore the authorities aren't going to
concern themselves too much with underlying motives and
all that. It's practically a closed case already. The law, you'll
find, is largely a matter of revenge. Punishment. And in
this particular case there's no one left to punish. Therefore

the county and the borough have nothing left to do. There'll be a coroner's inquest and that'll be about all."

"But not for Mrs. Kovy and her children, and Melba's boy," said George.

"I'm glad to hear you say that," said his father. "It's the first time you ever showed any signs of any feeling of responsibility. I've been quite worried about that, and inclined to blame it on the Psi U fraternity. The only other member of that fraternity in our family was a Congregationalist minister, and I doubt if you have many of them in your chapter."

"One boy's the son of an Episcopal bishop," said George.

"Yes. Well, several of us had a meeting this afternoon, unofficial, informal. The widow and children are all going to be taken care of. Most likely Mrs. Kovy will want to move to some other town. Father Kelly was at the meeting. He's her pastor, and he's going to suggest to her that for the good of the children they ought to be brought up somewhere else. She'll get the money, whether she agrees or not, but the children shouldn't have to bear the brunt of what happened. And that's one of the things that money is for, to protect the young."

"I know. I just heard, recently, about Mrs. Tatnall," said George.

His father remained calm, but the calmness lasted too long. "How recently?" he said at last.

"Today," said George.

"I'm not going to pump you, George. You didn't hear it from your mother, did you?"

"No."

"Then it doesn't matter who you heard it from, as long as she didn't tell you. Well, how did it feel to discover that your father wasn't the little tin god I pretended to be?"

"I never thought you were a little tin god."

"No? What *did* you think I was?"

"Well—I wouldn't have been surprised if there'd been others besides Mrs. Tatnall."

"You're inclined to judge others by your own standards. But it so happens that the lady you mentioned *was* the only one. There shouldn't have been any, but there was one." He pointed his cigar at George. "And it was all my doing, not Mrs. Tatnall's. Never forget that. That's why I can't pass any harsh judgment on that policeman. I haven't heard a good word for him all day, but by God I can't say anything against him. And neither can you. Don't forget that, George. Well, you won't. This'll be with you the rest of your life. I broke up a marriage, and you—you're the only one that knows what you said to Kovy. Or didn't say. If you want to call it like-father, like-son, go right ahead. But don't ever make excuses for yourself. When they examine that woman's body, remember whose seed they're going to find in her."

"I wore a rubber," said George.

"You're making excuses already," said his father. "You haven't learned a God damned thing."

There was nothing more to be said. Theodore Munson got up and poured himself a drink of whiskey, and his son left the room.

THE JOURNEY TO
MOUNT CLEMENS

We finished up at Number 4 in time for supper. The dining-room closed at seven o'clock and we just made it. There were five in our party and we all sat at the same table. The food was good; the hotel had a reputation for good food, and we all knew that the next place where we would be stopping had no such reputation. Nevertheless we were not sorry to be on our way. Nothing had gone right during the two weeks we had been at Number 4, on a job that should have taken much longer. Carmichael, the chief of our party, had been putting the pressure on us because he wanted to get back to the main office in New York. He would have two days in New York and then he would be off to another assignment in the Sudan, where the Company was building a dam. Carmichael was known as a slave-driver anyway, but during the two weeks at Number 4 he had outdone himself. Breakfast every morning at seven, lunches packed so that we could eat on the job, supper at the hotel, and then night work, and no time off on Saturday or Sunday. Carmichael wanted to have the Number 4 job all cleaned up before he went abroad, and he thus had an incentive that we had not had. It was characteristic of

him that he had not a word of praise or thanks for the extra
work we had been putting in, that made him look good but
that did nothing for us.

Our work was not easy to explain. We were a valuation
crew, which meant that we were putting a valuation on the
entire physical property of an electric power corporation.
Every item, from a box of paper clips to a steam turbine,
had to be inspected and a price put on it. The purpose of
the valuation was to enable the financial people in the
main office to show what was being done with the corporation's capital. This information was doubly important: it
was helpful when the corporation asked the power com-
missions for an increase in rates; and it showed the public
that the corporation was a substantial enterprise when a
new stock issue was offered. I was the only member
of our party who did not hold an engineering degree,
but even I had learned to identify such unusual items as a
mercury arc rectifier and a Coxe traveling grate and a continuous rail joint. I was eighteen years old, knew nothing
about electricity, had just been kicked out of prep school,
and had got the job because Carmichael had been a patient
of my father's. I was paid seventy-five dollars a month, but I
was living on an expense account a good deal of the time,
and I could count on at least five dollars a week from shooting pool with the other members of the party. They were
not very good, and I was just enough better to win. But
during the two weeks at Number 4 we had shot no pool,
drunk no whiskey, chased after no girls. We had been working twelve-hour days, seven-day weeks; and we hated Carmichael, he knew it, and seemed to enjoy it.

Our bags were packed and waiting in the lobby as we
ate our last supper at Dugan's Hotel. "Well, gentlemen,
this time next Saturday I should be passing through the

Strait of Gibraltar. No, not quite. I'll still be in the Atlantic a week from tonight. King, you've been to that part of the world. How long before I get to Gibraltar?"

"Depends on the boat. Eight or nine days. You stop at the Azores, more than likely, but I doubt if you go ashore. I didn't."

"I have no particular curiosity about the Azores, but I would like to see Gibraltar."

"See it is all you will do. You won't be going ashore there either, according to my recollection. You keep right on till you get to Naples. You can go ashore there."

"I've been to Naples," said Carmichael.

"Yes, I was a lot younger then," said King. "You can have a high old time in Napoli. Is your wife going with you?"

"Oh, no. Not on this trip. I'm afraid she's had her share of the tropics."

"Well, not me. One more winter in the North Temperate Zone and I'll be ready for the Sudan. Keep me in mind when you're out there, Carmichael."

"I'll do that," said Carmichael.

We all knew that King had once been Carmichael's boss, and that their positions had been altered by Carmichael's ambition and King's fondness for the booze.

"I'd go there in a minute," said King. "I don't suppose you know that I was the first man the company sent out there."

"I didn't know you were the first," said Carmichael.

"Well, I had another fellow with me. Ken Stewart. But he died while we were out there. Got one of those tropical bugs. But the original survey was done by me. I learned to speak Swahili. It's not hard."

"I didn't realize they spoke Swahili in the Sudan."

"I didn't say they did. I just said I learned to speak it.

There's no damn use learning to speak those other languages. There's fifty of them, from one tribe to another. But if you learn Swahili you can get along. It's like French. You go anywhere in the world and if you speak French you'll find somebody to understand you."

"Swahili is like French? Come now, King."

"For Christ's sake, Carmichael. The French language isn't like the Swahili dialect. But if you speak Swahili in that part of Africa, it's like speaking French in the rest of the world. Now have I made myself clear?"

"Now you have, yes," said Carmichael.

King was the only member of our party who ever spoke that way to Carmichael. Indeed, I doubted that anyone else in the entire organization, regardless of rank, would be so disrespectful. The man was so austere, so inseparable from the tradition of efficiency and hard work, that no matter how much he was hated, his personal dignity was inviolate. We could share King's dislike of Carmichael, but I think we all felt that his behavior toward him was foolishness. But then there was a great deal of foolishness to be tolerated from King. To me, working at my first real job, one of the most fascinating things about the Company was that it could include and retain a Carmichael and a King in the same organization. Could it be that there was someone back there in an office on Lower Broadway who remembered that King had once learned to speak Swahili and remembered also that Carmichael had not always been King's boss? Reluctantly, inexplicably I was discovering that my pity for King could be changed into pity for Carmichael. The Company had got all it could out of King, and was now getting all it could out of Carmichael. I, eighteen years old, could see that Carmichael would some day be another King, bled dry, burnt out, and kept on the payroll in some minor job where former underlings would be dis-

respectful to him. In those days, on that job, I was fascinated by many things, but most of all by the subtleties and
complexities of the relations among my superiors—and they
were all my superiors. They were all anywhere from five to
thirty-five years older than I; educated, experienced men
who had, among them, been in just about every country on
earth. Working with them, living with them, was rather like
being a very junior officer in the regular army. As it happened,
I was in home territory, never more than seventy-five miles
from the place where I was born, but for the others in our
crew Eastern Pennsylvania was only less strange than
Shanghai or the Sudan or Ecuador. Indeed, they were more
at home in the distant places, where they had spent more
time, than in the mountains where I lived. One night before Carmichael arrived to deprive us of our free time, I had
sat with them in the lobby of Dugan's Hotel and listened
to King and Edmunds trying to carry on a conversation in
Chinese, but they had made no sense to each other because
King spoke one kind of Chinese and Edmunds another, and
a word that meant duenna in King's dialect meant prostitute
in Edmunds's. Then they had turned to me and asked me to
spell shoo-fly as in shoo-fly pie, which we had had for supper.
Then we all went down the street and I beat them at pool. It
was a great job, just great.

Now it was time to get in the two Company cars and
drive the twenty-eight miles to Mount Clemens, where there
was a new sub-station. When we got outside the ground
was covered with new snow. "Oh, dear," said Carmichael
to the driver of his car. "How long has this been coming
down?"

"A good two hours or more, ever since you was in the
hotel," said the driver. "It's all right, though. I got the chains
on."

"The chains? Will we need chains?"

"We'll need chains all right," said the driver. "We'd of needed them anyway, without this extra snow. Once you get off the main highway the road to Mount Clemens'll be slow going."

"Well, it's only about thirty miles," said Carmichael.

"*Only,*" said the driver.

"What?"

"You said it was only thirty miles, but I'm glad it ain't any more."

"How long do you think it'll take us?"

"Well, we better allow about an hour and a half."

"To go thirty miles?"

"I seen it take six hours, when there was big drifts. If I was you, Mr. Carmichael, I'd bundle up warmer than that. Don't you have a pair of arctics?"

"Not with me," said Carmichael. He was wearing a topcoat, fedora, and low shoes. "I've put away all my winter clothes. I'm on my way to Africa."

"Try Dugan. Maybe he has a pair somebody left behind. And maybe you could get him to give you the loan of his fur coat. He has a big fur coat he wears. You ought to have a muffler to go around your ears. And warm gloves. You want *me* to ask Dugan?"

Carmichael hesitated.

"Mr. Carmichael, I know you only think it's thirty miles, but it's liable to be five below zero by the time we get to Mount Clemens. And if anything happens to the car we could be out there all night."

"It's been nowhere near that cold here," said Carmichael. "I haven't needed anything heavier than this coat."

"Yeah, but your office was only two-three doors away from the hotel."

"Well, I don't want to hold up the parade," said Carmichael. He returned to the hotel, having paid no attention to the rest of us who had stood waiting for him to assign us to the cars.

"Pig-headed son of a bitch," said King. "While we stand here freezing." He turned to me. "You and Edmunds might just as well get in the Studebaker. He'll want me and probably Thompson with him in the Paige."

Carmichael came back wearing a bearskin coat, arctics, and sealskin cap. He was accompanied by Dugan bearing three Thermos lunch kits. Dugan gave one to Edmunds and me. "Don't know how long the coffee'll stay hot, but it's better than nothing," said Dugan.

"You don't happen to have a couple of pints of whiskey," said Edmunds.

"You know I don't handle it," said Dugan. "But you know where you can get it. There's two ham sandwiches in there for you."

"What about our driver? Doesn't he rate anything?" said Edmunds.

"Mr. Carmichael didn't say anything," said Dugan.

"I'll be all right," said our driver. He held up a pint of whiskey. "But thanks for askin'."

In a few minutes we were under way, and the moment we left the town we were in almost total darkness, broken only by the dashlight and the beam from the Studebaker's headlights. We lost sight of the Paige. "Carney must be in a hurry," said our driver.

"Carmichael," said Edmunds.

"No, I mean Carney. That's the other driver. But I ain't gonna try and keep up with him. I don't want to break a cross-link. The hell with that. You warm enough back there?"

"Fine, so far," said Edmunds.

"The secret is get one blanket under you and one over

you. The best thing is if you have a dame with you. That keeps the old circulation going."

"The best thing is to stay home and have the dame in bed with you," said Edmunds.

"Well, you won't have a hard time finding them once we get to Mount Clemens. Lithuanian. Polish. Irish. But this being a Saturday night, some of them went to confession. Some of them won't go out with you Saturday night, or if they do it's a waste of time. They won't even have a beer with you after twelve o'clock midnight. Sunday night, that's an altogether different story. Talk about your hypocrites, them Catholics."

"You're talking to one right now," I said.

"Oh. Well, if you want to offer me out when we get to Mount Clemens."

"I will," I said. My stomach fell at the thought of having a fist fight at the end of our journey, but I had not learned to keep my mouth shut.

"I don't have anything against all Catholics. Carney's my best friend."

"Ah, shut up," I said.

"Both of you shut up," said Edmunds.

Conversation was suspended, but the absence of talk did not produce quiet. Now we listened to and thought about every sound, and most of the sounds were ominous, beginning with the rising and falling of the wind and the frequent changing down to second gear as we left the main highway. The side curtains were secure, we were not uncomfortable, but any minute we could expect the isinglass in the curtains to crack, and when that happened the wind and snow would rush in. Edmunds and I were dressed warmly in sheepskin-lined reefers, woolen helmets that rolled down over our ears and throats, and six-buckle arctics, the cold-weather clothes we had brought with us to Number 4. Our driver wore a plaid mackinaw and a helmet like ours. If the car broke down we would not freeze to death so long as we stayed inside—and the wind did not tear the curtains to shreds. We were moving slowly, very slowly. We came to a mining patch called Valley View—every county in Pennsylvania, I suppose, has a Valley View—which I knew to be less than ten miles from Number 4, and it had taken us half an hour to get that far. And the worst was yet to come. I had been over that road many times, in summer and winter, and one thing I remembered about it now was that between Valley View and Mount Clemens the road cut through practically virgin forest. There was no settlement large enough to be called a hamlet. My superiors, who had lived in jungles and spoke Swahili and Cantonese, probably had no idea how close they were to a wilderness. The bear and the rattlesnake were hibernating, but there were other hazards and the worst of them now was the cold. Every winter, in that part of the country, we would hear of men who had been found frozen to death and of others who had lost a foot by frostbite.

"You're not very talkative," said Edmunds.

"You told me to shut up," I said.

He laughed. "Well, I give you permission to talk now," he said. "I want to stay awake. I learned that in Wyoming and Montana. Don't fall asleep in this kind of weather, or you may not wake up."

"We'll be all right as long as we keep going."

"How much longer have we got to go?" he said.

"A little over half way," I said.

"We got about twenty miles to go," said the driver. "If we don't get to Mount Clemens by ha' past ten Carney said he'd come back and look for us."

"Well, at least we won't be stuck out here all night," said Edmunds.

"That's providing Carney gets through all right. If Carney gets stuck, we're stuck too."

"That's a pleasant thought," said Edmunds.

"Well, it's not so bad," said our driver. "If Carney don't get there by ten they'll send a Company truck out after us. We got nothing to worry about."

I was not so sure. "How big a truck?" I said.

"It's about a two-ton Dodge. One of them they got for the maintenance crews. They got them fixed up so they can stay out here all night if they have to. For when they have to repair a high tension line. I seen them go out when it was ten below. I wouldn't have that job if they paid me a hundred dollars a week. Sixty-six thousand volts. You don't even have to *touch* the God damn line. You get too close and the juice jumps out at you. I seen a guy got too close and it pops a hole right through the top of his skull. That's what sixty-six thousand volts'll do to you. Right through the top of your skull, a hole about the size of a silver dollar. I wouldn't work around that stuff if they paid me *two* hundred dollars a week."

"Well, it's better than freezing to death," said Edmunds.

"Maybe you're right at that," said the driver. "I never thought of it that way. Uh-oh."

Up ahead, in the middle of the road, stood Carney, waving both arms, flagging us down. The first thing I noticed was that the smoke was coming out of the exhaust pipe, which at least indicated that the Paige had not stalled.

"Get in," said our driver. "What's wrong, Carney?"

Carney got in the front seat, turned and addressed Edmunds. "You got another passenger. Mr. King is riding the rest of the way with you."

"How does that happen?" said Edmunds.

"Well, I guess that's not for me to say, but they had a little argument and Mr. King wants to ride with you."

"That's all right with us. Tell him to bring his blanket and come on back," said Edmunds. "Are you all right otherwise?"

"Yes, I guess so," said Carney.

"You don't seem too sure," said Edmunds.

"Well, I guess I ought to tell you. King took a poke at him."

"At Carmichael, I suppose?" said Edmunds.

"He gave him a bloody nose."

"A little argument. So Carmichael ordered him to ride with us."

"No. I did," said Carney.

"*You* did?"

"I told them, I said one of them had to change cars. They were swingin' away at one another back there, and I stopped the car. As far as I know they're still at it. They're acting like a couple of God damn kids."

"So you took charge. Well, good for you, Carney."

"I guess it'll mean my job, but those two bastards, rassling around back there, they could send me into a ditch."

"Sergeant Carney, of the 103d Engineers," said our driver. "You tell 'em, Carney."

"Supposed to be gentlemen, but acting like a couple of God damn hoodlums. I'll get another job."

"Don't worry about that now," said Edmunds. "Tell King to come on back here."

We watched King, being pulled out of the Paige by Carney and dragging a blanket along the snow, staggering toward us. He was talking to himself; you could see him.

Our driver switched his headlight off and on to signal to Carney that King was safely with us, and the Paige got under way again. King climbed in with Edmunds and me, and the Studebaker began to move.

"At your age you ought to have more sense," said Edmunds.

"Sense? If I'd had more sense, you're right. I'd have given him a *good* beating twenty years ago. I don't know why I didn't. He gave me plenty of cause to. In Quito, twenty years ago, I found out he was going over my head, sending back his confidential reports to the home office. That's when I should have given it to him, when I could have wiped up the floor with him. But I got in a couple of good punches tonight."

"Yes, and you've cooked your goose," said Edmunds.

"Have I? We'll see. And what if I have? They can retire me on half-pay and I'll open up a gas station in Florida. Maybe I'll let you come down and join me there, Edmunds. You're not getting any younger either."

"*You're* reverting to second childhood."

"Well, I hope it'll be better than my first," said King. "I grew up in a Methodist parsonage and that wasn't much fun." He took a deep sigh and turned over on his side. He was sitting in the left corner, Edmunds was in the middle, I was in the right corner. Now the going got really rough, and instead of being excited, as I had been, I was afraid. Up ahead the Paige, a heavier low-built car, was breaking the path for us, otherwise we could not have gone on. Several times we dropped down into low gear and our driver was zig-zagging to gain traction and keep moving. He was a good snow driver, I had to say that for him; he knew how to use the momentum of the car to keep from getting wedged in. Our undercarriage was higher off the ground than that of the Paige, but even so I could feel the transmission scraping the false crown in the center of the road. There was, of course, only one path. At best, in summer conditions, the road was narrow, not wide enough for two big trucks to pass. Now, if a third car had come from the direction of Mount Clemens we would have had to get out and shovel snow to make the path wide—and I knew who would be swinging the shovels: the two drivers and I. Maybe Thompson would have helped out; he was younger than the others of our party. But I was sure that Carmichael would have ordered me, as the low-ranking member of the party, to pitch in. I hoped that if another car came from Mount Clemens it would contain five hard-muscled Lithuanians.

As the Studebaker zig-zagged we in the back seat were jounced and jostled. "I'm lucky Gaston—in the middle again," said Edmunds.

"Do you want me to change places with you?" I said.

"No, stay where you are. You two keep me warm."

"Is King asleep?" I said.

"Yes, and I'm going to let him sleep. We must be more than half way," said Edmunds.

"We got about twelve miles," said the driver. The last four miles is the worst, all uphill. We'll make it."

"You're doing very well. What's your name?"

"Stone. Ed Stone. They call me Stoney."

"Well, I'm going to give you a good report," said Edmunds.

"That'll help, in case they fire Carney," said Stone. "I ought to be due for a promotion, but there's no job for me as long as Carney's there."

"Don't raise your hopes on that score. Knowing Mr. Carmichael, I doubt if Carney'll be fired."

"Well, maybe you could see I got some overtime," said Stone.

"That's not my business, but I'll give you a good report," said Edmunds. The car lurched, and I could not guess whether Stone was taking out his disappointment by mistreating the car or was making an honest zig-zag. In any case, King was thrown across Edmunds's chest and Edmunds impatiently pushed him back in his corner. I laughed.

"Lucky Gaston," I said.

"Don't get fresh," said Edmunds. "We've had enough for one evening, without a fresh kid to boot."

On the uphill climb I could almost literally follow each revolution of the wheels by the sound. The windshield wiper, operated by hand, gave Stone a view of the road ahead, but I could no longer tell where we were except to estimate by the steepness of the grade how far up the mountain we were. I had also lost track of time, and I was not sufficiently curious to take off my gauntlets and look at my watch. Over and over again I resigned myself to my fate, but the pessimistic composure did not last; the slightest change in the speed of the revolutions of the wheels put my imagination to work again. I had the disadvantage over Edmunds of knowing that the last mile or so was dangerous in daylight in any season; a car could drop three or four hundred feet before being stopped by timber, and here, of course, the wind was at its worst. I very nearly prayed, and my refusal to pray probably was prayer of a kind.

Then we were there. Out of the black darkness of the valley and the mountain road, and on the summit of Mount Clemens. Even through the isinglass and iced-over windshield we could discern the lights of the town, and we could feel the level progress of the car.

"Well, we made it," said Stone.

"Good work," said Edmunds. He reached over and shook King. "Wake up, fellow. We're almost there."

"You want to go right to the hotel?" said Stone.

"I sure do," said Edmunds. "Do you realize we never thought about the coffee? I'll bet it's still warm. But I'm going to have a drink."

"That's why I asked you," said Stone. "There's a couple places open where you can get booze. You can't at the hotel."

"No thanks, I have a quart in my suitcase," said Edmunds. "Come on, King. Wake up. I'm surprised he didn't wake up when I said I had a quart. King!"

But King was dead.

THE MECHANICAL MAN

They finished up their work shortly after six o'clock in the evening, and then in two company Buick touring cars they departed for Oakdale, about thirty-five miles away. That was Mackenzie's way of doing things. He got the most he could out of you, and then a little more, by making you travel on your time, not the company's. Gibbsville was only thirty-five miles from Oakdale, but it was hard going; up, then down, then up and down over two mountains, on roads that were nothing much in the summer and were now likely to be sheeted with ice and made narrow by snow piled up at the sides.

Mackenzie was coming by train the next day. The men all knew that he would be working until midnight and would have to get up at five-thirty to make the train connections, but he would be in a steam-heated office while they were riding in the touring cars, with the mountain temperatures somewhere near zero degrees Fahrenheit. In the morning, too, he would be riding in a railway coach, warmed by a coal stove. Tonight, although he would be working late, he could take time off to have a half-way decent meal in a restaurant at a half-way decent hour. They, on the other hand, would have to take what was left at the hotel in Oakdale. Their room reservations had been made, but the men who had been in Oakdale on earlier field trips knew what the food would be like after seven o'clock, and no one expected to get to Oakdale much before eight. You made no time on those roads in this weather. If you tried to make time, cheated a little bit on safety, you were liable to end up in a ditch or a snowbank, or upside down in the middle of the road. You drove up the mountains in second or low gear, and all the way down in second. There were five-mile stretches without a house or a store on either side of the road. If you ran into any kind of trouble you could still not be sure that the next house would have a telephone. That could be very bad if someone broke a leg or fractured his skull. Most of the men had worked in the Far West, in the mountains and in the tropics of South America and Africa, and this was only Pennsylvania, within a 120-mile radius of New York City and closer than that to Philadelphia. But they had learned to respect these mountains. It might be more spectacular to go to your death in the Rockies or to drown in the Nile, but these mountains were cold and wild, and their lakes were cold and deep. Here you might even lose out to an angry bear. It had happened, and what you had endured in Montana and the Sudan and Chile did not really make you tougher; you bled or strangled or were just as uncomfortable here as anywhere else.

They had all come to work that day in the clothes they would be wearing to Oakdale, and had felt self-conscious in their corduroy suits and high-laced shoes and sheepskin coats and woolen caps that would roll down over the cheeks and ears. (They overlooked the fact that in Gibbsville mining engineers in hobnails and pacs were seen every day.) Now, as the Buicks took them to Oakdale, they wished the sheepskins and mackinaws were heavier, although five men in a tightly side-curtained car created a warmth of its own. After the first ten miles it was not so bad inside the cars. The cars kept well in sight of each other, actually within the hearing range of each other's Klaxonettes, so that neither car would get too far ahead or behind. It was reassuring to know that that arrangement had been made by the two drivers, especially when the cars left the last good-sized town and approached the mountains. Conversation stopped. The isinglass windows of the side-curtains were translucent and no more. There was no moon, and nothing to see but the lights of other cars, fewer and fewer of them as they put more distance between them and the last town. The dashlights of the Buicks were like binnacle lights in a small boat, and there was even a ship-like roll as the cars encountered frozen ruts and patches of snow.

They made only one stop in the mountains; when a cross-chain and then another parted on the left hind wheel of the leading car. A single broken cross-chain would have been ignored, but when the second one broke it left too much unguarded space on the tire. The two drivers got out to fix the chains; the members of the engineering party stayed inside the cars. Hewlett, the chief-of-party, got out briefly to confer with the drivers, but he did not linger in the cold. He explained the delay to the men in the second car, then returned to the leading car and went to sleep.

They reached Oakdale just before eight o'clock. "I put you all at the one table," said Murphy, the owner of the hotel.

"Will there be time to wash up?" said Hewlett.

Murphy, coatless, looked at his large hunting-case watch. "If you don't take all night at it," said Murphy. "I'm paying the girl extra to wait on you fellows."

"You can put it on the bill," said Hewlett.

"Don't you worry about that," said Murphy. "But she

lives down the other end of town. Will one of your drivers get her home?"

"I'll see to that," said Hewlett. "What are you giving us for supper?"

"Pork chops, mashed potatoes, lima beans, red beets and the endive salad. There'll be your choice of two kinds of pies, the raisin and the coconut custard."

"That sounds pretty good. No soup?"

"Not this late. Soup'd take that much longer. The other suppers there'll be soup, but not tonight. You been here before, Mr. Hewlett. You know we start serving supper at ha' past five."

"No use asking for a drink, I suppose?" said Hewlett.

"You come back in my office I'll give you a shot, but I don't know them other fellows with you. And I ain't taking no chances. I won't start paying no graft when there's no profit in it for me. I could lose my hotel license and then where would I be? But I got a bottle in my safe, if you wish to partake."

"Never mind, thanks," said Hewlett. He joined the others of his party, who were warming themselves around the coal-burning heater. "We eat right away," he said. "Check in later. You can hang your coats and hats in the hallway, outside the dining-room. Your luggage'll be safe here."

"Any chance of a drink?" said Ames.

"No. Unless you brought your own," said Hewlett.

"I have a quart in my suitcase," said Ames.

"No, there won't be time. Let's not hold up the parade the first night," said Hewlett. "There's a place down the street you can get a drink after supper."

The food smelled good and it was hot. A small problem arose when Hewlett counted the places at table. "There should be nine," he told Murphy. "You only have places for seven."

"Seven is what they told me's in your party," said Murphy.

"They forgot the drivers," said Hewlett.

"Well, I'll put them at a table by themselves," said Murphy. "Are they staying the night?"

"Yes. I hope you have room for them," said Hewlett.

"Is the company paying for them?" said Murphy.

"The company pays for everything, for everybody," said Hewlett. "Even cigarettes. But not personal phone calls. You ought to know that by his time."

"They never said a damn word about the drivers," said Murphy.

"Oh, it's not your fault," said Hewlett. He was embarrassed at having to tell the drivers they would be sitting by themselves, but the drivers did not seem to mind. At last the entire party of nine men were seated and the serving dishes passed. They ate in comparative silence. McDonnell, the expert on turbines and generators, and somewhat of an expert on Oakdale, answered the questions put to him by Ames, who was a new man and an auditor.

"What about gash?" said Ames.

The others laughed. McDonnell was a strait-laced man whom the others teased by talking dirty. "Find out for yourself," said McDonnell.

"I am, but you could make it a little easier for me," said Ames.

"Don't expect me to get your women for you," said McDonnell.

"All right, Mac, if that's the way you feel about it," said Ames.

"Lay off," said Hewlett. He liked McDonnell; he did

not like auditors, or efficiency men, or Mackenzie, who combined certain features of them all. Dessert was being passed around, and it was time for an announcement. "As you all know, there'll be a certain amount of night work while we're here," he said. "Mr. Mackenzie would like us to be all finished up by the end of next week, Friday at the latest. I'll be working with the electrical and construction men. The bookkeeping men will get their orders from Mr. Mackenzie, direct, but I'm responsible for what goes on in his absence. So you office men might as well get used to the idea of a fourteen, sixteen, hour day. Eight in the morning to ten o'clock at night. There's plenty to drink in Oakdale, but I don't want anyone showing up with a hangover that'll —uh—impair his efficiency."

"What about Sunday? Do we get Sunday off?" said Ames.

"No. We all work Sunday. The company was hoping to deliver power by the first of October, but we had a run of bad luck last spring with the weather and that fire at the dam. New turbines and all that. We had to practically start from scratch, as Mac will tell you. Now we're just about all set again, and this we hope will be the final inspection trip, as far as we're concerned. You office men know what you're supposed to do and I don't. But Mr. Mackenzie will take it out of my hide if you're not all finished, and the only way I'll know you're working is if I see you in the office. Your nice, warm office."

"How long is Mackenzie going to be here?" said Ames.

"Two or three days, I guess," said Hewlett. "But you never know about him. He may stay the whole time we're here, or he may take a train at Mauch Chunk and be in New York for the next two months. He doesn't tell me his plans. If there are no more questions, meeting's adjourned."

"Who'd like to play some poker?" said Ames.

Mackenzie arrived the next morning by car. He went directly to the company offices, a new small brick building off the main street of Oakdale. The car, befitting his rank, was a Cadillac, and in spite of the cold and the few pedestrians, it was quickly surrounded by men and women who did not often get close to such a big automobile. The chauffeur, carrying two large briefcases, followed Mackenzie into the office.

Mackenzie, carrying a briefcase and an attaché case, was wearing a sealskin cap and an old coonskin coat that had frogs instead of buttons. Michaelson, the branch manager, greeted him and helped him off with his coat. "We gave you the same office you always use," said Michaelson.

"Thank you, Michaelson. Where are the rest of my people?"

"They're in the back room on the second floor."

"No," said Mackenzie. "Move them down here so they'll be near my office. Have you seen Mr. Hewlett?"

"He was here but he went out," said Michaelson.

"Call him at the plant and tell him I'd like to speak to him," said Mackenzie.

"He won't be at the plant," said Michaelson. "He'll be here any minute."

"Where is he?" said Mackenzie.

"I'd rather he told you himself, Mr. Mackenzie."

"What are you so mysterious about?" said Mackenzie.

"Well, I don't think it's my business to say anything."

Mackenzie, exasperated, gave up. "All right, all right," he said. "Now go tell Mr. Ames and Mr. Daley to come to my office, and meanwhile you can find some space for them here."

"Mr. Ames isn't here either," said Michaelson. "He's with Mr. Hewlett."

"Ames is with Hewlett? Oh, never mind, Michaelson.

I'm sure you're going to say it isn't your business to say anything," said Mackenzie. He hesitated. "Is there anybody doing any work around here today? Any of my people?"

"Mr. Daley's here," said Michaelson.

"Tell him I want to see him right away," said Mackenzie.

At that moment Ames and Hewlett entered the office. "Good morning," said Hewlett. "I see you drove up. I was expecting you on the train."

"So I gather. Let's go in my office. Not you, Ames. I want to talk to Mr. Hewlett," said Mackenzie. "Ames, you and Daley will move downstairs. Mr. Michaelson is finding space for you."

Mackenzie went to his desk. "Close the door, please," he said to Hewlett. "Thanks. Well, Joe, if we were back on the Duke Power job I'd say you and Ames had gone out for a Dr. Pepper. But I don't think they ever heard of a Dr. Pepper in this part of the country."

"No. We had a little trouble last night. At the hotel. Some of our party started a poker game after supper. A stranger, traveling salesman, wanted to get in it. They wouldn't let him. And there was a fight. Ames gave the fellow a bloody nose, and he had Ames arrested for assault and battery. Ames spent the night in the cooler. I got our local lawyer, Southard, and we went to the borough hall this morning and the salesman agreed not to press charges."

"Half the morning shot to hell. Do you want me to fire Ames?"

"That's not for me to say, Dave."

"Yes it is," said Mackenzie. "I'll keep him on till we finish up here. We're pressed for time, as you well know. But I'll get rid of him if you say so. I trust your judgment in such matters."

"Well, I wouldn't have hired Ames, but I only hire technical men. Ames is an accountant."

"An auditor, strictly speaking. That's hair-splitting, but in our organization an auditor gets a little more money than an accountant. You can put up with him for another two weeks, can't you?"

"Sure. As a matter of fact, he probably was in the right last night. That nosy bastard, the salesman, barged in where he wasn't wanted, and I gather he got what was coming to him. I wasn't there. No, Dave, I'm not going to tell you to fire Ames. If you want to fire him, you have the authority."

"I guess that's pretty well understood," said Mackenzie.

"Oh, sure. We all know you're the boss, Dave. Even the new men."

"There you go again, Joe," said Mackenzie. "You always like to see how far you can go. You never seem to understand that as long as you do your work as well as you do, our personal relations don't matter. You can say what you please, to me or about me, and it's water off a duck's back. In plain language, I will never fire you. But I'll give you a small piece of advice, my friend. You may irritate yourself to the point where you'll want to throw up your job, and good jobs are scarce."

"Yes," said Hewlett. "And there's another possibility that I haven't overlooked, Dave."

"What's that, Joe?"

"That you may deliberately irritate me to the point where I have to quit. Sometimes I think that's what you've been doing."

"No, I don't think that's fair. However, as you say, it's a possibility. In other words, I pile the work on you until you crack under the strain?"

"Yes. You did it to George Ferris."

"That's a God damn lie! You weren't even there when George was killed. You were a couple of thousand miles away. George Ferris was drinking on the job, had been drinking on the job before that, and I'd warned him. He was seen drunk, staggering, coming out of the shack, just before he fell. That was a four-hundred-foot drop to the bottom of the canyon. I kept George Ferris on even after I'd warned him twice."

"Well, the dam wasn't quite finished. Were you going to keep him on after you finished the dam?"

"I most certainly was not," said Mackenzie.

"Did he know that?"

"If he didn't he was a bigger damn fool than I thought he was. I can see what you're thinking, but it won't do, Joe. I worked twice as hard as Ferris, and I had *all* the responsibility. But Ferris wasn't my responsibility, not his death anyway." Mackenzie looked at his strap watch, a gesture which for him involved a small ceremony every time he did it. He would extend his arm, bend it at the elbow, and bring his wrist back toward his face. Hewlett had seen him do it in a sleeveless shirt, in the tropics; in fiercely cold weather, in a Canadian mackinaw; and in the lobby of the Palace Hotel in San Francisco, in a beautifully cut tweed suit. Mackenzie was a native of Evanston, Illinois, but whenever he flourished his wristwatch Hewlett imagined him a British colonel and half expected him to say, "In thirty-four minutes we shall attack." The watch had a gunmetal case and a strap of webbing, and Hewlett had never seen him without it.

"Are you having lunch at the hotel?" said Mackenzie.

"No. My men and I had lunches packed for us," said Hewlett.

"Well, that'll save *some* time," said Mackenzie. "Your men are all out at the plant?"

"Yes," said Hewlett.

"I'll be out there sometime this afternoon. I'll want to talk to McDonnell."

"All right," said Hewlett.

"No, it's not all right," said Mackenzie.

"Why?"

"You ought to know, Joe. Don't tell me Mac hasn't confided in you. That *is* a surprise."

"I guess it is," said Hewlett. "I don't know what you're talking about."

"He's had an offer from J. G. White."

"It's not the first time," said Hewlett.

"No, but it's the first time I've had to worry about losing him. I was hoping you'd be able to use your influence on him, but if he hasn't confided in you, I'll have to do it myself."

"If he hasn't said anything to me, I doubt if he's considering it."

"Precisely because he hasn't is why I think he is considering it," said Mackenzie. "If he hasn't told you, he hasn't told anyone. But he's had the offer, it's a good one, and my information is completely reliable."

"I don't look so good, do I?" said Hewlett.

"No, not in this matter. You don't look as bad as I did in the George Ferris matter, but you've always been known for your ability to handle men, and my reputation's been just the opposite. It must be quite a comedown for you, when you have to find out about Mac from me. The slave-driver. The cold fish. The mechanical man. That was a lousy God damn thing you said about me and George Ferris."

"Yes, I guess it was," said Hewlett.

"Don't say it again, or anything like it."

"No matter how good my work is?" said Hewlett.

"No matter how good your work is. In this case, you're no good to me or to the company if you imply that I was in any way responsible for George's death. The picture of me as a slave-driver is nothing new. Not even unique. In our profession we rather pride ourselves on our toughness, and the soft-hearted don't last long in jobs like mine. If they ever get jobs like mine. But I don't want anybody in my organization saying I was responsible for a drunken accident or a suicide, whichever it was. You happen to have a lot of influence among my men—*my* men, Joe, get that. *You* are one of my men. So don't undermine me, because if you do, that impairs the efficiency of my organization."

"Would you like to have my resignation, Dave?"

"No. I wouldn't ask you to resign, Joe. I'd fire you. I might even go so far as to ask you to take off your coat and put up your dukes, but I wouldn't ask for your resignation. When you and I part company let's do it like men, not ribbon clerks."

"No time like the present, Dave," said Hewlett.

"Oh, yes there is. We have a lot of work to do, and I know you're not the kind of man that would walk out on a job. You'd spend the rest of your life kicking yourself in the behind if you did that."

"Don't worry. I won't walk out on you now," said Hewlett. "But maybe in about two weeks the two of us ought to take off our coats."

"I can wait another two weeks," said Mackenzie. "Having waited quite a few years. Not just to take a crack at you, Joe. All of you. Ames. McDonnell. Ferris. All the way back to the first boss I ever had."

"Remarkable self-control, all these years," said Hewlett.

"Haven't you ever wanted to knock a few heads together? How did you feel about Ames this morning?"

"To tell the truth, I didn't even like him last night," said Hewlett.

"Well, in that case you and I ought to have quite a rough-and-tumble. You've been holding in as much as I have."

"At least," said Hewlett.

"All right, Joe. Get up to the plant. We're on company time," said Mackenzie.

CHRISTMAS POEM

Billy Warden had dinner with his father and mother and sister. "I suppose this is the last we'll see of you this vacation," said his father.

"Oh, I'll be in and out to change my shirt," said Billy.

"My, we're quick on the repartee," said Barbara Warden. "The gay young sophomore."

"What are *you*, Bobby dear? A drunken junior?" said Billy.

"Now, I don't think that was called for," said their mother.

"Decidedly *un*-called for," said their father. "What *are* your plans?"

"Well, I was hoping I could borrow the chariot," said Billy.

"Yes, we anticipated that," said his father. "What I meant was, are you planning to go away anywhere? Out of town?"

"Well, that depends. There's a dance in Reading on the twenty-seventh I'd like to go to, and I've been invited to go skiing in Montrose."

"Skiing? Can you ski?" said his mother.

"All Dartmouth boys ski, or pretend they can," said his sister.

"Isn't that dangerous? I suppose if you were a Canadian, but I've never known anyone to go skiing around here. I thought they had to have those big—I don't know—scaffolds, I guess you'd call them."

"You do, for jumping, Mother. But skiing isn't all jumping," said Billy.

"Oh, it isn't? I've only seen it done in the newsreels. I never really saw the point of it, although I suppose if you did it well it would be the same sensation as flying. I often dream about flying."

"I haven't done much jumping," said Billy.

"Then I take it you'll want to borrow the car on the twenty-seventh, and what about this trip to Montrose?" said his father.

"I don't exactly know where Montrose is," said Mrs. Warden.

"It's up beyond Scranton," said her husband. "That would mean taking the car overnight. I'm just trying to arrange some kind of a schedule. Your mother and I've been invited to one or two things, but I imagine we can ask our friends to take us there and bring us back. However, we only have the one car, and Bobby's entitled to her share."

"Of course she is. Of course I more or less counted on her to, uh, to spend most of her time in Mr. Roger Taylor's Dort."

"It isn't a Dort. It's a brand new Marmon, something I doubt you'll ever be able to afford."

"Something I doubt Roger'd ever be able to afford if it took any brains to afford one. So he got rid of the old Dort, did he?"

"He never had a Dort, and you know it," said Bobby.

"Must we be so disagreeable, the first night home?" said Mrs. Warden. "I know there's no meanness in it, but it doesn't *sound* nice."

"When would you be going to Montrose?" said Mr. Warden. "What date?"

"Well, if I go it would be a sort of a house party," said Billy.

"In other words, not just overnight?" said his father. "Very well, suppose you tell us how many nights?"

"I'm invited for the twenty-eighth, twenty-ninth, and thirtieth," said Billy. "That would get me back in time to go to the Assembly on New Year's Eve."

"What that amounts to, you realize, is having possession of the car from the twenty-seventh to the thirtieth or thirty-first," said his father.

"Yes, I realize that," said Billy.

"Do you still want it, to keep the car that long, all for yourself?" said his father.

"Well, I didn't have it much last summer, when I was working. And I save you a lot of money on repairs. I ground the valves, cleaned the spark plugs. A lot of things I did. I oiled and greased it myself."

"Yes, I have to admit you do your share of that," said his father. "But if you keep the car that long, out of town, it just means we are without a car for four days, at the least."

There was a silence.

"I really won't need the car very much after Christmas," said Bobby. "After I've done my shopping and delivered my presents."

"Thank you," said Billy.

"Well, of course not driving myself, I never use it," said Mrs. Warden.

"That puts it up to me," said Mr. Warden. "If I were Roger Taylor's father I'd give you two nice big Marmons for Christmas, but I'm not Mr. Taylor. Not by about seven hundred thousand dollars, from what I hear. Is there anyone else from around here that's going to Montrose?"

"No."

"Then it isn't one of your Dartmouth friends?" said Mr. Warden. "Who will you be visiting?"

"It's a girl named Henrietta Cooper. She goes to Russell Sage. I met her at Dartmouth, but that's all. I mean, she has no other connection with it."

"Russell Sage," said his mother. "We know somebody that has a daughter there. I know who it was. That couple we met at the Blakes'. Remember, the Blakes entertained for them last winter? The husband was with one of the big electrical companies."

"General Electric, in Schenectady," said Mr. Warden. "Montrose ought to be on the Lehigh Valley, or the Lackawanna, if I'm not mistaken."

"The train connections are very poor," said Billy. "If I don't go by car, Henrietta's going to meet me in Scranton, but heck, I don't want to ask her to do that. I'd rather not go if I have to take the train."

"Well, I guess we can get along without the car for that long. But your mother and I are positively going to have to have it New Year's Eve. We're going to the Assembly, too."

"Thank you very much," said Billy.

"It does seem strange. Reading one night, and then the next day you're off in the opposite direction. You'd better make sure the chains are in good condition. Going over those mountains this time of year."

"A house party. Now what will you do on a house party

in Montrose? Besides ski, that is?" said Mrs. Warden. "It sounds like a big house, to accommodate a lot of young people."

"I guess it probably is," said Billy. "I know they have quite a few horses. Henny rides in the Horse Show at Madison Square Garden."

"Oh, my. Then they must be very well-to-do," said his mother. "I always wanted to ride when I was a girl. To me there's nothing prettier than a young woman in a black riding habit, riding side-saddle. Something so elegant about it."

"I wouldn't think she rode side-saddle, but maybe she does," said Billy.

"Did you say you wanted to use the car tonight, too?" said his father.

"If nobody else is going to," said Billy.

"Barbara?" said Mr. Warden.

"No. Roger is calling for me at nine o'clock," said Barbara. "But I would like it tomorrow, all day if possible. I have a ton of shopping to do."

"I *still* haven't finished wrapping all *my* presents," said Mrs. Warden.

"I haven't even *bought* half of mine," said Barbara.

"You shouldn't leave everything to the last minute," said her mother. "I bought most of mine at sales, as far back as last January. Things are much cheaper after Christmas."

"Well, I guess I'm off to the races," said Billy. "Dad, could you spare a little cash?"

"How much?" said Mr. Warden.

"Well—ten bucks?"

"I'll take it off your Christmas present," said Mr. Warden.

"Oh, no, don't do that?" I have ten dollars if you'll reach me my purse. It's on the sideboard," said Mrs. Warden.

"You must be flush," said Mr. Warden.

"Well, no, but I don't like to see you take it off Billy's Christmas present. That's as bad as opening presents ahead of time," said Mrs. Warden.

"Which certain people in this house do every year," said Barbara.

"Who could she possibly mean?" said Billy. "I opened one present, because it came from Brooks Brothers and I thought it might be something I could wear right away."

"And was it?" said his mother.

"Yes. Some socks. These I have on, as a matter of fact," said Billy. "They're a little big, but they'll shrink."

"Very snappy," said Barbara.

"Yes, and I don't know who they came from. There was no card."

"I'll tell you who they were from. They were from me," said Barbara.

"They were? Well, thanks. Just what I wanted," said Billy.

"Just what you asked me for, last summer," said Barbara.

"Did I? I guess I did. Thank you for remembering. Well, goodnight, all. Don't wait up. I'll be home before breakfast."

They muttered their goodnights and he left. He wanted to—almost wanted to—stay; to tell his father that he did not want a Marmon for Christmas, which would have been a falsehood; to tell his mother he loved her in spite of her being a nitwit; to talk to Bobby about Roger Taylor, who was not good enough for her. But this was his first night home and he had his friends to see. Bobby had Roger, his father and mother had each other; thus far he had no one. But it did not detract from his feeling for his family that he now preferred the livelier company of his friends. *They* all had families, too, and *they* would be at the drug store

tonight. You didn't come home just to see the members of
your family. As far as that goes, you got a Christmas vacation to celebrate the birth of the Christ child, but except
for a few Catholics, who would go anywhere near a church?
And besides, he could not talk to his family en masse. He
would like to have a talk with his father, a talk with his
sister, and he would enjoy a half hour of his mother's
prattling. Those conversations would be personal if there
were only two present, but with more than two present
everyone had to get his say in and nobody said anything
much. Oh, what was the use of making a lot of excuses?
What was wrong with wanting to see your friends?

The starter in the Dodge seemed to be whining, "No
. . . no . . . no . . ." before the engine caught. It reminded
him of a girl, a girl who protested every bit of the way, and
she was not just an imaginary girl. She was the girl he would
telephone as soon as he got to the drugstore, and he probably would be too late, thanks to the conversation with his
family. Irma Hipple, her name was, and she was known as
Miss Nipple. She lived up the hill in back of the
Court House. The boys from the best families in town made
a beeline for Irma as soon as they got home from school.
Hopefully the boys who got a date with her would make a
small but important purchase at the drug store, because you
never knew when Irma might change her mind. A great
many lies had been told about Irma, and the worst liars
were the boys who claimed nothing but looked wise. Someone must have gotten all the way with Irma sometime, but
Billy did not know who. It simply stood to reason that a
girl who allowed so many boys to neck the hell out of her
had delivered the goods sometime. She was twenty-one or
-two and already she was beginning to lose her prettiness,
probably because she could hold her liquor as well as any
boy, and better than some. In her way she was a terrible

snob. "That Roger Taylor got soaked to the gills," she would
say. "That Teddy Choate thinks he's a cave man," or "I'm
never going out with that Doctor Boyd again. Imagine a
doctor snapping his cookies in the Stagecoach bar." Irma
probably delivered the goods to the older men. Someone who
went to Penn had seen her at the L'Aiglon supper club in
Philadelphia with George W. Josling, who was manager of
one of the new stock brokerage branches in town. There
was a story around town that she had bitten Jerome Kuhn,
the optometrist, who was old enough to be her father. It
was hard to say what was true about Irma and what wasn't.
She was a saleswoman in one of the department stores; she
lived with her older sister and their father, who had one
leg and was a crossing watchman for the Pennsy; she was
always well dressed; she was pretty and full of pep. That
much was true about her, and it was certainly true that she
attracted men of all ages.

The telephone booth in the drugstore was occupied,
and two or three boys were queued up beside it. Billy
Warden shook hands with his friends and with Russell
Covington, the head soda jerk. He ordered a lemon phosphate and lit a cigarette and kept an eye on the telephone
booth. The door of the booth buckled open and out came
Teddy Choate, nodding. "All set," he said to someone.
"Everything is copacetic. I'm fixed up with the Nipple. She
thinks she can get Patsy Lurio for you."

Billy Warden wanted to hit him.

"Hello, there, Billy. When'd you get in?" said Teddy.

"Hello, Teddy. I got in on the two-eighteen," said
Billy.

"I hear you're going to be at Henny Cooper's house
party," said Teddy.

"Jesus, you're a busybody. How did you hear that?"

"From Henny, naturally. Christ, I've known her since

we were five years old. She invited me, but I have to go to these parties in New York."

"Funny, she told me she didn't know anybody in Gibbsville," said Billy.

"She's a congenital liar. Everybody knows that. I saw her Friday in New York. She was at a tea dance I went to. You ever been to that place in Montrose?"

"No."

"They've got everything there. A six-car garage. Swimming pool. Four-hole golf course, but they have the tees arranged so you can play nine holes. God knows how many horses. The old boy made his money in railroad stocks, and he sure did spend it up there. Very hard to get to know, Mr. Cooper. But he was in Dad's class at New Haven and we've known the Coopers since the Year One. I guess it was really Henny's grandfather that made the first big pile. Yes, Darius L. Cooper. You come across his name in American History courses. I suppose he was an old crook. But Henny's father is altogether different. Very conservative. You won't see much of him at the house party, if he's there at all. They have an apartment at the Plaza, just the right size, their own furniture. I've been there many times, too."

"Then you do know them?" said Billy.

"Goodness, haven't I been telling you? We've known the Cooper family since the Year *One*," said Teddy. "Well, you have to excuse me. I have to whisper something to Russ Covington. Delicate matter. Got a date with the Nipple."

"You're excused," said Billy. He finished his phosphate and joined a group at the curbstone.

"What say, boy? I'll give you fifty to forty," said Andy Phillips.

"For how much?" said Billy.

"A dollar?"

"You're on," said Billy. They went down the block and upstairs to the poolroom. All the tables were busy save one, which was covered with black oilcloth. "What about the end table?" said Billy.

"Saving it," said Phil, the house man. "Getting up a crap game."

"How soon?"

"Right away. You want to get in?"

"I don't know. I guess so. What do you think, Andy?"

"I'd rather shoot pool," said Andy.

"You're gonna have a hell of a wait for a table," said Phil. "There's one, two, three, four—four Harrigan games going. And the first table just started shooting a hundred points for a fifty-dollar bet. You're not gonna hurry *them*."

"Let's go someplace else," said Andy.

"They'll all be crowded tonight. I think I'll get in the crap game," said Billy.

Phil removed the cover from the idle pool table and turned on the overhead lights, and immediately half a dozen young men gathered around it. "Who has the dice?" someone asked.

"I have," said Phil, shaking them in his half-open hand.

"Oh, great," said someone.

"You want to have a look at them?" said Phil. "You wouldn't know the difference anyway, but you can have a look. No? All right, I'm shooting a dollar. A dollar open."

"You're faded," said someone.

"Anybody else want a dollar?" said Phil.

"I'll take a dollar," said Billy Warden.

"A dollar to you, and a dollar to you. Anyone else? No? Okay. Here we go, and it's a nine. A niner, a niner, what could be finer. No drinks to a minor. And it's a five.

Come on, dice, let's see that six-three for Phil. And it's a four? Come on, dice. Be nice. And it's a—a nine it is. Four dollars open. Billy, you want to bet the deuce?"

"You're covered," said Billy.

"You're covered," said the other bettor.

"Anybody else wish to participate? No? All right, eight dollars on the table, and—oh, what do I see there? A natural. The big six and the little one. Bet the four, Billy?"

"I'm with you," said Billy.

"I'm out," said the other bettor.

"I'm in," said a newcomer.

"Four dollars to you, four dollars to Mr. Warden. And here we go, and for little old Phil a—oh, my. The eyes of a snake. Back where you started from, Billy. House bets five dollars. Nobody wants the five? All right, any part of it."

"Two dollars," said Billy.

When it came his turn to take the dice he passed it up and chose instead to make bets on the side. Thus he nursed his stake until at one time he had thirty-eight or -nine dollars in his hands. The number of players was increasing, and all pretty much for the same reason: most of the boys had not yet got their Christmas money, and a crap game offered the best chance to add to the pre-Christmas bankroll.

"Why don't you drag?" said Andy Phillips. "Get out while you're ahead?"

"As soon as I have fifty dollars," said Billy.

The next time the shooter with the dice announced five dollars open, Billy covered it himself, won, and got the dice. In less than ten minutes he was cleaned, no paper money, nothing but the small change in his pants pocket. He looked around among the players, but there was no one whom he cared to borrow from. "Don't look at me," said Andy. "I have six bucks to last me till Christmas."

"Well, I have eighty-seven cents," said Billy. "Do you still want to spot me fifty to forty?"

"Sure. But not for a buck. You haven't got a buck," said Andy. "And I'm going to beat you."

They waited until a table was free, and played their fifty points, which Andy won, fifty to thirty-two. "I'll be big-hearted," said Andy. "I'll pay for the table."

"No, no. Thirty cents won't break me," said Billy. "Or do you want to play another? Give me fifty to thirty-five."

"No, I don't like this table. It's too high," said Andy.

"Well, what shall we do?" said Billy.

"The movies ought to be letting out pretty soon. Shall we go down and see if we can pick anything up?"

"Me with fifty-seven cents? And you with six bucks?"

"Well, you have the Dodge, and we could get a couple of pints on credit," said Andy.

"All right, we can try," said Billy. They left the poolroom and went down to the street and re-parked the Warden Dodge where they could observe the movie crowd on its way out. Attendance that night was slim, and passable girls in pairs nowhere to be seen. The movie theater lights went out. "Well, so much for that," said Billy. "Five after eleven."

"Let's get a pint," said Andy.

"I honestly don't feel like it, Andy," said Billy.

"I didn't mean you were to buy it. I'll split it with you."

"I understood that part," said Billy. "Just don't feel like drinking."

"Do you have to *feel* like drinking at Dartmouth? Up at State we just drink."

"Oh, sure. Big hell-raisers," said Billy. "Kappa Betes and T.N.E.'s. 'Let's go over to Lock Haven and get slopped.' I heard all about State while I was at Mercersburg. That's why I didn't go there—one of the reasons."

"Is that so?" said Andy. "Well, if all you're gonna do is sit here and razz State, I think I'll go down to Mulhearn's and have a couple beers. You should have had sense enough to quit when you were thirty-some bucks ahead."

"Darius L. Cooper didn't quit when he was thirty bucks ahead."

"Who? You mean the fellow with the cake-eater suit? His name wasn't Cooper. His name is Minzer or something like that. Well, the beers are a quarter at Mulhearn's. We could have six fours are twenty-four. We could have twelve beers apiece. I'll lend you three bucks."

"No thanks," said Billy. "I'll take you down to Mulhearn's and then I think I'll go home and get some shut-eye. I didn't get any sleep on the train last night."

"That's what's the matter with you? All right, disagreeable. Safe at last in your trundle bed."

"How do you know that? That's a Dartmouth song," said Billy.

"I don't know, I guess I heard *you* sing it," said Andy. "Not tonight, though. I'll walk to Mulhearn's. I'll see you tomorrow."

"All right, Andy. See you tomorrow," said Billy. He watched his friend, with his felt hat turned up too much in front and back, his thick-soled Whitehouse & Hardy's clicking on the sidewalk, his joe-college swagger, his older brother's leather coat. Life was simple for Andy and always would be. In two more years he would finish at State, a college graduate, and he would come home and take a job in Phillips Brothers Lumber Yard, marry a local

girl, join the Lions or Rotary, and play volleyball at the
Y.M.C.A. His older brother had already done all those things,
and Andy was Fred Phillips all over again.

The Dodge, still warm, did not repeat the whining
protest of a few hours earlier in the evening. He put it in
gear and headed for home. He hoped his father and
mother would have gone to bed. "What the hell's the matter
with me?" he said. "Nothing's right tonight."

He put the car in the garage and entered the house by
the kitchen door. He opened the refrigerator door, and
heard his father's voice. "Is that you, son?"

"Yes, it's me. I'm getting a glass of milk."

His father was in the sitting-room and made no answer. Billy drank a glass of milk and turned out the kitchen
lights. He went to the sitting-room. His father, in shirtsleeves and smoking a pipe, was at the desk. "You doing
your bookkeeping?" said Billy.

"No."

"What *are* you doing?"

"Well, if you must know, I was writing a poem. I was
trying to express my appreciation to your mother."

"Can I see it?"

"Not in a hundred years," said Mr. Warden. "Nobody
will ever see this but her—if she ever does."

"I never knew you wrote poetry."

"Once a year, for the past twenty-six years, starting
with the first Christmas we were engaged. So far I haven't
missed a year, but it doesn't get any easier. But by God,
the first thing Christmas morning she'll say to me, 'Where's
my poem?' Never speaks about it the rest of the year, but
it's always the first thing she asks me the twenty-fifth of
December."

"Has she kept them all?" said Billy.

"That I never asked her, but I suppose she has."

"Does she write you one?" said Billy.

"Nope. Well, what did you do tonight? You're home early, for you."

"Kind of tired. I didn't get much sleep last night. We got on the train at White River Junction and nobody could sleep."

"Well, get to bed and sleep till noon. That ought to restore your energy."

"Okay. Goodnight, Dad."

"Goodnight, son," said his father. "Oh, say. You had a long distance call. You're to call the Scranton operator, no matter what time you get in."

"Thanks," said Billy. "Goodnight."

"Well, aren't you going to put the call in? I'll wait in the kitchen."

"No, I know who it is. I'll phone them tomorrow."

"That's up to you," said Mr. Warden. "Well, goodnight again."

"Goodnight," said Billy. He went to his room and took off his clothes, to the bathroom and brushed his teeth. He put out the light beside his bed and lay there. He wondered if Henrietta Cooper's father had ever written a poem to her mother. But he knew the answer to that.

ABOUT THE AUTHOR

Son of a doctor and the eldest of eight children, John O'Hara was born in Pottsville, Pennsylvania, January 31, 1905; he died at his home in Princeton, New Jersey, on April 11, 1970.

After graduation from Niagara Prep School, he worked at a great variety of jobs. His career as a reporter was also varied. He worked first for two Pennsylvania papers and then for three in New York, where he covered everything from sports to religion. He also was on the staff of *Time*, and, over the years, wrote columns for *Collier's*, *Newsweek*, the Trenton *Times-Advertiser*, *Newsday* and *Holiday*.

His first novel was *Appointment in Samarra*, published in 1934, and with its appearance he became, and continued to be throughout his life, a major figure on the American literary scene. He published seventeen novels and eleven volumes of short stories, in addition to plays, essays and sketches, many of which he never got around to collecting for books. Because of his prodigious energy and productivity, he left behind a considerable body of finished work not yet published in any form.

His novel *Ten North Frederick* (1955) received the National Book Award for 1956, and in 1964 the American Academy of Arts and Letters presented to him the Gold Medal Award of Merit.

TE PU